When all

the days

have gone

Also by Lars Boye Jerlach

The Somnambulist's Dreams

2017 Angry Owl Publishing © All rights reserved

Copyright © Lars Boye Jerlach

Printed in the United States of America

Cover design and artwork by Kyle Louis Fletcher www.usklf.com

ISBN-13:978-1975746124

ISBN-10: 1975746120

When all the days
have gone

A Novel
By

Lars Boye Jerlach

For Jesper

Chapter 1

He was staring at the surprising amount of nearly translucent blowfly larvae writhing in the fading sunlight on the moistened dirt.

Although the distinct smell of decay was completely at odds with the surroundings, he was nevertheless reminded of the first time he had been sitting in the crammed hull of his uncle's small boat while a glistening heap of herrings, having been abruptly released from the net, slid across each other with flapping tails, desperately seeking an escape from their constricted newfangled element.

He had been quite a lot older than most of the other boys in the village when his mother had finally relented and allowed his uncle to take him out to sea, and although he had always been familiar with the tools of the trade and equally with the catch, he had nevertheless been caught woefully unaware of how fish behaved when hauled up from the deep.

He was instantly ashamed by the lewd images the squirming creatures conjured up in his mind, and even as he blushingly looked away, he secretly savored the continued lubricity behind him and wondered if Fromm could tell where his mind had strayed when he attended church the following Sunday.

The image of the tall gaunt priest standing in the shadowed doorway of the small village church, disapprovingly inspecting his entering congregation, darted through his mind and even after all this time had passed, he instinctively pulled his free hand closer to his body as if to forestall the cool and bony grip.

Father Fromm had had the most unpleasant tendency to hold on to his hand a fraction too long looking at him with bloodshot eyes from hollowed sockets as if he was searching for a sign of weakness in his soul, and though the priest always smiled, revealing a large set of stained yellowed teeth more befitting the mouth of a horse, he had nonetheless suspected that the grip from the hand of death itself would be not too dissimilar.

He inadvertently flexed his fingers a couple of times and rubbed his hand against his trouser leg.

He looked down at the animal on the ground.

The fox had been lying perfectly still.

Only when he had nudged it with the tip of his left boot had he realised that it must have been dead for some time, camouflaged as it was in the golden hues of the leafy blanket. The tissue beneath the fur was a little too soft and the pressure of his foot caused the gasses in the decaying carcass to send forth a stench with which he was all too familiar.

He took a step back and wafted at the cool air with his hand, then he swung the shovel off his shoulder and pushed it under the carcass.

The ground underneath the dead animal was all but macerated with decaying juices and it made a rich squelching sound when he separated the shovel from the viscous surface.

He lifted the shovel off the ground, and the head of the fox rolled over the edge swinging gently from side to side, drooping like a ripened pear waiting for the right moment to let go.

Part of the snout and most of the soft tissue around the mouth had been pecked away by buzzards and other scavengers. They had left behind a hideous toothy grin that made it look as if the fox was permanently sneering at its own misfortune.

With its yellowing bared teeth and its empty eye sockets the head of the fox was an effigy of the grotesque painted face on one of the marionettes he had seen hanging behind the puppet master's stall at the local market.

Although he had never once seen it being used in the play, he had nevertheless assumed it represented death.

He had been standing with the fox as a counterweight at the end of his shovel left to his own thoughts and he almost jumped when a cacophony of croaky sounds broke the evening stillness.

A small coven of crows, appearing like small black paper cut outs silhouetted against the darkening sky, watched his movements from a large maple tree across the path.

Then they all took off from the branches, leaving the crown of the tree like an undulating murky stream in the evening sky.

He watched them fly towards the woods dragging behind them a cacophonous chorus until they dissolved in the air like drops of ink in a bowl of water.

When all movement stopped and the quietness returned, he grabbed the smooth head of the well-worn ash handle, expertly turned the shovel sideways to get the smell of death away from his body and carried the remains of the fox and most of its teeming ocean to the edge of the cemetery and into the woods.

The heat from the decomposing flesh left a faint misty trail in the cool evening air.

He looked around for a suitable spot on the near to lightless ground and eventually deposited the remains in a small hollow close to the base of a small white pine tree.

He bent down and gathered a handful of pine needles that he scattered over the carcass and the still grinning face.

A few of the needles got stuck upright in the reddish fur, looking like tiny brown lances sticking out of a red haired giant. He grabbed a few more handfuls and spread them until the fox was completely covered, then he turned around and silently walked back towards the path. When he reached the edge of the woods he stopped and wiped the shovel on a tuft of long dried out grass while looking back over his shoulder.

At first glance he imagined he saw one of the fox's ears protruding, like a small white sail in a darkened sinuous sea, but the light must have been playing tricks with his eyes because when he attempted to locate it again, it had disappeared in the dense undulating network of needles covering the ground.

He removed his threadbare black cap and ran his hand across the top of his head feeling the bristly hair that although thinning, still covered most of his crown.

The branches of the naked trees cast their elongated finger-like shadows over the gravestones in an almost osculating embrace as the closing glow of the setting sun barely illuminated the ground around him.

He put his cap back on, slung the shovel over his shoulder and began walking down the path towards the cottage.

His gait was slow and methodical and the gravel made its familiar anhydrous sound as he continuously pressed his heavy work boots against the ground.

His legs were slightly bowed under his short thickset body and his free, still powerful arm moved like an adipose pendulum in unison with his steps.

He was as always dressed in black, but for the colourless cotton shirt that, although he had put it on clean the same morning, was already grubby at the cuffs and neck.

When he reached the cottage he walked to the end of the small garden and opened the creaking door to the tool shed.

Although the inside was nearly pitch black, he reached in and exigently hung the shovel in its appointed place on the wall before closing the door behind him.

Then he walked over to the chicken coop.

He quietly opened the small door in the fence. He bent down, gently pushed on the door to the coop and turned the small piece of wood that kept the door shut.

He listened as the initial cries of alarm from the disturbed birds within changed from cackling to soft throaty sounds of reassurance, before he slowly backed away closing the door in the fence and refastening the hook. The original coop had been a small half rotten ramshackle and had held only a few hens, so before winter set in he had rebuilt the coop to allow space for a few more birds. He had first dug a trench the width of a spade's blade, a foot and a half deep and twelve feet square around the coop. Then he had stapled new galvanized chicken wire to a cedar board at the bottom before filling the trench with granite and marble fragments to prevent larger predators digging their way in. He had collected the stone fragments from Mr. Svensson, a Swedish stone carver in the neighboring village who over the last couple of decades had provided a great deal of the grave markers and monuments now on permanent display at the cemetery. Not only was Svensson happy to get rid of the debris, but he had hired him on the spot to build a new fence around his own chicken coop as he had recently lost six hens of his own to what he claimed was a fisher cat. It had gotten under the fence and into the coop during the night quietly killing the sleeping birds leaving nothing but carnage behind.

Above and around the fence he constructed a low slanting roof structure that he covered with chicken wire and although the coop was mostly shaded by the long leafy tentacles of a small willow tree, he nevertheless inserted a boarded up old window frame to provide additional shade for the birds during the hot summer months.

He wasn't exactly a specialist when it came to the care of hens or even particularly knowledgeable of the distinct behavior of the different breeds, but when he was just a boy his uncle had shown him how to properly build and fortify a chicken coop and he was grateful for the advice, because so far he had never lost a bird.

In and around the cemetery he had however seen quite a few aftermaths of wild birds being taken.

Often the only evidence would be an artfully arranged array of bloodstained feathers lying on the ground and he always found it fascinating how the outcome of an action so utterly brutal could appear so beautifully tranquil. It strangely reminded him of the exhibition of Flemish floral paintings that his aunt had taken him to see so many years ago at the Museum of Art in the city of Copenhagen.

His aunt was the second daughter of a school teacher, who had not only been a compassionate autodidact artist, but also had instilled in her a love for the arts in all its multiplicity of forms. Much to her father's despair she went against his wishes and eventually married a fisherman, but even though her new husband shared very little of her enthusiasm for painting or music, she could never get herself to completely sever the ties to a world for which she had cultivated a deep seated appreciation. Instead she bestowed that continued passion on her nephew and took every opportunity to introduce him to the wonders of the world seen through the eyes of the painter, the elaborate words of the poet or the music of classical composers. She would occasionally bring him to concerts in the city, where the musicians would transform the enigmatic calligraphic marks on the sheets of paper in front of them to an elaborate mesmerizing ocean of sound, in which he would have happily drowned himself.

On the way home on the train, she would talk to him at length about the work they had encountered and always listened carefully and respectfully to his interpretations. She would often encourage him to think about why an artist had selected a certain element to include in a specific painting and would sometimes explain to him a particular religious or political motif that could be found in an object or subtly veiled form hidden in plain sight to reveal a secret message. She had from the very beginning demonstrated the world of art as a tessellation of images and sounds, that everything is interconnected and that new forms of expression can only be achieved if the artist has a comprehensive understanding and appreciation of history and the work produced by anterior artists.

She would illustrate her point by saying: 'Do not forget that however tall you build a tower; it is always reliant on the foundation to make it stand'.

She would frequently lend him books from her own small but refined library, first translations of Brontë, Austen, Conrad and Shelley and somewhat tattered copies of the writings of Ibsen, Gruntvig and Kierkegarrd. Although he sometimes found the writings difficult to comprehend, she always encouraged him to think about what he read and to expand his way of thinking about and interpreting a text. Through this private cultural education, he came to believe that everything created is part of a much larger collective movement, he also came to appreciate the world of art and literature equally as much as his enthused teacher.

For inexplicable reasons he was from the beginning especially drawn to the Flemish flower paintings and would return to those paintings, or paintings like them, repeatedly to see if he could subtract some kind of information or direction from them. However, he found that the longer he stared at the images the further he was from understanding them. There was no florid fragrance, no corporeality or tactility exuding from the two dimensional plane, in fact he could find absolutely nothing alive in the paintings, and yet they had an unnatural almost spellbinding grip on him that he found both mysterious and inexplicable, as he had never been especially interested in the world of flora.

When looking at real flowers, he could hardly distinguish one from another, but when faced with a painting he found himself drawn to counting the number of petals in a crown or the number of leaves on a stem. He noticed the subtleties in the colouration, acknowledged the way the light had been seamlessly captured and the way the illusion of texture had been flawlessly applied. He carefully observed how the flowers had been arranged, how many different samples of flowers were represented and the type of vase in which the bouquets were displayed. He could spend hours staring at these images.

He found the flowers forever trapped in time a strange illusion of a perfect paradise. They were obviously a representation of something incomparably alive, and yet he couldn't help thinking about the fact that the flowers inside the real vase themselves were long dead.

He mulled over the actuality of death while looking at life.

The flower paintings were in many ways similar, if somewhat antipodal, to the feathers left behind after the attacks.

In the beginning when he encountered one of these grisly but picturesque tableaus, he would often lose track of time. He found the images strangely haunting and while he could quite easily recall them later on, it was as if they had left only a faded flocculent imprint on his mind and no matter how hard he tried to bring them into focus, the images remained somewhat nebulous. So he started carrying around a small black notebook and a short square carpenter's pencil and began to draw the scenes whenever he encountered them. He wasn't especially good at drawing and at first his sketches were nothing but a jumble of unorganised lines. However, he learned that time and persistence are invaluable tools when you want to learn something new and over time he became, if not exactly prodigious, at least proficient at rendering the morbid yet beautiful tableaus.

He discovered that he was most intrigued by the smaller nondescript assemblies of feathers or tufts of fur. If there were any recognisable parts of the animal left or the smell of decay was still polluting the air, the image on the ground immediately lost its appeal and he never found the urge to sketch it.

What he especially enjoyed drawing were the aftermaths of hawks having taken a bird in mid-flight. The way the white downs had fallen and been deposited like soft cloudy flowers, sometimes in the long grass and sometimes on the bare dirt, he found particularly satisfying When he revisited those drawings he was often brought to images of the sea and remembered the times he had been sitting in a sandy dune on the beach, resting his chin on his knees looking at the seabirds that like small white specks were bobbing up and down on the ever moving fluid surface. Occasionally the birds completely dissolved in the blinding light and other times they would appear like a handful of white pebbles strewn carelessly across a dark sandy beach. When he closed his eyes he could sometimes recall the smell of the rotting seaweed, feel the sharpness of the long hardy grass that grew in disarray amongst the sand dunes or hear the desperate cries of the large grey backed seagulls, lacerated by the howling wind until only a clamorous mutilated chorus of crazed sirens satiated the air.

He had never once showed the drawings to anyone, but he would often spend an evening in the yellowing light from his candlelit lamp, perusing one of the many small notebooks.

Looking at his less than adequate sketches he could often remember the exact time of day he had traced the image, the way the light had illuminated the hollow shafts of the small feathers and how the wind had played in the delicate fibrous downy barbs.

He bent down and picked up a small downy feather and brought it to his eyes. It was difficult to see in the fading light, but he felt the almost imperceptible softness brushing against his fingers. He gently blew the feather away and checked the door again before slowly walking back towards the cottage.

The small stone cottage sat on the edge of the woods that surrounded the cemetery near the somewhat larger caretaker house and close to the boulevard that connected the cemetery to the city.

There were no carriages or automobiles on the road at this hour and everything was quiet. Though the city had grown to almost fifty thousand souls and expanded well beyond its original borders, out here the city had yet to install the street lamps that for more than a decade had illuminated the streets downtown and only the faint flickering lights in the small cluster of houses in the distance showed signs of life.

Across the road the golden dome of the convent of the Sisters of Mercy caught the very last of the sun's orange rays, fittingly making it appear as if an eternal flame was burning within its core. Otherwise the great brick building sitting in the grass behind the tall iron fence was equally as still as its inhabitants.

He slightly shook his head and walked up to the front door where he stopped and habitually ran the bottom of his boots against the cast iron boot scraper to the left of the steps.

Not that it was necessary.

This time of year the muck was not usually wet enough to stick to his boots in the compacted layers that sometimes made it difficult for him to keep his balance. Nevertheless, he methodically went through the well-rehearsed motions while looking at the distinct red rimmed scars on the surface where the thick hardened black paint had flaked off.

He couldn't actually make them out in the dark, but he still knew they were there.

He repeated the action three times for each boot before fishing out a large iron key from his coat pocket to insert it in the keyhole.

He pressed down the heavy iron handle on the weather beaten

oak door and turned the handle. The door disapprovingly creaked on its hinges and swung open to let out a stream of warm air.

When he had been offered the position, the caretaker, Mr. Galloway, had pointed through the office window and indicated a small grey stone cottage nearby. It was almost hidden from view by a cluster of young willow trees. Thin leafy tentacles playfully cascading like a green shimmering waterfall in the afternoon sun nearly obscured the dark slate shingled roof underneath.

"So, Mr. Moerk let's go have a look shall we?" The caretaker jovially patted him on the back. Although his Scottish accent was still quite prominent, it was infused with a tonal nasality that betrayed an already long stay on the American East Coast.

He was a relatively small slender man with a head full of flowy hair the colour of aged ivory and an impressive set of white fluffy sideburns that framed his broad somewhat fleshy face. His high deeply furrowed forehead was matched by his prominent cheekbones and though he was no longer young, his lips, under his quite formidable nose, were rather large and the colour of budding roses. Combined with his well-fitting dark green velvet coat, matching vest and plain but tasteful white cravat, it gave him a somewhat dandyish look that was strangely conflicting with his position. His large heavy lidded eyes sat under a pair of bushy white eyebrows and were almost colourless, like a slightly hazy frozen pond in the early morning light.

They had walked side by side through the knee high grass and Ambrosius must have looked somewhat apprehensive when they reached the cottage because McCullum looked at him and nodded knowingly.

"I know it's not much," he said in a rather apologetic tone, "but at least it's a place to call home." The caretaker then handed him the key and he unlocked the door to the cottage and pushed open the creaking door.

He had put down his dilapidated brown suitcase on the single slab of grey speckled granite that served as a threshold and looked into the cottage, that apparently was as old as the cemetery itself.

It was a simple natural stone structure with two square southeast facing windows placed about three feet apart on either side of the heavy weather beaten oak door.

A small deep fireplace centered on the opposite wall was framed by two plain square wooden pillars upon which sat a fairly wide dark varnished shelf. There were no signs that the shelf had recently held anything but for the coating of dust that was currently spread evenly across its surface. In the center of fireplace stood a heavy, slightly corroded ash covered crate that overcrowded the darkened recess.

On the right hand side of the fireplace a small but broad headed shovel and a broom with long feathery black bristles were leaning against the wall.

To the left of the room a small iron-cast stove had been rather hastily installed on an almost square platform of slate, and the mortar around the black pipe in the wall looked relatively fresh.

The blackened silhouettes of an assembly of pots and pans dangled above the stove from what looked like blunt fishing hooks fastened with thin pieces of rope nailed to the rafter above. Next to the stove stood a large grey soapstone sink held up by four metal legs with square bases that had been screwed into the floor with heavy, now rusty screws and on the wall across from it a fairly wide but thin red pine door revealed a narrow but wide larder with six heavily mottled thin pine shelves.

A small square pine table, marked by a number of jagged yet fluid rings, reminiscent of fiery celestial bodies, occupied the center of the space.

Four chairs were pushed underneath the table so only the spindly curved backs showed. The chairs were all slightly darker at the top where countless grimy hands had grabbed them and no matter how many times they had been scrubbed, it had left a permanent murky stain in the soft light wood.

Above the table hung a small square lantern from a long, rather brutal looking iron hook.

The frame of the lantern was made of thin strips of redwood, expertly joined together to form a hollow rectangular box. Although it was difficult to be certain due to the lack of light, he had thought it peculiar how the frame appeared to have been painted an almost identical colour to the wood itself.

Two strings of what appeared to be thin copper wire were running across the small sooty sheets of glass covering the sides, cutting them into three equidistant sections. The top of the lantern was made of what looked like a copper alloy and shaped like a low pitched square roof with small domed windows on each side. A curved ornamental band had been engraved beneath the windows creating a symmetrical four pointed wave and through the chimney at the pitch of the roof a small copper ring had been inserted, from which the lantern was now attached to the hook. The two visible windows were perforated with tiny symbols, one with a small X and the other with a small circle. From where he was standing it appeared as if the two symbols were exactly the same circumference.

He had been intrigued by the only unexpected object in the room and had immediately walked across the floor and around the table to see if there were perforations in the windows on the two other sides. His curiosity had been rewarded.

Across from the circle sat a small three pointed crown and across from the X was a vertical symbol that looked like two semicircles turned away from each other but connected by a small band.

Although he recognized three of the markings, he had never seen the sign of last perforation before and didn't quite know what to make of it.

He placed his finger underneath the delicate frame and gently opened the small sooty glass covered door and peered inside the lantern.

The semi opaque wax in the shallow tray formed a solid sheet and a now frozen stream had at one point flowed from the small gap under the door and left a small yellow tinted waxy island in the center of the table.

He thought it strange that no one had removed it. He reached out, ran his finger across the slightly lumpy but smooth and waxy surface and removed a thin coating of dust revealing a slight shine underneath.

He was about to ask Galloway if he knew anything about the history of the lantern when he turned and caught a view of the narrow door at the other end of the cottage. It had apparently received a number of treatments similar to that as the shelf above the fireplace, and although the varnish had been excellently administered it couldn't completely hide the badly dented wood underneath. The bottom of the door was inflicted with a number of indentations varying in depth that had left the lower part with a distinct pockmarked appearance, almost like the door had been imprinted with a dark shiny image of the moon. He walked across the creaking floor, bent down and studied the lower panel that had borne the brunt of the abuse. The slightly oval indents were deeper and more prominent on the right hand side and as he ran his fingers across them they felt cool and smooth to the touch almost like flowing water having been brought to a standstill.

He stood up and opened the door to the adjacent room. It was equally as sparsely furnished as the main room.

A thin striped mattress lay on a simple but sturdy looking bed frame shoved up against the wall. Opposite the bed a tall dark wardrobe, reminding him in both shape and colour of a casket, loomed heavily in the corner. He walked across the floor, gently opened the door and peered in half expecting to find evidence of the cottage's former occupant, but apart from a wooden rail and a couple of small brass hooks on the back of the door the cupboard was utterly empty.

He pushed the door shut and walked over to the small square window above the bed and looked into the overgrown garden.

A tunnel spider had spun its elaborate web in the deep window sill, and a large iridescent fly buzzed in vain in the silky contraption.

The desperate sound reverberated in the otherwise quiet room, but was quickly quenched by the rapid arrival of the owner.

The stillness it left behind was remarkable.

He stood in the doorway between the two rooms and looked around to see if he could spot any personal effects.

There were no pictures hanging on the walls, no clothes, shoes or blankets, no trinkets or ornaments and besides the few pots and pans there was nothing left behind that told him anything about the former occupant.

He walked back across the floor leaving a set of reverse prints in the heavy dust on the floorboards and looked up at the crawl space above the bedroom. He stepped on the low rung of the steep wooden ladder to make sure it could carry his weight before taking a few more steps. Although the ladder creaked loudly under his foot, it held his weight and he nimbly climbed to the top and peered into the space.

As far as he could tell it had been unoccupied for some time.

There was a small round window split into four sections on the back wall and judging from the patchwork of red bricks and fresh mortar surrounding it, the window had been inserted fairly recently.

Although the glass was somewhat obscured by cobwebs and the mummified remains of a variety of flying insects, there was still enough light for him to see, but besides a few dusty potato sacks lying in the corner where the rafters joined the wide rough floorboards there was nothing else in the space.

He stepped down from the ladder and walked over to Galloway who had respectfully remained in the doorway observing his ruminations.

"Yes," he said in a voice neither sad nor happy, "it's a place to call home."

Then he stepped outside, bent down, grabbed the brown suitcase and carried it into the cottage. He walked across the floor into the bedroom, laid it in the center of the mattress and looked at the eruption of miniscule dust particles dancing in the fading shaft of sunlight spilling into the room.

Chapter 2

"......and the most frightful thing about all of this: That it appears as if a large number of the population is completely hypnotized and could be made to do terrible things without them ever once thinking that the things they were doing were terrible."
The voice trickled like a small collection of brightly coloured beads, rolled over the edge and into the bottom of the grave where he crouched.
He was sifting through the dirt with his calloused hands and looked as it disappeared between his fingers and fell on the ground in small granular piles. The palms of his hands each had their own individual system of dried out riverbeds running across them and he often felt as if the dirt that continuously flowed through them had only assisted in embroidering a more profound system of trenches in his flesh.
He had almost finished digging and had finally reached the level where the dirt had shifted from the soft porous dark particles to the more compact layer of reddish clay upon which the entire cemetery sat. He had spent most of the day digging his way through the heavy moist top layer and the second layer filled with pebbles and rocks before reaching the sandier layer that preceded the heavy viscous layer of clay roughly five and a half foot down. He had just allowed himself to take a short break before starting on the last impediment.
He leant the newly sharpened spade against the narrow seven stepped ladder and reached for his light green water bottle when the unexpected bright but somber voice of a young woman reached him.
"....and the worst of it is, that all these terrible things are often powered by some form of dark self-interest that goes way way back, perhaps even to the beginning of time."
Although it was nearing the end of November and the ground had been covered in frost when he began digging the same morning, he was now sweating profusely and a thin wisp of steam rose from his bare arms and the back of his shoulders. He watched it dissipating in the clear afternoon air as he lifted the bottle, removed the cork and

put the cold rim against his parched lips. He rinsed his mouth with a bit of water, spat it out and watched as the small pool slowly dissipated on the slightly viscose ground. He then drank greedily from the bottle feeling the familiar yet slightly peculiar coolness of the water as it passed through his throat, down his chest and then into his stomach. He waited as the sloshing water came to rest in its new fleshy cavity before he put the bottle back on the ground in the corner beneath the ladder. Then he reached for his shirt that hung on the last step of the ladder and carefully pulled it over his head trying not to dirty it more than it already was. He rolled up the sleeves and tucked the shirt into his trousers before taking a step up the ladder.

He had to stand at the second to last step to peek over the mount of dirt that now surrounded the grave. He looked up at the emerging specs of lights in the cloudless sky and though he totally accepted the futility of the action he still crossed his fingers and hoped that it wouldn't start raining during the night as he knew that a good part tomorrow would be occupied by moving the dirt to one side to make space for the funeral attendees.

He put the thought of rain out of his mind and tried instead to locate the place from which the voice had originated.

The sun was nearly setting and its orange glare blanketing the ground, making it appear as if parts of it was on fire, was still intense enough that it forced him to shield his eyes with his hand as he looked around. Even then it was difficult for him to discern more than the expected static shapes of the grave markers and the massive trunks and heavy branches of the nearby oak trees.

At first he didn't notice anything out of the ordinary, but then he caught a slight movement out of the corner of his eye perhaps only fifteen feet away.

A young girl, about the age of fourteen, was sitting on the steps leading up to a family plot.

In the center stood a fairly imposing square two step bevelled gravestone holding a large draped urn. He knew the design was influenced by the vases of ancient Greece and he had learned from Svensson that the image of the veiled urn had been a particularly popular motif amongst the more affluent members of the North American public during the last couple of decades.

He had always found the selection of the veiled urn slightly peculiar. Perhaps not so much because of the design itself, as most of them were in fact quite beautiful. It was more the strangely conflicting fact that so many Americans had chosen to have a draped urn standing on top of their earthly remains for all eternity since none of them, as far as he knew, were Greek nor had chosen to be cremated. It was a bizarre fashionable appropriation that for a reason, unbeknownst to him, had been popularized and during the last couple of decades seamlessly had been integrated into the landscape of the North American cemetery.

In his rough estimation this cemetery alone held somewhere between thirty-five and fifty of such urns, although he suspected there might be more if he one day took the time to count them all. Most of them were carved in white marble, some of them in granite and a few, like the one standing on its large square platform behind the girl, in sandstone. While they were all different in materials, shapes and sizes they all told the same story: The urn symbolically held the ashes of the departed and the drape, much like the shroud that had covered the son of God, represented death and sorrow. Though, perhaps, according to the conversations he had overheard between funeral attendees, the drape could additionally symbolize the veil that supposedly separates earth and heaven.

Looking at the rather large example on top of the gravestone he wondered if the family who owned the plot had had any misgivings about their choice. After all the family name, carved into the center of the gravestone in big capital letters, read 'TRUE'.

The plot itself, about twenty feet in either direction, was surrounded by a low sandstone wall with a small square stone positioned at either corner, upon which sat a smaller replica of the draped amphora although these were without arms.

He squinted and looked at the girl, not sure if she was aware that he was watching her.

She was dressed in a light blue summer dress with a small white shawl draped over her shoulders. A pair of long white stockings covered her legs and her shoes shone like pieces of polished marble on her small feet. Her long unnaturally straight hair, the colour of ebony, was held in place by a white hair band and framed her slightly elongated but perfectly symmetrical face. She had large dark almond shaped eyes above which sat a pair of eyebrows that, if put together, would have formed a perfect circle. Her nose was small and straight and her rose coloured lips was very nearly the shape of a small heart.

Her features were so exquisite that he at first thought he was looking at a large doll, but then she made a small movement with her head and a strangely unsettling image of Snow White flashed through his mind. He wondered if she was a character in a play and looked around to see if anybody was accompanying her, but there was nobody else in the vicinity.

If he had been surprised by her appearance, it was nothing compared to the shock he felt when she suddenly looked up, raised her long pale arm and waved at him.

"There you are!" Her excited voice rang out like a silver bell in the still evening. It was like she was greeting a dog she'd been looking for, yet somehow always expecting to find. "I was beginning to fear that you would never emerge."

She stood up and somewhat carelessly brushed at the fabric at the bottom of her dress.

In contrast to her voice that was clear and joyful, her movements were slow and gracious like long broad leafed kelp moving in the current.

She looked at the leaves at her feet and for a moment it seemed like she had forgotten he was there, but then she looked up and raised her hand and waved once more.

"Are you coming out?" There was a slight note of impatience in her voice.

He nodded in affirmation and carefully walked up the last two steps of the ladder.

He steadied himself with one hand on the dirt covered ground, picked up his jacket from the last rung and stepped out of the grave.

No matter how many times he had emerged from a grave, he still found the transition from the interior to the exterior space somewhat strange. Although he was a lot more accustomed to the confined working environment than when he had first started digging graves almost two decades ago, it still took a bit of time for his body to accept that he could once again swing his arms freely without bumping into the wooden boards or inadvertently knocking over the ladder when he took a step backwards.

He wouldn't necessarily describe the feeling as oppressive or even uncomfortable, it was just a bit peculiar and would often wear off fairly quickly, depending on how long he had been digging. Sometimes working through exceptionally difficult layers could take quite a long time and in cases like that, it would often take a little longer for his body to shake off the sensation of confinement.

If anybody had ever asked, he would have likened it to the feeling of stepping off a boat onto dry land. For a while everything would feel like it was still in motion even though he knew he was not.

He put his left arm in the sleeve of his jacket and slowly walked over to where the girl was standing.

She folded her delicate hands in front of her, cocked her head and smiled at him while he clumsily took a half circle dance step searching for the other sleeve with his right hand. When he finally managed to find it, he pushed his arm through, pulled the jacket close and buttoned the three large multi-hued buffalo horn buttons.

"You do realize that you have been digging almost continuously for quite a considerable amount of time?" She didn't wait for a reply and paused only briefly before continuing:

"For a moment I thought that you would never finish and that you would disappear without a trace into the bowels of the earth." While she looked at him searchingly with one of her dark eyebrows slightly raised, her voice was light and pleasant with no noticeable accent.

"Was that your plan? To disappear into the depth of the earth?"

She looked up at him with quite a serious look on her face. Two small wrinkles had appeared in the otherwise smooth pale surface just above her nose.

"No, I can't say that it was." He looked into her eyes. They were like obsidian so dark that it was impossible to distinguish the iris from the pupil. He leaned forward, turned his head ever so slightly and focused on one of her eyes to see if he could detect a variation in the darkness, but all he saw was a distorted reflection of his own searching face.

"I'm glad to hear that," she said. "I spend a lot of time here, but I have never seen you before. Did you arrive recently?"

"Well, everything is relative, but I suppose you can say that I did."

He answered her question wondering where her parents might be and if they knew where she was. Judging from her behaviour and the quality of clothes she wore, he deduced that she must be from a rather well to do family.

She was certainly a far cry from the ragamuffins straying like feral cats near the town center holding up their scrawny dirty hands begging for alms.

"Where are you from? You don't sound like anybody else I know. Are you from somewhere in Europe like the caretaker? He's from England isn't he?" She reeled off her questions in rather a quick sequence, but stopped abruptly waiting for him to reply.

"Yes, but I am not from England, I am from a small country in Scandinavia called Denmark," he answered, "and by the way, in case you meet him some day, the caretaker Mr. Galloway is from Scotland, not England. I think he would be quite upset if you mistook him for an Englishman. The Scots are quite proud of their heritage you know." He smiled at her.

"I shall remember that in case he ever notices me," she said solemnly, "but do tell me; are you really from Denmark? Just like the author who wrote all those marvelous stories about the mermaid and the emperor who walked around in public with no clothes on, oh and the one about the ugly duckling that became a beautiful swan, his name is quite long and has a Christian in it if I remember correctly?"

For the briefest of moments, he thought he caught a tiny spark in the depth of her eyes.

"Hans Christian Andersen," he said.

"Yes that's it," she said. "Are you really from there? Is that not very far away?"

"I am," he said, "and yes it is indeed very far away."

"Is it always snowing there? I have heard that it is frightfully cold and that you have polar bears walking in the streets at night, standing on their hind legs looking through the windows into people's houses."

She had an inquisitive look on her face.

"That, I'm afraid, is a misconception," he replied smiling. "There have not been wild bears of any kind in Denmark for hundreds of years, and the polar bear that you are referring to lives much further north near the arctic circle. Actually, the only bear I ever saw was in the Zoological Garden in Copenhagen and that was a very sorry sight indeed. It was sitting in a corner of a tiny cage, slowly rolling its head back and forth, looking more like an old toothless man covered in a filthy tattered blanket than a bear."

"That sounds incredibly sad," she said. "Why would anyone want to look at something like that?"

"That's a very good question." He paused for a moment. I suppose it's because most people want to experience something new and exotic, and a bear, no matter what condition it's in, is still something that most people don't see every day, so it becomes a unique experience for them, something they will remember for a long time."

He looked at her face as he spoke. Her eyebrows once again moved closer together and the two small wrinkles reappeared.

"So what you are saying is that most people would like to see a suffering animal trapped in a cage because it's a unique experience to them? That's very disturbing don't you think?" She tilted her head and looked up at him. There was a somewhat defiant look in her obsidian eyes.

"Yes, I suppose it is," he answered, thinking that whoever she was, she was no ordinary girl. She certainly had a mind of her own and even though some of the information she had received was flawed, it was obvious that she was well educated.

He decided to leave the image of the dilapidated dying bear behind and steer the conversation in a somewhat less depressing direction.

"By the way, in my experience it's actually much colder here than in Denmark, and although it does sometimes snow during the winter over there, it is hardly anything compared to the amount of snow that falls here."

"Don't think that changing the subject will make me forget about the plight of the bear," she said. "You were the one who planted the image in my mind and it will take a lot more than a conversation about the weather to rid my mind of it."

She placed her hands on either side of her narrow hips to emphasize the poignancy of her statement.

Although there was no wind he could feel the cold beginning to move stealthily up his legs. He tugged at the collar of his jacket and stomped his feet on the ground.

The girl however did not seem to notice the cold.

"Yes, I am sorry about that," he said. "I realize I probably shouldn't have told you. I did think it was quite a dreadful image and not something I should have shared with a young lady."

He removed his cap and bowed his head.

"Please accept my sincere apology."

"Apology accepted," she said smiling and once again folded her delicate, nearly porcelain white hands in front of her.

"However, in the future please remember that anything and everything you ever tell someone stays in their mind forever and that the horribly sad image of the bear waiting for death in its dirty small cage now has become part of the infinite number of other images forever floating around inside my head. Like one of those fluffy white seeds from the dandelion letting themselves being carried by the wind with no true destination. One day the seed will land in just the right spot and it will begin to grow and another dandelion will emerge."

She looked at him making sure that he was paying attention.

"You understand why it is important that we think about what we say before we share that information with one another?"

He had been confounded by the weightiness of her analogy, but he didn't let it show.

"Yes I understand," he said, "and I promise I will take that into consideration in our future conversations."

She nodded in approval and smiled again, revealing two almost symmetrical rows of teeth that glinted like tiny pearls behind her parted lips.

"Good," she said.

"So tell me: If it's much colder here than it is there, why do people think that your country is a frozen desolate land covered in snow dunes, with polar bears running around all over the place?"

"That's another very good question."

He scratched the side of his bristled skull.

"I suppose it's because people presume that Scandinavia is one big country and that it's quite remotely placed in the northern hemisphere. Also, there are wild polar bears living in the freezing inhospitable northern parts of both Norway and Sweden, so I guess it's an easy assumption to make that Denmark would have the same climate as its northern neighbors and that polar bears would also be found there."

She again nodded her head in approval.

"I think that's a great explanation."

"I'm glad you like it, though I can't promise it to be true."

"Don't worry about that, it makes perfect sense to me." She cocked her head, and her hair flowed like a melanoid velvet river around her alabaster neck and came to rest like an elongated inkblot on her white shawl covered shoulder.

"What's your name?" She asked.

"Ambrosius Moerk, but Moerk will do."

"That is a very handsome name," she said. "A name fit for a king that is lucky enough to already have so many devoted subjects in their kingdom."

She made a grandiose sweep with her hand and he turned and looked at the numerous grave markers surrounding them, casting their long dark shadows on the ground.

"In his role as caretaker, I believe Galloway is the true ruler of the land," he answered, "but as his right hand man I promise I will do my best to serve both his kingdom and his subjects."

"I am glad to hear it," she said, "I am sure they will all appreciate his gentle and thoughtful rule."

She lifted her skirt ever so slightly and curtsied. In return he gave a solemn bow of his head.

"Is Ambrosius Moerk your full name or do you have a middle name? Everybody I have ever known has had a middle name." She puckered her lips and gave him a suspicious look.

"I do have a middle name, but I only use it when signing my name, and it is not that often I get asked to do so." He took a deep breath, exhaled slowly and watched his breath form a small misty cloud in the air.

"I have not shared this information with anyone for a long time, but since you asked I will tell you. My middle name is Clemens. I suppose the reason I didn't tell you from the start is that I'm not terribly fond of the name and that I never liked saying it out loud."

She gazed at him wide eyed with a stunned look on her face.

For a while she didn't move a muscle, she just kept staring at him unblinkingly, as if she had been caught in a ripple in time. When she finally recovered, she closed her eyes and slowly shook her head from side to side.

Then she leaned forward, opened her dark mirrored eyes and slowly whispered: "What did you say?"

She gazed into his eyes as if the answer to her question could be found inscribed on his retina.

"I said that I have never liked saying my middle name out loud."

"That is the strangest thing." She put her hands together in front of her face and in small rapid movements bounced the end of her index fingers against her lips.

"I believe that is about the strangest thing I have ever heard."

"Why is that so strange?" he asked. "It can't be that uncommon. I am certain you can find quite a number of people who are not happy with the name their parents gave them and amongst those there will definitely be some who have chosen never to use it."

"Yes, I am sure you're right about that," she said. She still had her hands clasped together in front of her face. "However, that is not what is strange. What is strange is that Clemence was one of three Christian names given to my late father, and that I heard him utter the exact same words you just did."

She paused and looked at him with a most serious expression.

"You see, he too was not fond of the name Clemence and would never speak it out loud. Indeed, he took a great care to hide the fact that he even bore the name. He was in fact so set on not being a Clemence that he had even left instructions not to have the name included on his gravestone."

She turned and pointed at the gravestone that held the large urn behind her.

"You can go see for yourself," she said. "Where it should have read Anthony Edward Clemence True it instead reads Anthony Edward True. Don't you think it is a strange coincidence that I meet someone here, in my late father's eternal resting place who also has an uncommon dislike for the name Clemence?"

He detected a bit of rattled disturbance in her voice. Like a slight layer of tarnish having momentarily appeared on the silver bell.

"Yes," he replied. "I have to admit that is very strange. Although my adversity to the name is not as severe as that of your late father. I just don't like saying the name out loud."

He again began wondering what this remarkable girl was doing on her own in the cemetery so late in the evening. If she was here to visit her father's grave, surely she would have been accompanied by other relatives.

He once again scanned the perimeters, but there was nobody else in sight.

By now the sun had set and the long dark shadows, before so stark against the ground, had quietly and effectively been obnubilated by the creeping dusk.

As if she had read his mind, she slowly turned and with elegant languid movements she walked up the four stone steps.

At the last step she stopped, folded her arms across her chest and looked over her shoulder. In the fading light she looked uncannily like a small statuette. "I have to go now," she said in a voice almost free of the earlier agitation, "but I promise I will come back soon to continue our fascinating conversation."

"It is not advisable for a young lady to be walking around alone so late in the evening, so if you don't mind I would like to walk you home, to make sure that you arrive safely."

"It is very kind of you to offer, but I assure you that won't be necessary. I don't have far to go and the cemetery is nearly always empty at this time."

She lifted her small hand and waved, then she walked across the grass past the imposing monument. She jumped down from the low wall without slowing her pace, and her slight frame was soon swallowed up in the circumambient darkness.

Just before she vanished he called after her:

"What is your name?"

At first he thought she hadn't heard him but then, some distance away, a faint voice called out of the darkness.

"Veronica." One by one the syllables dissolved in the air until all that was left was the sound of his own breathing.

For a moment he gazed into the space he imagined her voice had been coming from.

Then, as the abundant darkness enfolded him in its infinite cloak he walked over to the almost ready grave, picked up the shovel, put two strips of wood down across the opening and placed the large template on top, to prevent people and animals falling into the crevice. When he was satisfied that no one could tumble into the cavity, he began walking back towards the cottage.

Chapter 3

He opened the door and the cold sifted through the opening like an invisible force and swiftly wormed its way into the entire fabric of the cottage. He quickly closed the door behind him and rubbed his upper arms. Small wisps of breath briefly consolidated around his face before quickly dematerializing in the cool still air. He blew a larger plume into the air. It was a bit like a faint milky replica of those of the fire breather who entertained the crowds at the market with his daring and dangerous performance.

The first snow of the season had coated the ground in a thin white sugary blanket that made soft satisfying sounds under his boots as he walked from the cottage to the chicken coop. He opened the door, bent down, turned the handle and opened the hatch.

Normally the hens would be eager to escape their overnight confinement and rush out in a pandemonium of ruffled feathers and a babel of noise.

This morning however, only a couple of hens came to the hatch.

They stood on the threshold, turning their heads in small convulsive motions, tentatively exploring their surroundings. He took a couple of steps away from the coop and the remaining birds appeared to perform their distinct gambol down walkway, stretching and contracting their long squamous feet under their feathery ovoid structures, while clucking loudly and pecking at each other.

Then he spread a couple of handfuls of grains on the lightly snow covered ground and watched as the birds began their frantic and relentless pummeling. Then he walked behind the coop and opened the small wooden hatch at the back and surveyed the nests. He picked up the four perfectly formed light brown speckled eggs and carefully deposited them evenly in each of his side pockets. He closed the hatch behind him, walked out of the coop and back to the cottage.

He placed the bag of grains by the door, reached up and released one of the small pots hanging from a hook above the stove, removed the eggs from his pockets and put them in the pot. He then stood the pot near the center of the barely warm surface and fetched a plate from the small cupboard to use as a lid. Normally he would have put the eggs in the pantry, but it was stocked for the winter and there was not enough space for the pot.

When he was satisfied that the eggs were relatively safe he picked up the grains, walked out to the shed, opened the door, put the bag of grains in the small metal bucket by the side of the door and placed the heavy, slightly damaged brick on the dented lid. When he had made sure it wouldn't slide off and couldn't be moved by a rat or other vermin, he surveyed the interior.

On the wall to the left seven different types of shovels and large spades were hanging side by side. He had arranged them according to height of handle and width of blade.

They had recently been cleaned, polished and sharpened and the thin curvy lines of the greyish blue steel edges glinted in the morning light, creating quite an anomalous pattern against the wall, of seven levitating smiles of the Cheshire cat.

On the wall opposite hung three types of long narrow spades with heavy oak handles, two of them with serrated rust coloured blades.

The longest spade, with a blade about two feet in length, was the shape of an elongated shield, flat on top with slightly inward curved sides and a raised ridge on the back. It was bluish black and shone like the wing of a raven. Although he had never shared the information with anyone, it was the only tool he had ever had an immediate impulse to name and the only one he had never had the urge to use.

For a while he stared at the head of the spade.

Even in the murky shadows it appeared like a planate aperture containing nothing but pure emptiness.

After a while he averted his eyes and looked instead at the several boards of differing sizes, leaning up against the back wall. Next to the boards a couple of large pickaxes were placed upside down on ground, and a heap of well drubbed heavy wedges lay in a corner beside a low cart with wide iron rimmed wheels.

He grabbed one of the red spades, lifted it off the two parallel nails and leaned it against the outside wall. Then he picked up the eight heavy planks of oak from the back of the shed, placed them on the bed of the small low cart and dragged the cart outside.

He was sixteen years old when he had been offered to assist the local gravedigger.

Mr. Gravesen who was getting on in years, and in dire need of younger stronger arms, had made a pledge to Ambrosius's aunt to take him on as an apprentice and to teach him the tools of the trade. Although his aunt had had high hopes for his continued education there was very little money to support such an endeavor, and since both of them loathed the idea of him following his uncle's trade hauling fish from the tempestuous sea, they had agreed that the job as the local gravedigger wouldn't be the end of the world. He would still be able to live with them and with his meager earnings from the church and the contributions from the families of the deceased, he would be bringing much needed income to the household.

 On the very first day on the job, his former master Mr. Gravesen had taught him that the construction of a grave was much more than just digging a hole in the ground, and that an accomplished gravedigger would have to employ any number of devices in order to successfully accomplish his task.

He learned that digging a grave required a number of varying tools: A spade, a shovel, a pickaxe, a six-foot ladder, six to eight sturdy boards for shoring and a number of heavy wedges. Most importantly he learned that digging required an understanding of the conditions of the soil and a sincere respect for the weather. He learned that everything he did with the soil could change in an instant. That a heavy consistent downpour could turn a newly dug grave into a pool of murky water and rapidly turn the dirt in an uncovered earthbox into a rectangle of solid mud.

He learned that an exceptionally dry pocket of sandy soil could collapse a grave and potentially trap and suffocate the digger, if he had been careless and hadn't shored the grave properly, and he was taught to recognize when it was futile to dig in the frozen ground and the deceased would have to be placed in a receiving vault or in the undercroft of the church to wait for interment until spring when the frost subsided.

In extreme winters the ground could be frozen almost four-foot-deep and he would have to wait well into spring before digging could commence, often bringing about further distress for the grieving family, when they had to go through a second funeral service.

In addition to digging the grave, Gravesen would show him how to build a template of heavy wood to place on the ground over the intended grave and how to weigh it down with four heavy rocks, before using a serrated sod-cutter to cut the outline of the grave. He would show him how to carefully cut the loosened top layer into smaller square sections and place them in small stacks some way from the grave before removing the dirt itself.

Gravesen also taught him how to build a large rectangular box, that he referred to as 'the earthbox', out of eight heavy oak planks joined together in the corners by large mortise and tenon joints. The box would be placed about four to five feet from the grave to hold the soil they dug up. After it was filled, the box would be covered with a piece of waxed or tarred tarpaulin or linen depending on the wishes of the family. Immediately after the funeral rites, the fabric would be removed and the grave refilled.

He learned that it is advisable to dig a grave slightly deeper than the minimum, depending on the level of the groundwater, and to allow for a maximum of three coffins to be buried in the same grave as it was customary for family members of the deceased to be buried in the same plot when they passed away, and he quickly discovered the agonizing truth that in cases of epidemics the grave could be reopened more than once in a matter of weeks to accommodate yet another eternal resident.

When he had been taught all that could possibly be learned about grave digging, it was only befitting that Mr. Gravesen, a year and a half after Ambrosius began his apprenticeship, became the first person for whom he single-handedly dug his very first grave.

He hauled the loaded cart up to the path and began walking towards the nearly finished grave. The cart's iron wheels were almost soundless against the snow and the morning stillness was only broken by the occasional rattle from the planks, caused by the uneven surface of the gravel path. The long shadows from the trees cast a vast entangled pattern on the unblemished snow, like colossal drawings on an immense piece of paper.

He noticed how the drawings morphed in the sunlight. How the sharpened outline of the trunks of the trees changed in the brightness and how the softened plicature of their extremities interlaced on the ground. He removed the small black notebook from his right side pocket, sat down on the planks and attempted to draw the scene before him. However, there was something about the situation and the scale of the image, that somehow eluded him. He found it impossible to replicate the image before him and after having spent a good part of the morning drawing, it altogether appeared as if a child had absentmindedly made a jumble of lines of contrasting thickness.

He put the book back in his pocket, grabbed the handle of the cart and continued on his way, adding his own dissonant tracks across the large image.

He had found it difficult to eliminate the image of the girl from his mind.

The reasons for her being alone in the cemetery late in the evening had occupied his thoughts since she had disappeared into the night, and after his return to the cottage he had in fact been thinking a great deal about their serendipitous encounter and the perplexing conversation they had had about his and her father's shared middle name. There was something about her that gave him a feeling he couldn't quite place or put into words. Something slightly unfamiliar that besides her appearance and mannerism added to the enigma. While he realized that it was unlikely that the girl would be back to visit her father's grave the following day, as even the most yearning visitor to the cemetery allowed a week or more between visits, he very much hoped that she would return sometime soon, so that they would have an opportunity to continue their conversation.

He continued his walk across the snow covered grounds and a while later he dragged the cart up to the grave and placed it near the mound of dirt. He removed the planks, and put down two side panels and two end panels on the ground next to the mound and joined them together with the use of a battered wooden mallet.

The rhythmic sounds of beating bounced off the nearest headstones and arrived back as a profusion of muted echoes merged with the telltale resonating noise of a large woodpecker searching for larvae in the rotting bark, and although it sounded like the bird was near, he couldn't make it out in the interlacing network of branches above.

When the box was assembled, he grabbed the large shovel by its smooth ash handle and began the arduous task of filling the earthbox. Fortunately, the overnight frost had not been too severe and the mound of dirt was quite accommodating and yielded easily to the head of the shovel. It took him a couple of hours to shift the mound and even though he had removed his jacket and rolled up his shirt sleeves, he perspired like it was a warm summer day and the sweat made his shirt cling to him like a second clammy layer of skin. When he had finished he drank a bit of water from the flask and wiped at his brow with the shirt sleeve. Then he picked up a large decrepit metal bucket and threw it down the hole, picked up the small serrated spade from the bed of the cart, turned his back to the grave, stepped down the ladder and descended into the hollow.

When he had worked for Gravesen it had been his job to haul the filled bucket out of the grave with a rope and empty it before handing it back, now he had to fill the bucket, walk it up the ladder and deposit the clay rich dirt in the earthbox. Walking up the ladder with a heavy clay filled bucket was a precarious and strenuous procedure that caused quite a considerable amount of pain to his carrying shoulder, neck and upper legs. Thankfully he only had to remove about half a foot of material from the bottom before he reached the required depth.

He had intentionally made the ladder eight feet tall and had additionally cut a notch at either end so he could always tell when he was deep enough.

Not that he needed it.

These days he could often sense where he was in the earth, as if his body received a personal external stimulus from the surrounding walls that told him exactly when it was time to stop.

After the last load, he sat down on the upside down bucket, took a sip of water from the bottle and looked up at the clear blue sky above.

Framed by the edges of the grave it seemed like he was looking at a giant infinite painting. Only the greyish white specks of pair of seagulls suspended in the air high above ruined the otherwise sublime canvas.

"The question is: if solitude increases the perception of self and grant us something valuable, why is it then that we choose not to be alone?" The girl's questioning but exuberant words tumbled over the edge interrupting his reverie.

He immediately pricked up his ears to see if he could make out a reply, but as far as he could tell, no one else seemed to be speaking.

After a brief pause he again heard the animated voice of the girl:

"But If you really enjoy solitude, can you ever claim to be fully alone? Surely the feeling of aloneness is intrinsically connected to how you relate to, or not relate to other people? If you are truly happy in your solitude does that not exclude the feeling of being alone?"

Her words, although spoken like a glorious gallimaufry in the buoyant voice of a child, conveyed a solemnity well beyond her years.

He waited for a reply, but when that failed to materialize he got up from the bucket, and slowly walked up the steps of the ladder. He looked over the edge of the grave and immediately spotted the girl.

She was sitting in the same place on the steps leading up to her family's plot.

She was dressed in the exact same attire as the day before and her long black hair shimmered like the surface of an inkwell in the midday sun.

It was as if she had been waiting for him to reappear, and as soon as his head was above the ground, she promptly waved her delicate milky arm in the air and called out:

"What were you doing down there? I was afraid you might have tricked me yesterday and chosen to disappear anyway." She smiled and made a small flick of her head, causing a subtle luminous oscillation in her long dark hair.

He stepped out of the grave, rubbed his dusty hands against the legs of his trousers and walked over to where the girl was sitting.

"As a matter of fact I was spending some time looking at the sky," he said, when he reached her. "Somehow I perceive it very differently from the bottom of a grave, than when I look at it from up here."

"That's quite interesting." She looked up at the sky using her left hand to shield her eyes and then looked at him.

"Why do you think it is so different for you to watch the sky from down there?"

"I admit that is a bit of a conundrum," he said, pausing briefly. "Honestly, I cannot give you a reasonable explanation for why I perceive it differently."

"Why don't you give it a go? I am interested in hearing what six feet underground can possibly do to change one's perception."

She cocked her head, pulled her legs up, folded her hands on her knees and looked at him expectantly.

"Very good then," he said, thinking about how to best explain the sensation. "I think that not having the full immensity of the sky in view gives me an opportunity to better observe it. It's like watching it in smaller segments somehow allows me to see it better." He looked at the girl who returned his gaze with eyes wide open.

"Like plucking a single flower from a boundless field of buttercups and holding it close to your face so you can smell the scent of the flower and see how it is constructed?" she asked, showing the rows of small pearly teeth behind her smile.

He noticed two small symmetrical dimples appearing on her cheeks. In the sunlight they looked like tiny rounded chisel marks, purposefully carved into her translucent flawless skin.

"Yes, I suppose that is a very good comparison," he said, once again marvelling at this remarkable young girl. "Although, when I'm looking up through the opening of a grave, it's not only to admire the composition of the sky, but also an attempt to grasp the aspects of the indeterminable. In truth I wonder what lies out there in the infinite beyond the moon and the stars."

The girl didn't respond. Instead she pursed her lip and looked at him with one of her eyebrows raised. Then she slowly nodded her head in agreement and her hair once more swayed in the air like a tenebrous waterfall.

"That is by no means surprising," she said. "I find it is quite the difficult task thinking about the infinite."

She got up from the steps and performed a slow pirouette, waving her arms halfway in the air. There was something disparate about her unconstrained leisurely gestures that reminded him of a creature deep beneath the sea, and he again had the feeling that she was moving in slow motion.

"May I ask you a question?" he said.

"By all means," she said cheerfully, "ask away."

Who were you talking to before I came up from the grave yesterday and again today? I clearly heard you converse about something, but as far as I could see there was nobody else around."

Although the girl immediately stopped twirling, a slight almost unnoticeable oscillation occurred in the space around her. Like something unseen touching the surface of an otherwise unstirring lake. It disappeared in the blink of an eye and Ambrosius thought that the brightness of the sun, and the changing wind must have caused the disturbance.

"That is rather difficult to explain," the girl said, studying the perfectly shaped polished fingernails of her right hand.

"Don't you worry," he said. "I can assure you, I've heard some peculiar tales in my time. People talking to their loved ones heretofore alive and well, now dead and buried deep in the ground is not at all an uncommon occurrence. In my experience it is rather the opposite."

"Even so, you must surely think me mad if I told you."

The girl paused, looked down at the ground at her feet and grasped at her own hands. Then she looked back up at him and her unblinking obsidian eyes found his.

"If I do tell you, you have to promise me you won't think of me as crazed or that I keep company with the devil." There was an inflection in her voice that did not invoke supplication. In fact, it sounded rather like a command.

"I promise I will not think of you in that manner, whatever it is you tell me."

He looked straight into the girl's pitch black eyes and placed his right hand over his heart.

"I trust that you won't," she said.

Chapter 4

The immutable coven of crows transmitting their raspy caterwaul from high up in the conifer they had chosen for the night drowned out any other sounds.

After the final dig, he had carefully removed the lower shoring boards, carried them up the ladder and placed them on the cart. Then he had put down a pair of two inch square pieces of wood on the ground about three and a half feet apart, to allow for the rope used to lower the coffin to slide unobstructed underneath. As a final act he slid the template over the opening of the grave satisfied that it was ready to receive its new occupant the following day. He would have to come back early in the morning to remove the template and make sure that the earthbox was uncovered so that the content was available for the member of the family who, when handed a small flat silver shovel, would hesitantly scoop up a small amount of dirt, walk over to the edge and then drop the coarse dark particles onto the pristine lid of the coffin that now inhabited the cavity, while the grandiloquent voice of pastor Godfrey droned the prerequisite words in the background.

The sky already lay like a vast interwoven orange and purple blanket across the landscape as he began trudging back the same way he had walked in the morning. The melting tracks he had left in the virgin snow earlier that morning, were now so horribly misshapen that it looked like a giant with large deformed feet had been strolling around the grounds. He barely noticed however, because he couldn't stop thinking about the incredible story the girl had told him.

It had been such a capricious tale told with such remarkable equanimity and candour that, although he knew that he was supposed to understand it purely as a figment of the girl's extraordinary imagination, he nonetheless found it too elaborate to be cast aside as mere inventiveness.

As he retraced his steps following the now wider footprints, he attempted to recall the entire conversation as it had happened.

At first he could tell the girl was hesitant to tell him as she had begun her narrative quite cautiously to assess his reaction. However, when she was assured of his willingness to listen and when he had obviously gained her trust, her narrative became altogether an effusion of words and images that, though fairly easy to comprehend, he could not easily understand.

"What you have heard are not truly conversations," she said, "it's more like a variation on a theme of thoughts. It's difficult to put into words exactly what happens, but I think it's comparable to how a composer creates a new piece of music from an older already well known musical piece, or constructs a musical piece in the style of their personal paragon."

She paused, sat down on the steps, pulled her legs up under her and hugged her knees.

"I suppose if you listened to it from a distance it would appear as if I am partaking in a conversation, but really I am only rephrasing and putting into words what has already been thought by somebody else. Does that make sense to you?"

She lifted her gaze and looked at him for signs of distress.

"I am not exactly sure that it does," he replied hesitantly.

"I thought as much." It appeared as if she was looking for the right words to continue.

"You do recall I asked of you not to bring into question my mental state or make assumptions about witchcraft and that you gave me your promise that you wouldn't do that no matter what I told you?"

"Yes of course I do," he answered, curious to know where this mystifying conversation was heading.

"Alright then, although I do not fully understand it myself, I'll nevertheless tell you what transpires when these conversations as you call them takes place."

He could tell by the tone of her voice and her demeanor that she had made up her mind and that she was determined to share with him whatever was happening regardless of how aberrant it might sound.

"There's a cat who loiters in the cemetery, I wonder if you have seen it? It's rather large and its coat is black as coal and shines like a piece of granite in the sunlight. Frankly, it would be a perfect representation of a sending, if you were gullible enough to believe that such a thing exists. It comes and goes as it pleases and it doesn't seem to care much about catching anything. When I first came across it, I assumed it was here to catch some of the mice or the small birds that are so abundant around here, but I was wrong to make that presumption, because when it's here it usually just sits in the grass or on the top of a gravestone and gazes into the air with its piercing blue eyes.

He wondered if the girl was avoiding the original topic and had chosen to steer the conversation in an entirely different direction, but he was mistaken.

"The most laconic explanation I can give you is this: When the cat visits the cemetery, I can hear what it's thinking and I transmit its thoughts into a spoken language."

She stopped talking and watched him closely as he considered what she had just relayed. He could feel he was being watched very carefully and although his first impulse had been to laugh, he immediately stopped himself when he saw the look on the girl's face.

The look in her eyes told him that this was no laughing matter so he quickly covered his mouth and instead ran a calloused hand across his chin. He could feel and hear the sound of bristled stubble rubbing against the palm of his hand while he considered what the girl had just said.

"Did you understand what I just told you, or are you pretending not to have heard?" There was a slight accusatory note in her voice.

"No, I did hear you. I am just not quite sure what you told me is possible. How can you possibly hear what a cat is thinking? It seems very uncanny."

Although he attempted to keep his voice calm, there was a certain potency in his reply that set her on edge. She stood and cocked her head.

"Are you implying that I'm crazy?" She said defiantly.

"No, no," he said, putting his hands up apologetically, "that's not at all what I meant. I was merely saying that it sounds very unusual to be able to hear anyone's thoughts, not only those of a cat, but I suppose that's only because I have never heard the thoughts of anybody else."

"So let me get this straight;" she said, "you do not believe that I am crazy per se, but that being able to hear others' thoughts is at least abnormal, that is until you hear them yourself? That somehow seems contradictory don't you agree? I bet you wouldn't tell your physician that you were able to hear the thoughts of other people for fear of being diagnosed as mentally impaired, unless of course you were absolutely certain that the physician could also hear your thoughts, whereby the entire exercise would be rendered pointless."

She looked at him waiting for a reply.

"First of all; I do not believe that you are crazy and second of all; I essentially agree with what you just said. However, if it was indeed the case that we could all hear each other's thoughts, I don't think you would find many people spending a lot of time thinking."

He offered her a benevolent smile and he was relieved to see her smile back.

"You're absolutely right," she said. "The most intricate parts of the mind are indeed a dangerous maze full of pitfalls and perilousness not to be shared lightly and believe me when I say that there are a lot of thoughts in the world that are better left alone in the deepest darkest depths of their lairs never to see the light of day."

"I believe you," he replied in earnest.

"I am glad you do."

"So tell me, what exactly is the cat thinking?"

"That's also a somewhat difficult question to answer," she said.

The way in which she twisted a lock of her hair between her fingers reminded him of a blackadder slithering through the fingers of the hand of a marble statue.

"Though I realize how peculiar this may sound, I believe the cat to be some form of conduit. You see, it doesn't think about things a cat would normally think about, like where to best catch mice or find a warm lap on which to take a nap. It mainly has thoughts about art, ethics, religion and more complex thoughts about what it means to exist. Sometimes it thinks about extremely plain things, like which day of the month it's best to plant barley and sometimes it thinks about concepts I don't fully comprehend, like the formation of the stars in the sky for example, and of the behaviour of light or space and time."

She gazed at him with her dark glass-like eyes to see if he was paying attention.

"Yesterday I believe the cat was thinking about writing an article about an art exhibit. However, the person who had viewed the exhibit was obviously deeply disturbed by something relating to the history of the human psyche and was thinking about how to put those thoughts into words when the cat intercepted them and I repositioned them and spoke them out loud."

She pushed her hair away from the side of her face revealing an impeccably shaped ear, behind which she eloquently deposited the strands of her ebony coloured hair.

"Earlier today the cat intercepted the thoughts of what I believe is someone who has chosen to live in solitude and has been doing so for a long time."

"But why do you speak out loud what the cat thinks?" he asked, trying not to sound too sceptical.

"That is another difficult question to answer." She briefly gazed into the distance.

"In truth I believe I am some sort of designated repositioner. I believe my task is to adjust the motley collection of words that are disseminated by the cat and speak them out loud. I am still not entirely certain why I need to do this, but I think that the cat somehow retransmits them to the original thinker."

"But if the cat can read other people's thoughts, surely it would be able to read yours as well," he replied somewhat apprehensively.

"You would think so, but that's definitely not the case. Believe me, I have tried to communicate with the cat by other means, but apparently speaking the words out loud is the only way it works. I have tried to ask it why this thought-transference is happening, but all I have gotten so far is simply more thoughts to sift through."

"Why do you think it's happening?"

"Honestly I do not have the faintest idea. Before I met the cat, I never even considered having such an implausible ability. I was by all accounts a perfectly normal girl mostly concerned with learning and reading. Although, I suppose that could also be perceived by some as quite unusual."

"I would imagine that could quite easily be the case." He thought about how his aunt had struggled against an entire village that essentially believed that all a woman needed in life was a good husband and a good home with lots of children to raise. In most people's minds there was no good reason for a woman to have ambition beyond her station, and to actively pursue culture or knowledge was still frowned upon as an act of sheer folly by most.

"Do you have any idea what happens to the words you are speaking?" he asked.

"Not entirely. I assume that when the cat sends them back, they're perhaps written down or spoken by somebody, although I cannot possibly be sure. Conceivably they're just rethought and retransmitted. There's really no way to be certain."

"I'm still curious why you are doing this," he said. "As I understand it nobody asked you to translate the thoughts of this cat, correct?"

"That's not entirely correct," she said, "the cat did ask me, or at least I believe it did."

"But why do you do it?" There was a suggestion of bemusement in his voice.

"It passes the time." She answered solemnly and looked at him with unblinking eyes.

He heard the murmuring sound of voices behind them and he turned around to see six nuns walking by in consummate synchronicity on the path about thirty feet away. Although he couldn't quite make out what they were saying, they were deep in conversation and paid little attention to him or his companion as they glided by, each face framed by a wide white wimple, feet hidden beneath their long black cowls.

He waved in their direction as he usually did to see if he could possibly force a response, but either none of them saw him or they pretended not to, because they continued their evening stroll uninterrupted. He followed their floating progress until they rounded the corner and then turned around to find that the girl had vanished. He looked around, called her name a couple of times and strained his ears to hear if she answered, but when he got no other response than that of the choir of raucous crows overhead, he walked over to the grave, stepped down the ladder and once more disappeared from view.

Chapter 5

He was still deep in thought when he returned home and he went through his evening ritual of checking the hens, putting the tools back in the shed, removing the dirt from his boots at the bootscraper and hanging up his jacket on the back of the door without really noticing.

The girl's story had left him completely baffled and there were only two possible explanations for her narrative. Either she had an incredible imagination and had been making the whole thing up as a form of entertainment or she actually believed that she was translating the thoughts of a cat, in which case she had questionable mental faculties.

Whatever the case it was as strange as anything he had ever heard, not even the ancient story of The Golden Ass or any of the Nordic myths were as peculiar as the story this prodigious young girl had told him. A cat being some form of mind reading receptacle and a girl being a decipherer was as nutty as a fruitcake. He realized he could never tell anybody about their encounter, as any person with a modicum of reasoning would immediately proclaim her deranged, and quite possibly question his own sanity as well.

However, the fact that she had made him promise not to think of her as mad, made him uneasy.

It was obvious that she was self-conscious and aware that her explanation could cause quite an upsetting response, hence the cautious manner with which she had originally broached the subject.

He loaded the stove with firewood from the bucket, put a lump of the butter from the pantry on the small frying pan and was just about to crack one of the eggs that he had collected in the morning, when there was a knock on the door.

The noise made him drop the egg in the pan. Fortunately, it landed softly in middle of the lump of butter and he picked it up, scraped off the clinging butter with a knife, put the egg back in the pot and placed the frying pan near the edge of the stove so it wouldn't overheat, before walking over to open the door.

Galloway was standing on the doorstep holding what looked like a small package in his left hand. His face appeared somewhat eldritch in the dim glowing light from inside. The illusion was aided by the large sideburns and unruly hair framing his furrowed face and the addition of Robert the Bruce, affectionately known as Brucy, the great black dog sitting on the ground beside him with its large spotted tongue lolling from its grinning mouth and its eyes, like two shining marbles suspended a couple of feet in the air, glowing green in the dark.

However, Galloway's manners were as impeccable as ever and he seemed quite free from tension judging from the sound of his throaty but nasal voice.

"Good evening Moerk, I hope you don't mind me disturbing you so late," he said stretching out his hand, "but I have something here that I think you might find quite interesting."

He held out a small grey metal box that Ambrosius accepted. It had no identifying features and was so light that it could have been empty.

"It's quite alright, it's not really that late and I wasn't doing anything that can't wait. Do you want to come in?" He gestured behind him with the hand that was now holding the box.

"Some other time perhaps, my wife's busy preparing supper and I'm already in trouble for running over here against her wishes."

He smiled showing his collection of small badly disarranged teeth and the image of a gargoyle flashed through Ambrosius' mind.

Mrs. Galloway was a large big hearted woman whom Galloway adored as much as any man can adore anyone. As far as Ambrosius could remember she was of either German or Austrian descent and had resided in a small town in one of the more unmemorable states near the center of the country, before having been introduced to Galloway at a family event that he had attended many years ago. She was quite a formidable woman that chiefly reminded Ambrosius of Brunhilde from Wagner's Volsunga Saga, with a rosy plump face, a high and wide forehead under which sat a pair of large cobalt blue eyes and a wide mouth that was nearly always smiling showing her strong white teeth. She also had the most impressive amount of golden hair that he believed he had ever seen. It was normally fashioned into two large braids that flanked either side of her head in large golden buns, but occasionally she could be seen hanging washing in the garden and her loose golden mane blowing in the wind would have made any male lion envious. She also had a tendency to laugh a lot and very loudly and her vociferous voice could often be heard calling out for her husband across the cemetery when his supper was ready. Ambrosius found her to be a very kind and approachable woman who seemed genuinely happy with her lot in life.

"I just imagined you would like to receive this as soon as possible. My wife found it earlier this morning when she went through some of the items we collected from your predecessor. I'm afraid to say that there was not much that was worth saving, but we put those that were in a box and placed in in the crawl space under the stairs. I must admit I had completely forgotten about it until my wife handed me this box of letters this morning."

He pointed to the small metal box Ambrosius was holding in his hand.

He opened the lid and looked inside.

At the bottom of the box lay a small bundle of smudged greyish envelopes tied together with a piece of thin black string. The writing on the envelope on top spelled the Danish word for beginning; *Begyndelsen* in diminutive but elegant cursive letters.

"I'm afraid we already opened that one," Galloway said, gesturing to the envelope on top of the bundle. "No good that did us though, since it's all written in a language neither me nor the wife can understand. However, Mrs. Galloway recognized some of the letters and said that it looked like it was written in your native tongue or one like it, maybe Norwegian or Swedish and that I should give the letters to you to see if you could read them."

"That's very kind of you, but are you sure you don't want to hold on to these. These letters were never meant for me and I somehow feel it would be intrusive to read them."

He picked up the letters and held them out, but Galloway waved his hand dismissively. "Well, they were most certainly not meant for me either and it can't really harm anybody since the letters were never sent and apparently never read. Also, the fact that the author passed away quite a while ago should ease your worry about being unduly intrusive."

He paused, pressed his lips together and grimaced slightly.

"Besides that, you have a lot more in common with the man who wrote these letters than both Mrs. Galloway and I, so it seems only fitting that you should be the one to read them. However, I would be interested to hear what they say, so perhaps you can let me know when you've read them, eh?"

"That's a promise," he said and shook Galloways hand.

"That would be great. Well good evening to you Moerk."

He began walking, but stopped a couple of steps from the cottage and looked up at the late evening sky. A blanket of low hanging hoary clouds had formed overhead, nearly obscuring the glowing light of the quarter moon.

"Winter is coming," he said, "I'll give it another week before the top layer is too hard to break even with the pickaxe. You think you have enough time for Johnson and Timble? If you need help I can call upon Svensson's sons to come and give you a hand."

"I don't think that will be necessary, but thank you for the offer. I believe I have sufficient time for both gentlemen if the frost doesn't get any worse and if it doesn't start snowing too heavily."

"Ok then, but don't hesitate to let me know if you need help. It would be good to have both interred for the sake of both families. They've suffered enough already. No reason to prolong that if we can help it."

"Of course."

"Well, good evening to you Moerk."

"To you as well and give my best to Mrs. Galloway."

"I shall."

Galloway and Brucy were almost completely swallowed by the darkness before reappearing silhouetted against the soft radiant light of the opened front door of the caretaker house. He watched as they were greeted at the door by Mrs. Galloway before he closed the door, walked over to the table and put down the box containing the small collection of letters.

Then he walked over to the larder and crouched down to check the two traps he had placed in the darkened corners at the ground level. The traps were of slightly different sizes but principally worked the same. The rodent was attracted to the bait, a small piece of smoked sausage, that was placed on the trap's pedal and when it unsuspectedly stepped on it, a U shaped metal bar shut close with a force that pinned the invader against a wooden block.

When the trap slammed shut the mice usually died instantly having their backs broken and their internal organs smashed, but with some of the bigger rats it often took awhile for them to succumb. Occasionally when the trap snapped, he could hear the rat scuttle about trying to free itself from the tormenting contraption while slowly suffocating.

In the morning, when he carried the traps outside to remove the cold stiff bodies, he could feel the small round beady eyes staring at him and although he knew it to be irrational, he could never get himself to meet that cold unblinking stare, afraid of what they might see.

Tonight both of the traps were empty but the bait had gone from the larger trap. It had most likely been removed by a shrewd mouse who'd been able to evade the deadly mechanism and he almost admired its enterprise.

He walked over to the sink, turned the tap and washed his hands. The water was exceptionally cold and his fingertips were almost numb before he shut off the water and dried his hands on the well-worn towel hanging from the hook on the larder door.

He wondered if the water pipe would freeze up and burst at any point during the winter months and whether he should begin to store water in the large barrel at the back of the cottage. It probably wouldn't be the worst idea.

He walked back to the pantry and picked up a small tin containing a small smoked sausage from the middle shelf, he cut off a small piece with his pocketknife and carefully put it down on the pedal, then he replaced the sausage in the tin and put the lid back on.

While he'd been talking to Galloway, the butter had melted and now covered the bottom of the small pan in a semi-opaque glistening mass, in which he could see a faint liquid delineation of his own face. He waited until the butter started to bubble and seethe before he cracked the first egg and released it over the pan. The gelatinous mass with its shining yellow cycloidal yolk briefly shimmered in the warm puddle before slowly turning from the colour of translucent melted glass to a colour much like the ivory keys on his aunt's small upright piano.

As the eggs simmered in the pan, he dropped the eggshells into the small metal bucket in the corner, stepped over to the pantry, opened the door and lifted the thick wooden lid of the breadbox. All around the edge he could feel the small but distinctive serrated marks made by the sharp tiny teeth of the ever present night visitors.

He removed the loaf and cut off a couple of thick slices with the large serrated bread knife before replacing the loaf in the box. Then he fetched the white porcelain salt and pepper shakers and the small bottle of Worcestershire sauce from the pantry and put them on the table next to the bundle of letters.

He put the two slices of bread on the plate and when the edges of the eggs began to blister and encrust the side of the pan, he slid them and the remaining juices onto the bread and carried the plate over to the table, sat down, drizzled a bit of salt and pepper over the eggs, picked up the Worcestershire bottle and splashed a generous amount of sauce on top.

Then he picked up the cutlery and began to eat.

He was a slow and methodical eater, chewing his food much like a cow masticating cud and allowed nearly the exact amount of time to pass between each bite. After every five or six bites, he would lift the glass and take a sip of water, before returning to the task at hand.

He preferred eating alone and although there was always a lot on his mind, he made every effort not to think too much while he ate, and though he very much enjoyed his food and the amalgamation of different tastes, he treated the actual act of eating much like a time of quiet reflection.

The imaginative girl, the thought grabbing cat and the letters Galloway had just delivered were all pushed to the outer periphery of his mind as he chewed, drank and swallowed deliberately giving up the centre of his mind to obliviousness.

When he had finished eating, he carried the plate and cutlery over to the sink and placed them in the bottom, put the black rubber stopper over the drain and poured a bit of the warm water from the kettle into the sink and mechanically scrubbed at the plate and cutlery with the long yellow bristles of a small crude brush, most likely made for cleaning surfaces. Then he dried the plate and the cutlery on the towel, put them back in the cupboard, refilled the kettle and replaced it on the stove, before picking up the small brown glazed teapot standing on the small cupboard. The creamy yellowish floral design on the surface was quite unique. It looked like the crown, stem and leaves of a flower having first been pressed between pages in a book, then dipped in a viscid liquid and applied to the surface, leaving a flowing almost ghostly rendering in the otherwise dark brown glaze.

When he had first spotted the teapot in a department store window downtown, he had been transfixed by the motif and was immediately struck by the similarities with his own production of drawings. When he went inside to have a closer look he discovered that teapot had the signature of the maker and the country of origin inscribed at the bottom. It looked like it was made by someone called Fadler in the country of England, and even though the price had been exorbitant, and quite a lot more than he had been willing to spend, he had nevertheless surprised the young man at the counter when he had counted his money and bought the pot on the spot.

After the store clerk had wrapped the teapot in white tissue paper and carefully placed it at the bottom of a brown paper bag with the name Porteous printed on either side in large swirly letters, he had carried it home like a delicate treasure.

However, at home he quickly discovered that he needn't worry about breaking it. The pot, being a low rather chunky potbellied vessel with a low centre of gravity, was as sturdy as it looked. Nonetheless, he attached a certain amount of importance to it, mainly due to the beautiful floral design, and was always careful not to place it too close to the edge of the table and to make sure that the lid was properly placed before pouring the tea.

He fished out the old tea leaves and threw them in the bucket, poured a bit of warm water in the pot, replaced the lid and put the pot near the center at the back of the stove. Then he walked over to the door, put on his jacket, opened the door, picked up the small kerosene lantern standing beside the bootscraper, lit it with a match and waited until the flame took proper hold.

Then holding it slightly above his head, watching his steps in the darkness, he walked around the cottage, down to the outhouse at the very back of the yard.

He opened the door, hooked the lantern over the large fishing hook that dangled on a rather substantial rusty chain from the square ceiling.

Then he unbuttoned his trousers and lifted his jacket, hesitating briefly before quickly lowering himself on the decidedly cold but mercifully smooth surface.

Although he loathed the feeling of the unwelcoming chilled grip of freezing wood on his legs and buttocks, one of the eminent consequences of the changing weather was that the suffocating acrid smell of accumulated excreta at the bottom of the pit was much less pervasive during the winter months, and that the number of obstinate susurrating bluebottle flies was greatly reduced. He altogether abhorred the feeling of them crawling around searching his exposed skin for unsavory victuals and did his best to keep the population down by putting up several strips of fly ribbons from which the desperate buzzing of multitudinous trapped insects could inevitably be heard.

After he had relieved himself he walked over to the shed to wash his hands. The handle squeaked loudly in the quiet evening and the water that came out in a sputtering stream looked murky and red, like a clay filled river, in the feeble light from the lantern.

He quickly rubbed his hands together under the running water, turned off the tap, dried his hands on his trouser legs, picked up the lantern and headed back towards the cottage, thinking about how the day's unexpected events had unfolded.

For months nothing out of the ordinary had occurred.

Each day had been so like the one before that it almost felt like they had melded together like one continuous stream of sunrises and sunsets interspersed with feeding the hens, digging, eating, drawing and sleeping, when suddenly out of the blue a number of miscellaneous but distinct parts had been presented to him creating an ambiguous composite that was as titillating as it was peculiar.

He wondered if the mysterious girl was indeed telling the truth and that the cat was really capable of reading and disseminating thoughts or whether the whole thing had been a premeditated and extremely well executed hoax. However, he couldn't think of a single reason why she would have made up such an elaborate and volitional lie other than to amuse or preoccupy and even that explanation seemed preposterous.

When he reached the door he scraped each boot three times against the iron before blowing out the flame in the lantern.

The darkness surrounded him like an impenetrable far-reaching blanket and standing with his back against the door he instinctively pulled his jacket close across his chest.

He looked up at the sky above him and saw nothing at all.

Chapter 6

He opened the pantry door, picked up the mustard coloured box of black tea from the shelf, put his fingertips under the rim of the small round lid and popped it open. The lid released with a faint but gratifying suspiration, and he lifted the box to his nose to breathe in the content. The aroma was moderately heavy with the typical sweet maltiness that characterized the teas from the Assam region in India. He cherished the smell of tea and briefly closed his eyes to let the scent fully enfold him and to fully savor the sensation, before depositing a couple of topped spoonfuls into the dark belly of the teapot.

Then he grabbed the towel, lifted the kettle off the top of the stove, poured the steaming water into the pot and watched as the tiny leaves spiralled in the hot liquid like a minute school of blackened fish in a dark fishbowl, before replacing the lid, enclosing the floating specimens to continue their saturated ambulations in complete darkness.

He then folded the towel and placed it over the teapot as a somewhat unresolved but fairly efficient tea cosy before crossing the floor, pulling out one of the small rickety chairs and sitting down by the table. The chair groaned in dissent under his weight but soon ceased to resist and fell quiet.

The lantern above the table cast its distinguishing pattern of symbols on the walls around him as he picked up the small bundle of letters from the box, pulled out his pocketknife and carefully inserted the blade between the envelope and the string. He made a small upwards movement with his wrist and the string that bound the envelopes together snapped releasing the long fibrous filament. It floated through the air and settled silently on the scuffed floorboards, creating what appeared to be a rather casually produced silhouette of a cat in a seated position.

He folded the knife, returned it to his trouser pocket, put the bundle of letters down on the table and laid out the envelopes in front of him in three rows of three.

The first of the nine identical envelopes had the word *Begyndelsen* written on it and on the last envelope the Danish word for the end; *Slutningen* had apparently rather rapidly been scrawled. The remaining seven envelopes were completely blank.

He slowly and systematically turned the envelopes over one by one looking for clues as to their chronology.

They were unadorned, nondescript and an almost colorless greyish white, and apart from the *Begyndelsen* envelope that had already been cut open with what he assumed was the letter knife, carved from the tooth of a narwhal, that was lying on the desk in Galloway's office, there were no other noticeable differences between them and no sign that any of them had ever been opened. He collected them one by one, starting with *Slutningen* working his way backwards arranging them in the same order in which they had been received and placed them in a small bundle at the center of the table hoping that the sequence would make sense.

He wondered why someone would have written nine letters, put them into closed envelopes never to mail them and apparently never intending for anyone to read them either. Also, he was mystified by the lack of letters or numbers on the rest of the envelopes and wondered how he could possibly know if they were read in the same order they had been written. It was all quite inexplicable.

He reached out and picked up the *Begyndelsen* envelope from the top of the pile, gently inserted the tip of his forefinger and thumb and pulled out two small sheets of diaphanous paper that had been flawlessly folded. He unfurled the sheets, spread them out on the tabletop and carefully smoothened them with his hands. Since the paper was remarkably delicate, the sheets instantly behaved as directed and only the thin striations where they had been folded prevented the sheets from lying completely flat against the surface.

Even if the writing hadn't been in Danish, the cross pattern on the paper instantly brought back memories of Dannebrog, the name of the red and white national flag of Denmark, and he felt an unexpected and quite powerful surge in the central part of his chest.

He got up from the chair, took a few deep breaths, walked over to the small cupboard to retrieve a small plain teacup the color of freshly whipped cream that he placed on the corner of the stove.

He removed the towel, lifted the teapot and made a couple of small rotating movements with his hand and felt the warm liquid swirl around inside the bulbous cavity. He stopped moving his hand and waited until the interior mass seemed motionless, before he attentively poured the steaming syrup coloured liquid into the cup.

He then gently returned the pot to the top of the stove, lifted the cup and carefully carried it back to the table making sure not to spill the contents.

A fine cloudy mist, like that of a hovering haze over a pond on a late summer's evening, formed on the surface of tea, and when he walked across the floor the wispy steam rolled over the edge of the cup and enshrouded his hand in something akin to the moist breath of a large animal.

The aroma of the tea enlivened the air in the cottage and he sipped cautiously at the hot liquid before putting down the cup close the edge of the table, some distance away from the unfolded letter and wiped his hand with his shirt sleeve before sitting down.

He looked at the small achromic sheets in front of him.

The manner in which the words elegantly flowed like small equidistant babbling streams across the paper proved that the letters had been written by someone with excellent penmanship. However, he found the tiny words difficult to decipher in the fairly dim light from the lantern, so he once again rose from the chair, this time to walk over to the shelf above the fireplace to fetch a small brass candleholder in which stood a small, already halved, white candle. He also picked up a small red and blue box of matches from the Diamond Match Company and carried the items over to the table.

He placed the candleholder on the table to the left of the letter, so that he wouldn't accidentally knock over the candle when he reached for the cup of tea, and sat down, struck a match against the side of the matchbox and, leaving an unmistakable whiff of phosphor in the air, watched as the flame took hold of the small narrow piece of wood. He then held it to the blackened wick of the candle and the flame soon cast its swaying glowing light on the nearly translucent sheets.

He blew out the match and put it in the bottom of the candle holder, where it lay smoldering, briefly sending a diminutive spectral smoke signal into the air.

He reached out for the cup and pensively sipped at the tea before he leaned forward in his seat and began to read.

Dearest E,

I am happy to tell you that I have arrived in the New World alive and well. I am writing this letter warming myself by a roaring fire in a small cottage on the outskirts of a cemetery in P, a city far up on the American East Coast near the Canadian border. Outside it is colder than I have ever experienced and the snow lies so high that it entirely covers the windows. When I opened the door to the cottage the other morning, I was met by a wall of snow and I had to dig a trench to the outhouse, once in awhile standing on a small stool to see where I was going.

So many things have happened since I left that I find it difficult to explain them all in one letter. They all seem to blend together in one long sequence of images, sounds and smells that are nearly impossible to differentiate. As a consequence, I have decided to place each letter in an envelope that you can then open whenever it pleases you. Hopefully that will give you a more detailed account of my experiences and while I will attempt to write the events in order and exactly as they happened, I realize that certain elements undoubtedly will float into one another and some will be near impossible to understand.

I often imagine the two of you, the ones I hold dearest in my heart, standing side by side like two minute immovable figures at the end of the world as I must have finally disappeared from view in the glare of the setting sun. Know that not a moment has passed when you do not enter my thoughts, and that I miss you more than can ever be expressed in words. Even writing this seems somehow spiritless and uninspired and not at all a representation of how I feel when I think of you. In truth, I constantly imagine I see your beautiful features in the bark of a silver birch tree, that I hear Lise's tinkling laughter in the chirping of the exotic birds, or see the reflection of your eyes staring back at me in the sparkling surface of the nearby creek. Sometimes when I close my eyes, I believe I can feel the light touch of your hand lightly brushing my face, only to reopen my eyes to discover that the touch is nothing but that of the flowing wind.

What is merely the tiniest imperceptible crack in the fabric of time, nevertheless feels to me like an enormous rupture. It is such a long time since I last laid my weary eyes on you and held you in my arms that those days seem like they took place in another lifetime entirely. I cannot describe how much I miss you, *suffice it to say that I long for us to be together again, as I have never longed for anything else on this earth.*

Crossing the Atlantic Ocean under sail was a somewhat harrowing but also an incredibly mesmerizing experience. Being confined on a large ship, that is thrown about by giant waves, like it was nothing but a small piece of cork, in the middle of the great sea with no land in sight, soon makes you realize just how small we all are.

I have encountered things you can hardly imagine: Monstrous whales covered in layers of barnacles, with heads as big as steam engines, shooting geysers of water tens of feet into the air from their blowholes. I have seen schools of grey dolphins as smooth as pieces of polished marble, playing in the spray of the ship like a flock of smiling children, entertaining the passengers and crew alike and I have stared into the infinite sky where giant white birds with wingspans as wide as the ship itself, silently floated like living kites in the sky above without moving their wings. Believe me, I am not making this up for your sake, these are all actual things I have seen with my own two eyes.

Due to the generous loan from my uncle, I was among the few lucky ones who could afford to travel in a second-class cabin and I must say I did not envy the passengers who were crowded together in the unsanitary, vermin-infested accommodations below deck. As far as I know those poor souls had no access to fresh food or clean water, or anywhere to go to relieve themselves other than a large wooden bucket, which malodorous reeking content would be carried up by the shipboy every morning and hauled over the bulwark. The condition those people were in meant that maladies were rampant and throughout the journey, we unfortunately had more burials than can be counted on one hand. One of the three clergymen aboard the ship would read the funeral rites over the unfortunate soul, whose travels to the New World had woefully been cut short, before the deceased was placed on a large wooden plank and tipped into the fathomless sea, wrapped in a piece of old canvas. Sometimes this ceremony would be accompanied by the wailing cries of a loved one, but most often all that was heard afterwards was the continuous sound of the howling wind and the everlasting waves slapping against the hull.

In those instances, I often had to remind myself of the great desperation and hope for a new beginning that has led them, and to a certain extent myself, into this abyss of terror and wretchedness. Let us not forget that the reason most of them are here, in these unfavorable conditions, is due only to the terrible circumstances they left behind. The many accounts I heard from my fellow passengers of parents screaming in the night over the loss of yet another child, wives shivering from lack of warmth with no wood to put in the hearth and proud strong men faltering in the middle of a field surrounded by yet another season of failed crops, made me acutely aware of how fortunate my circumstances were in comparison. Whereas those wretched souls, sitting cramped in the foul smelling bowels of the ship had nothing left but the dreams of a brighter future, I was not only in good health but could pay my way in life, which, as everyone knows, makes for a much brighter future. I am sorry if this account is upsetting, but I have found it difficult to eliminate the images of those penurious persons from my mind. I often wonder what became of them in the New World and if they ever found what they were so desperately seeking.

I made a few acquaintances amongst my fellow travelers and will tell you more of them and of my arrival in the great city of New York in my next letter.

I wish it was possible to gather all the love and affection I have for you and our daughter and enclose it in this envelope, so that you could open it and instantly feel yourselves surrounded by my circumambient love.

Yours Faithfully Forever,

C

He leaned back in the chair and it made a small objectionable creak that nonetheless broke the stillness. For a while he sat there staring into the dancing flame of the candle thinking about what he had just read.

The detailed and vibrant descriptions of the journey on the sea brought back memories that had been quelled for so long. He recalled the corresponding feeling he had had when standing on the deck of the ship, leaning over the bulwark staring searchingly into the horizon only to see the seemingly unceasing sea.

He distinctly remembered how the entire world appeared to have consisted purely of water and sky, against which the ship seemed only a grain of sand and he himself smaller than a speck of dust.

When looking into the ostensibly infinite weave between the elements, he thought that there was nothing quite like immensity that could make a person feel more inconsequential and it certainly explained why so many people the world over were looking for something other than themselves to answer the ultimate question of their existence.

He closed his eyes and could almost feel the salty spray on his face and hear the persistent unfaltering sound of the waves slapping against the hull. The images of large whitish grey albatrosses floating in the endless sky, the schools of dolphins tirelessly following the boat, apparently for no other reason than to amuse themselves in the parting waves, and the pungent miasma of tar, seawater, wet hemp and bile came back to him in vivid disorder like that of a broken mirror flung carelessly through an open space.

He opened his eyes, reached for the cup at the edge of the table, lifted it to his lips and took a sip only to discover that the tea was already lukewarm. He got up from the chair, walked over to the sink and poured the tepid liquid in the drain, placed the cup on the corner on the stove, lifted the teapot and poured a fresh cup of tea that he carefully carried over to the table. He sat down and, looking into the flickering solitary flame of the burning candle, he sipped at the edge of the cup wondering what narrative was yet to come in the remaining envelopes.

Chapter 7

When he woke up the next morning it was extremely cold and a collection of ice flowers spread their intricate bloom on the interior surface of his bedroom window. He sat up and looked at the formation of sublime ice structures covering the entire surface of the glass pane. By the small crack at the bottom of the window an inconsistency had appeared in the growth pattern. The tiny blemish in the otherwise flat surface had produced an entirely different flow with an elongated flowy feathery design and he immediately wanted to get out of bed to fetch the notebook from his coat pocket to see if he could replicate the image.

He testingly put his feet down on the floor.

The floorboards felt, as he had expected, like sheets of ice against his feet and he was forced to tiptoe through the room. He quickly went over to pick up a few pieces of kindling and a split log from the bucket by the fireplace, opened the stove door, put the wood down on top of the few pieces of granite coloured coal still glowing faintly in the grey dust, and crouched down to blow on the embers. They quickly changed colour from red to light orange, the wood began to smoke and in an instant, as if it had been conjured, a small flame appeared. He waited until the kindling was fully alight before placing the log in the stove. The fire welcomed the new arrival with silky caresses from its slender flexible appendages and he closed the door and opened the vent, making sure the fire had enough air to consume its victim.

He put the kettle on the stovetop, picked up the notebook and the small pencil from one of the outside pockets in his jacket and his watch from the other and flipped open the cover to check the time before tiptoeing back into the bedroom. The bed still retained some of the warmth from his body and he pulled the cover over his leg and opened the book. He gazed at the synthesis of ice crystals for a fair amount of time before he picked up the pencil and began to draw.

It was much later in the morning when he pulled up the collar, slowly buttoned his coat, tugged on the cap covering his head, put on the grey woollen gloves and patted the pockets one by one making sure that he had remembered everything before he opened the door. Although it had snowed less than an inch overnight, the temperature had dropped significantly.

The clear frosty air immediately enveloped him, stung the inside of his nostrils and almost made him gasp, bringing an instant chill to the chiffony fibers of his lungs, and though he was wrapped in several layers of fabric he could feel the cold stealthily creeping into the gaps and perforations in his clothing filling them with gelid air.

He coughed a couple of times, clapped his hands, squinted and looked around.

The brush and the branches of the surrounding trees were altogether covered in a thick layer of brilliant frost and the flashes of early morning light coruscating through the trees made them sparkle like they had been covered in thousands of tiny pearls, making it appear as if he was looking at the ice kingdom in a fairy tale.

To add to the anomaly of this notion there was a set of animal footprints in the snow leading up to and away from his door. Furthermore, it appeared as if the animal had been sitting down on the slab of granite, because it had left behind a small furry imprint in the snow.

He wasn't exactly an authority on animal prints, and had only been told how to recognize the paw print of a black bear by Galloway, who had made certain he understood the danger of the animal, especially in the months leading up to winter where they could often be found foraging for food adjacent to the cemetery.

The Galloways had themselves had a close encounter a couple of years ago when a hungry bear had banged against their door in the middle of the night and only the loud belligerent barking from Brucy had finally scared it away.

As a secondary warrant to Brucy, a large Winchester rifle had been placed on a shelf above the front door and since the visit from the bear, neither of the Galloways' ever went to the outhouse unarmed.

"Could you imagine a worse way to go?" Galloway had said, jovially slapping Ambrosius on the back. "Sitting there in the middle of the night with your kecks around your ankles minding your own business and then suddenly finding yourself waking up with your head in the jaws of a bear. No sir, there is not a chance I'm going out of this world as bear feed."

Galloway had encouraged Ambrosius to get a rifle of his own, but for one reason or another he had never gotten around to it.

Also, the fact was that he thought it very unlikely that any guileful bear would be attracted to the mephitis emerging from the depth of the pit in the outhouse and that it therefore would be one of the safest places to hide from a hungry predator.

He bent down to have a closer look at the pawprints in the fresh snow.

From the size of the paws and the small indentation in the snow, he surmised that the nightly visitor had been a fairly sizable cat. From what he could tell the animal had walked straight to the front door, sat down for a while and then walked away following the direction from which it came.

He headed down to the shed to fetch the chicken feed and walked over to feed the hens who were already prancing around in their pen, cackling loudly as if demented, now seemingly oblivious to the snow covered ground. When he had fed the hens, he opened the hatch and picked up three newly laid eggs, carefully placed them in his jacket pocket, closed the hatch behind him and walked back to the cottage, deposited the bag of chicken feed by the door, put the brown mottled eggs in the small pan that he covered with a plate, before placing the pan at the back of the stove.

Then he picked up the chicken feed by the door, closed the door behind him and walked back to the toolshed, put the chicken feed back in the bucket, replaced the brick on the lid, lifted the large shovel of the hook, picked up the compressor, a large rectangular piece of metal at the end of a long straight handle and made sure that the hasp was properly secure, before he headed back to the cottage and began walking, following the pawprints on the ground.

As far as he could tell, the cat, if that was indeed the animal he was tracking, had followed the exact route that he had walked the day beforehand without divagating. It had softly trod a more or less direct line in the snow between the newly dug grave and the cottage.

When he reached the grave, the paw prints disappeared in a small hollow under a new rather grandiloquent grave marker. It was an approximately ten feet tall speckled granite pillar in the Ionic style, standing on a large square pedestal. It held an expertly carved effigy of a globe on top, from which a small bird, perhaps a sparrow, was currently surveying its surroundings. The plot belonged to the family of a shipping merchant who'd indubitably had the means to display that he had once been a very important person in this world.

However, when Ambrosius had come to carry out the fill in, he had been surprised to see only three people present at the funeral and even more so when not a single member of their small company looked back as they quickly departed.

Not all is what it seems.

He looked around to see if he could pick up the cat's tracks anywhere else, but apart from a couple of smaller imprints of birds in the snow on the top of the earthbox, and those of his own boots, the surrounding area was otherwise unblemished.

He removed his gloves, and quickly picked out the watch from inside his coat pocket, flipped open the lid and checked the time. He still had approximately forty minutes before the funeral assembly arrived and after having redeposited the watch, he put his gloves back on and began the last preparations. First he brushed off the accumulated snow from the cloth covering the earthbox, picked off the stones holding the cloth in place, removed the cloth and folded it and placed it next to the box. Then he used the shovel to scrape a four feet wide path around the edge of the grave and clear a small footpath leading from the gravel road to the gravesite.

When he was satisfied that everything was ready for the funeral procession, he slung the shovel over his shoulder, picked up the folded cloth, stuck it under his arm, picked up the compressor and started walking away from the grave site down the gravel path in the opposite direction of the main road.

He knew from experience that the presence of a grave digger could make some of the funeral attendees uncomfortable. He had quickly learned never to meet the gaze of a mourner directly, and if he was standing in the close vicinity of the assembly he could sometimes feel their eyes on him as if they were viewing something disagreeable, like he was a bad omen that somehow had the power to send them to an early grave. That being the case, he had early on decided to always remove himself from the proceedings and only return to the grave site to execute the fill in, when he was absolutely certain everyone had gone.

He walked down towards the giant Oaktree at the crossroad, stopped and looked back towards the site.

At first he thought that there was nobody there, but then a small movement caught his eye and he saw the girl appearing from behind the large urn belonging to the True family. Though the morning was much colder, she was wearing the exact same clothing as yesterday, and only the thin white shawl, wrapped over her shoulders, protected her from the elements. Her long black hair caught the sun and shimmered in the clear crisp light. Although he was freezing and repeatedly had to stomp his feet against the frost covered ground to keep his circulation going, she didn't seem to notice the cold at all. As a matter of fact, she appeared to be completely impervious to the change in weather as she slowly walked over to the edge of the grave, and stood there with her dainty white shoes precariously close to the edge looking into the hollow.

She didn't look around and made no indication that she had noticed him. She just stood there at the edge of the grave and stared into the pit. A little while later there was another small movement behind her and a large cat as black as a piece of velvet joined her beside the grave. It walked over to the edge of the hollow, sat down next to the girl and looked into the grave.

The girl didn't move.

In fact, as far as he could tell from this distance, there was no discernable demonstration that she had even acknowledged the cat's presence on the edge and yet something changed. It was as if a small oscillation occurred in the air around them, like a large round shivering sheet of transparent material was being held by an invisible force in front of them. He could still see both of them clearly, but it was like looking at them through a suspended pane of flexible glass.

The mirage lasted only for a few seconds and afterwards he wasn't even certain that the whole thing had not been a figment of his imagination or an optical illusion caused by atmospheric conditions, like a Fata Morgana.

However, soon after the ripple dissipated the girl turned to look at the cat.

She said something that he couldn't hear and then she turned, walked back the way she came and quickly disappeared from view.

The cat stayed behind for only a little while longer before it also got up, jumped on top of the earthbox and down on the other side. He followed its tail as it vanished from sight behind a small gravestone about twenty feet from the grave.

He took off his gloves, rubbed his eyes, picked out the watch to check the time, breathed warm air into the hollow of his freezing hands, put his gloves back on and looked towards the main road. This time of day the traffic on the main road would normally be light and he didn't expect too much activity from either horse-drawn carts or automobiles and he was fairly certain the funeral procession would be conducted according to the established schedule.

As if it had been summoned, the horse drawn hearse appeared on the road some distance away. It was steered by a heavily wrapped coachman whose face was barely visible, and steadily made its way to the cemetery entrance. It was followed by a small black clothed assembly and turned down the narrower gravel road until it came to a stop by the gravesite. The large white plumes of air coming from the frost covered nostrils of the two black horses and the fine vapor rising from their bodies, made them appear as if they were fire breathing beasts and the snow almost completely smothered the sound of both hooves and wheels, making the hearse's progress eerily quiet.

The congregation was led by the imposing figure of pastor Godfrey who walked the assembly over to the grave and gently directed the members to take up their places around the hollow. When the small congregation had flanked both sides, pastor Godfrey took his place at the head of the grave and nodded in the direction of the hearse. A few heads turned to cast furtive looks, as two of the four pallbearers standing at the back of the hearse reached up to swing open the doors and slide out the darkly varnished Victorian style casket. The four men lifted it in concert and placed it on their shoulders, while two other men positioned the two pieces of rope at the end of the grave. Then the four men slowly walked in unison to the relevant spot and carefully set down the casket on the waiting ropes.

Although he couldn't hear much more than a couple of fragments of Godfrey's muffled voice Ambrosius kept his eyes on the funeral party. Because of the freezing cold, he could tell pastor Godfrey had to move rather quickly through the required rites and a lot quicker than Ambrosius had expected. Soon one of the women went over to the earthbox to scoop up a small collection of dirt, that she hesitantly carried over and threw into the grave. She repeated the action two more times, each time a little slower than the previous, before the man standing to the side of the pastor took the small silver shovel from her trembling hand.

The woman turned her back to the grave, put her head in her hands and began to wail.

Her voice was like a drawn-out inefficacious chant filled with lament and sorrow. It moved swiftly through the crystal air and reverberated against the snow covered gravestones until finally fading away like a desiccated echo.

The woman then fell to her knees and it was as if this desolate action brought the entire world to a halt. She collapsed in the snow and it took more than a few seconds before three of the people in the company rushed to her side, helped her to her feet and gently escorted the still lachrymose woman away from the scene.

After the convocation departed, pastor Godfrey lifted his hand indicating that it was all clear, and Ambrosius began trudging back towards the grave to commence the fill in.

As soon as he reached the grave it began to snow.

He looked at the thick layer of leaden flocculent clouds inauspiciously gathering in the horizon and pulled the collar of his coat close against the wind that had picked up significantly.

He looked into the grave.

The casket standing at the bottom was made of beautifully carved walnut, not, as it was common these days, of an alloy or steel. Even down there in the scant light, the surface shone like that of a grand piano. Only the small peppery particles of frozen dirt disrupted the otherwise burnished surface. He thought about the many hours the carpenter must have spent in creating this exquisite object and the pride he must have felt in putting the last finishing touches to an article that from the outset faced the unfortunate and inescapable outcome to be interred deep in the ground, soiled from the inside by decaying gaseous matter and attacked by beetles and grubs from the outside until finally disintegrating.

He walked over to the earthbox and as he lifted the shovel off his shoulder and stuck it into the mound of soil, he tried hard not to picture the man inside the casket, forever resting in total absence of light.

The frozen surface layer broke into small fragments that slid down the small hill, like a miniature avalanche, tumbled over the edge of the box and landed by his feet in a small disintegrated pile.

He expertly threw the first shovel of soil down between the wall and the casket. Although it was a fairly laborious task, he knew it was important to be meticulous and fill the grave slowly and systematically to ensure that there were no pockets of air that could cause unsightly droops on the surface later on.

He walked around the pit and deposited the soil evenly.

When the lid appeared as a small rectangular raft in a murky pond, he grabbed the compressor and, as he walked around the grave, lifted the tool and repeatedly thumped the soil around the casket. The exercise was gruelling and strained his entire body. Nevertheless, he kept going until the trench around the casket was reasonably compacted and the muscles in his shoulders and neck were burning with pain.

He let go of the compressor and it tumbled over and landed next to the earthbox.

Then he stretched his arms over his head to alleviate the burning sensation.

The snow had changed from miniscule pieces of ice to quite substantial flakes that nearly obscured his view. Judging from the already abundant accumulated mass it wouldn't take long before his route home to the cottage would be close to impassable.

He picked up the shovel and started shovelling.

He was an efficient and practiced worker and the grave slowly but surely filled in.

Though it was freezing cold the strenuous work made him sweat profusely.

He suddenly thought he heard the voice of a girl, coming from somewhere through the now dense snowfall.

He immediately stopped shovelling and listened attentively.

She was seemingly humming what he believed to be the first bars of Brahms' Requiem.

Her beautiful voice increased in strength as she got closer.

She finally appeared walking through the snow shower like an apparition and walked over to where he was standing. Although it was well below freezing and the wind had picked up significantly, she appeared completely unaffected by the change in weather, looking peculiarly lambent in the falling snow.

She stopped humming and looked up at him.

"Good morning Moerk. How are you today? It's an extraordinarily fine day to be interred, wouldn't you agree? Not only will this lucky individual be covered in soil, but a fine white duvet will be spread on top, so that he can rest properly in the apparently blissful oblivion of unending time."

She spread her hands and slowly twirled around in the falling snow and yet it looked like none of the falling flakes came to rest on her.

"I suppose so," he responded absentmindedly.

The piece of music she'd been humming was still resounding in his mind.

"What was the tune you were singing just now?"

"Oh, I don't know. It was just something the cat was thinking about earlier. I guess it got stuck in my mind. To be honest I wasn't really paying attention, there were a lot of subdued mutterings and repetitions of notes, so I did my best not to concentrate too hard."

There was a slight attitude in the tone of her voice, like someone who was clearly bored by recitals and whose mind would quite easily wander.

"So you don't actually know who wrote that piece of music?" he asked curiously.

"No I can't say that I do, though I must have done something right if it stuck in my mind, which I suppose is acceptable."

She made a small movement with her head that sent her long black hair cascading atop the white shawl covering her shoulders.

Once more, not a single snowflake got caught in the graceful manoeuvre.

"But I don't understand. How did you get to know this particular piece? I know that piece of music quite well. It's by a composer named Johannes Brahms and if I am not mistaken the tune you just hummed is the beginning bars to his Requiem."

"Oh," she said, "I didn't realize that. Like I told you: the cat was working through some thoughts, and the piece of music must have gotten stuck in my head. It's quite a nice tune though don't you think?"

"Yes I do, but that doesn't quite explain how the cat was thinking about a piece of music that was written more than thirty years ago."

"Is that important?" she asked.

"Is what important?"

"That it was written so long ago?"

"No, I suppose it's not really that important. I am just curious to know when you learned that piece of music. Have you ever heard it before?"

"No, the first time I heard it was just a moment ago, right before I came over here," she replied casually.

"Are you absolutely sure?"

"Yes of course I am sure. I told you I just heard it and that's the reason why I was humming it."

He stared at her ingenuous face through the flickering snow.

"That's quite incredible," he said after a while.

"Perhaps so," she said looking up at him with a somewhat preoccupied look on her face.

"Moerk, I came to tell you that we probably won't be seeing each other for quite some time."

"Why is that?" The few words scattered in a sudden gust of wind.

"What did you say?"

He shielded his mouth with his hand and leaned a bit closer to her.

"Why won't we be seeing each other?"

"Because of this." She spread out her arms and gestured to the descending snow. "You won't be digging graves for the foreseeable future, so that means I won't be seeing you." She tilted her head and looked at him through the now plummeting snow.

"I came to say goodbye Moerk. I know we have only just met each other and that I do not know you as well as I had wanted, but I truly hope you have a good winter and that your long dark days will be filled with adventure. Perhaps one day we shall meet again."

She looked straight into his eyes, and clasped her hands in front of her.

"I am so happy we became acquainted," she added somberly.

"But where are you going?" he asked, perplexed by the turn of events. "Are you not going to be around? I thought that you said you lived close by."

"Don't worry about me. I promise you, I am not going to be that far away."

She smiled and the sheen of her small perfect teeth commingled with the flakes of falling snow.

"Goodbye Moerk."

She curtsied, turned around and was rapidly absorbed by the snowstorm.

He had been too confounded by the latest event to reply.

"....ease ook a..er ..e cat." He heard the disintegrating words in the gusting wind.

"What?" He called after her. "What did you say?"

"The cat." Her voice was already coming from some distance away. "Look...for.....hecat."

"Look for the cat?" He shouted into the whiteout.

"Yehhs," came the affirmative whisper before her voice was drowned out by the flurry.

For a while he just stood there crestfallen, looking into the heavy snowfall. Then he finally woke himself from the light trance and went back to work.

He still had a couple of hours of shoveling left and he noticed a particular tension building. Not that the job was especially difficult at this point, even with the falling snow there was not much to think about, just one shovel after another being thrown into the open grave until it was filled. However, he hadn't planned for the intensity of the snowfall and after the fill in, he still had to disassemble the earthbox and go back to the toolshed to pick up the cart to haul the boards back. With the amount of snow falling that whole process might turn out to be quite an arduous task.

While he worked, he intermittently looked for the cat, but it was close to impossible to see more than about ten feet in front of him and so far he had seen no sign of it.

He wondered if it would even be possible to find the creature in this weather and genuinely hoped that the cat had found shelter somewhere else.

After another hour of work, he took apart the earthbox and continued the fill in until a smooth domed hill had formed above the grave. He had learned to leave about eight to ten inches of soil at the highest point assuring a proper fallback when the soil settled. If he had calculated correctly it might not be necessary to add any additional soil in spring when the saturated ground would begin to form a solid lock around the casket.

It took an additional hour to plod his way back to the cottage, fetch the cart and drag it through the already quite substantial drifts of snow to pick up the equipment.

He placed the boards, the piece of fabric, the compressor and shovel on the bed of the cart and looked around to see if he could spot the cat anywhere. He thought about calling out to it, but couldn't think of anything to say other than kitty kitty and when he couldn't see it anywhere in the close vicinity, he began instead the onerous task of dragging the heavy cart through the accumulated snow.

He could hardly see more than a couple of feet in front of him and with one hand shielding his face, he kept his eyes locked on the ground not to lose the earlier tracks that were now almost obliterated by the blowing wind.

As he fought his way through the whiteout, the almost inconceivable struggle Sir Franklin and his men must have faced when they decided to abandon Erebus and Terror to begin their doomed journey flashed through his mind, and influenced by the image of dead bodies scattered in a frozen wasteland, he pulled at the cart even harder than necessary to reach the toolshed.

Twice he stopped to catch his breath and each time he looked behind him to see if the cat was following him, but there was nothing but his own laborious tracks in between those left by the broad wheels of the cart.

When he finally reached the tool shed, he forced open the door against the blasting wind, carried the boards inside to lean them up against the back wall and dragged the cart still holding the piece of fabric and the compressor to the end of the shed. He then grabbed the shovel and shoveled a path from the chicken coop to the shed and from the shed to the cottage, before trudging back to the shed to pick up the chicken feed and back to the coop to clear the walkway and a fairly large spot on the ground on which he spread a generous amount of feed. He finally checked that the small water bowl that he had placed inside the coop was still liquid before he returned the feed to the shed.

He picked up a small square hammer and twenty or so long sticks pointed at one end with a fairly large hole drilled through at the other, left a bunch at the toolshed, carried a bunch of them to the front of the cottage, a bunch to the outhouse and the last bunch to the chicken coop and dropped them in the snow. He then proceeded to hammer the pointed end into the ground at about six to eight feet intervals between the cottage and the outhouse, from the outhouse to the shed and from the shed to the coop.

It was slow moving work in the swirling snow, but when he had finally constructed what looked like a somewhat makeshift fence, he grabbed a bundle of rope and fastened one end by the stick at the cottage and ran the rope through the rest of the sticks until he had created a secure connecting route between the buildings.

Then he went back to the shed, hung the hammer on the wall, closed the door and dropped the hasp. Although it was quite a heavy piece of iron, the metallic clatter was entirely smothered by the howling wind.

He turned around and had only taken about ten steps on the path to the cottage when something in front of him compelled him to stop. On the doorstep in the middle of a small snowdrift sat the large black cat. At first he thought that he was imagining things and that the black spot in the white snow was just a trick of his mind playing back a peculiar sequence of sibylline images. However, looking carefully at the image in front of him he most definitely saw that of a black cat in the white snow, and for the second time that day he had the feeling that he was looking at something that would only occur in an enchanted fairy tale.

He took a couple of steps closer to the cat, fearful that he might
scare it away, but when he reached the cottage, the cat, with eyes the colour of a cloudless sky, looked up at him as if it had already anticipated his arrival. It stood up, stretched its front legs, pointing its tail in the air and walked around on the spot making a fresh set of tracks in the snow as if circling an invisible pole, apparently waiting for him to let it in.

He removed his glove and fished the large key out of his pocket,
unlocked and opened the door and before he had taken a single step, the cat had already jumped over the drift of snow and disappeared into the cottage.

Chapter 8

The presence of the cat inside the cottage was incontrovertible.

It purposefully moved around the room like it was recording the surface area and features in the space to somehow construct a detailed cognitive map. When it was seemingly satisfied with its findings, it disappeared into the bedroom where it performed a similar examination, then it jumped up on the bed and walked back and forth on the faded cover before lying down in the middle of the bed with its head on its paws.

Even from where he was standing he could see its eyes sparkle and he very much had the feeling he was being watched.

He had the distinct impression that something in the cottage had changed, beyond the obvious presence of the cat. There was something imperceptible in the air, like a slightly charged atmosphere as if the cat had instantly permeated the space with its being much like warmth emanating from a fireplace.

As he removed his gloves, hung the jacket and the cap on the hook at the back of the door, and proceeded to the fireplace to light a fire, he could feel an unmistakable difference in the room and wondered if an ordinary cat could have such an intense effect on its surroundings. His limited knowledge of felines was mainly based on the farm cats from his youth, and then only the younger ones who would allow him to pet them. They had all been mousers and none of them had had an unequivocal personality.

This cat was however unquestionably different.

He bent down and struck a match. The kindling had already been placed in the form of a small tepee at the bottom of the grate and all he had to do was hold the small flame to the curled up piece of newspaper in the center.

The fire took hold of the dried out branches and quickly covered the walls in a flowy glow.

While he prepared his meal, a couple of slices of bread with fried eggs and dried sausage, he thought about the girl and her whereabouts. For reasons he could not quite explain, he was concerned about her and her rapid disappearance gnawed at him like a nanoscopic rodent. He was also curious why she had said that they wouldn't see each other for some time. Even though the ground was frozen and he couldn't dig, he would still be performing other duties around the cemetery. Galloway had informed him that although the cemetery had a tendency to slow down in winter, he could always find something to do.

He could cut down brush and make sure that the paths were properly cleared or help Svensson repair the chipped or cracked grave markers.

While he understood that the girl might not have known about the other duties that came with the job, he still couldn't help wondering, why she had been so sure that they wouldn't meet again.

It was almost as if she had had a feeling that something was about to happen.

Something imminent.

While the eggs were simmering in the pan, spreading their pervading aroma in the cottage, he found a small ceramic bowl, filled it with water and placed the bowl on the floor between the sink and the fireplace, then he walked over to the pantry to look for something for the cat. He really had no idea what to feed it, but in the back of one of the shelves, he found a piece of beef jerky. It was the colour and texture of a corrugated piece of iron and nearly as tough so he put it on a plate, poured a cup of lukewarm water over it and left it to soak. He filled the kettle, put it on the stove, picked up his food and a glass of water and walked over to the table. Although it was early in the afternoon, the low light of the stormy day darkened the cottage, so he put the plate and the glass down on the tabletop before striking a match to light the candle in the lantern.

The flame flickered slightly before growing in strength, sending a warm amber light through the space, casting the quotidian ethereal shapes on the walls around him.

The lantern had, according to pastor Godfrey, at some point in the past likely belonged to a theologian, although he couldn't be certain of the denomination. The structure of the lantern itself and the configuration of the small cutouts were allegedly a nexus of ideograms, that at some point had carried a kind of shrouded secret. Like a cryptic signal between brothers to distinguish themselves from others. Godfrey thought that it was most likely fabricated and used by a Carmelite, Franciscan or an Augustinian to communicate a particular allegiance to the true faith.

Although he had paid attention to Godfrey and genuinely appreciated the mystery, Ambrosius wasn't especially concerned with the possible code or with the supposedly secretive communication, he merely enjoyed the way the illuminated images floated on the walls as the lantern slowly turned on the hook.

He sat down and began to eat.

As per usual he attempted to empty his mind while he slowly masticated, yet he was somewhat distracted by the melodious vibratory sound coming from the other room.

When he finished eating, he put the plate and cutlery in the sink, poured a bit of warm water in the teapot, slushed it around a couple of times before using it to rinse the dishes. Then he fetched the square canister from the pantry and prepared the tea.

He prodded at the piece of jerky with his finger. It had absorbed some of the water, and now had the consistency of a slightly dried out earthworm. He removed it from the plate, cut the meat into small pieces on the chopping board, grabbed another ceramic bowl from the cupboard, put the meat in the bowl and placed it on the ground next to the water bowl.

He looked at the now quiet, sleeping cat through the open door.

He poured a cup of tea and carried it over to the table, gently placed it near the edge and picked up the blank envelope lying on the top of the pile. For a moment he thought about choosing another, but he pulled out his pocketknife, sliced open the envelope, folded the knife and deposited it in his trouser pocket, before removing five small pieces of paper that he put on the table and carefully flattened with the palm of his hand.

The small studious writing snaked across the page like miniscule pathways.

He lifted the cup and sipped at its hot contents, replaced it on the table, leaned forward and began to read.

Dearest E,

I cannot possibly express in words how much I miss you. You and my dear little one are forever in my thoughts and as I count the days without you by my side, they seem to go by so incredibly slowly, like time itself is slowly being pulled apart, with us positioned as antithetical poles at either end.

Here the days are long and cold. The snow keeps falling and seems to never end. To be perfectly honest, I never imagined there could be that much snow outside of the arctic circle. The roads in or out of this place are covered in a new layer of snow almost daily and are nearly impossible to keep open, which has made it difficult for me to travel anywhere. I spend the majority of my time drawing and reading or writing. I don't see many people, as the cottage is quite remote and few are bold enough to make the trip out here, and then only to pay their respects to their beloved departed. I have attempted to speak with a few of the visitors, but they seem to regard me with a certain weariness and the conversations often stall when I tell them why I am here.

If I remember correctly, I promised you in my last letter that I would tell you more of my fellow travellers and of my encounter with the great city of New York. While I assure you that I will get to that soon enough, something else occurred on board the ship, that I really must tell you.

I am fully aware that what I am about to write down will sound utterly outlandish to you, and I can assure you that it was, and still is, extremely perplexing to me. I have nevertheless decided to share it with you, not only because I have no one else to share it with, but because I believe you will trust that I am not making any of it up. I promise you that I have not been drinking too much wine or consuming any other form of remedies or opiates. What follows below is indeed a truthful account of my experiences.

One evening, or perhaps it was already early in the night, about three weeks into my journey, I was standing alone on the deck at the back of the ship. I had found it especially difficult to sleep due to the constant creaking of the wood and the slapping of the waves against the hull. The unabating sounds would keep me awake well into the night, and even though I was dog tired, I often took to wandering around the ship appeasing my fatigued mind until I could fall into a restless slumber.

This particular night was clear and cool with millions of stars shining in the sky above, each casting its radiant light on the waves below, thereby turning the entire ocean into a colossal illuminated fluid spectacle. I was staring into the firmament above, wondering about our inherent vulnerability against the vastness, when I suddenly became aware that I wasn't alone.

I looked around to see if anyone had joined me on the deck, but except for the large white ship's cat sitting some feet away, there was no one there. Yet I had an unmistakable feeling that someone else was present in the space. So I did what I would normally do in circumstances where I suspect that there is someone around that I can't necessarily see, and although I felt somewhat foolish at the time, I nonetheless whispered: 'Hello, is anybody there?' into the night.

At first everything was quiet and I thought that I had been imagining things, but then from somewhere indistinct came an answer. It was loud and clear, spoken with a tonality that unveiled nothing of the person who did the speaking and with no discernable accent or dialect.
As a matter of fact, what sounded like a perfect voice had answered.

'Yes,'' it said.

I must confess to be rather shocked by this unexpected utterance and I immediately looked around to see if I could spot the source of the voice, but apart from the sailor standing by the wheel at the helm quite some distance away, I could see no one. Somewhat mystified as to who would be playing this trick on me, I called out: "Please show thyself, whoever you are."

The sailor at the helm waived his hand.

"Good evening Sir," he shouted across the ship. His voice was gruff from too much wine and tobacco and not at all like the voice I had just heard. I waved back informally, pretending to be on my way down to the cabins, when I heard the voice once more.

"You asked if I was here, and here I am. You thought there was somebody else around, and there is." It sounded like a peculiar riddle materializing from somewhere indeterminate.

"Where are you?" I said turning around looking for the source of the voice.

"Right here." Again the voice appeared to be coming from a place right in front of me.

"*How is it that I can't see you?*" *I asked somewhat nervously.*

"*But you can see me.*" *The voice was perspicuous, but entirely unpretentious.*

"*I am afraid I cannot,*" *I said, now slightly alarmed that someone was performing a prestidigitation purely for their own entertainment.*

Then I suddenly realized that I had been looking at the cat the entire time I was talking. I stopped and stared at it and it turned its head and looked back at me with eyes that were like a pair of large polished sapphires. If I told you they were glowing in the night, it wouldn't be far removed from the way they appeared to me.

"*I told you, you could see me.*"

It was a voice devoid of gender, without accentuation or social implication and without personal or geographical history. It was utterly immaculate and unambiguous, and though the cat was sitting on the deck right in front of me, it was clear that it wasn't actually speaking.

I don't know how to fully explain this, without sounding like I have lost my facilities, but the fact is that the cat seemed to speak inside my head, as if it was transferring whatever it was thinking directly to my mind.

"*This is not possible,*" *I said aloud.* "*It is not possible. This is not actually happening. I must be more exhausted than I realised and this episode is just a figment of my anxious mind.*"

I rubbed my face with my hands and took some deep breaths trying to retain my focus.

"*No,*" *said the cat,* "*I am not a figment of your imagination. I am here and what you hear is real.*" *It stood up and walked around in a circle before sitting down again.*

"*This cannot be happening! I am clearly losing my mind,*" *I said, fearful that that was indeed the case.*

"*You are not losing anything,*" *said the cat staring at me with its large azure eyes.* "*You are in fact gaining something. Something of great value.*"

"*What can I possibly gain of great value from a talking cat?*" *I responded somewhat truculently, at the same time thinking that I could never share this conversation with anyone. I was at that point convinced that I was showing symptoms of a deranged and unbalanced soul.*

"Time," the cat said rather cryptically, "you will be gaining time."

"That's preposterous," I said contemptuously. "No one gains time, it's a physical improbability. Even a small child knows that time only moves forward, and no matter what you do there is no stopping it."

"Is that so?" said the cat.

"Yes it is," I said defiantly. "You can't possibly gain time; it goes against the natural physical laws. There's no escaping time and you most certainly can't gain it. How could you even gain something that is continual if you can't contain it or stop its flow? It's simply not possible."

In my discountenance, I was completely forgetting that I was having an argument with a cat on a ship in the middle of the ocean.

The cat stared at me with eyes as blue as a mountain lake. I had the strangest feeling it was smiling in the starlit night.

"We shall see," it said.

Then it ran across the deck and disappeared down the stairs.

"What shall we see?" I called after it.

The only response was the eternal sound of the sloshing waves.

I stood on the deck looking at the spot where the cat had disappeared, thinking that I must have fantasized the entire event. There was no rational explanation for what had just occurred, other than that my mind was so exhausted from the journey and lack of proper sleep that I had imagined the cat talking to me as an illusion, or worse: That I was slowly entering into a state of madness, which I very much hoped was not the case.

I decided that the former explanation was probably the cause for the disconcerting deviation and immediately retired to my cabin to get some rest. For the first time in many weeks, I at once fell into a deep sleep and had one of the most bizarre and vivid dreams I have ever had.

I dreamt that I was smaller than anything but also that I wasn't made of anything and therefore bigger than everything. I had no substance or colour. It was as if everything that is and everything that was, was happening at the same time and moved around effortlessly in a gigantic fluctuant space. I felt like I was moving in all directions, but that there was no before or after, everything was happening both to me and in me. I saw the earth, the moon and the sun from *somewhere far away and I was in the center, and at the same time on the edge of everything. I was the ocean, the land and the sky and I felt very happy, and I can remember thinking: 'Yes, this is exactly where I was always supposed to be.'*

I awoke rather late the next morning confused about what I had dreamt, but also strangely refreshed by finally having been able to sleep. I was thinking that the talking cat most likely had been part of the dream, and I almost smiled to myself thinking about the absurdity of having had a conversation about the design of time with a ship's cat in the middle of the night. I felt better than I had in weeks, and it was only when I returned to the deck a little later in the day, that the incontestable proof of the previous night's encounter was presented to me. The cat was sitting in exactly the same spot as the night before, staring into the distance with its clear blue eyes. When I cautiously approached, it cocked its head slightly and looked at me knowingly.

I knew then that the event from the previous night was not something that I had imagined. As a further matter, the cat looked at me and, although it didn't speak, it almost imperceptibly nodded its head, subtly but plainly confirming our earlier encounter and also unequivocally making me aware that it knew what I had dreamt. I don't know what to say about these events, other than that I have described them to you in the exact way that they occurred. At this point I don't know what they mean or what exactly the cat is seeking to communicate, all I know is that it's somehow talking to me, and that I had an extremely vivid dream following our encounter. I promise you that I am not losing my mind and that everything else around me is exactly as usual, but as you can probably imagine, I have been somewhat preoccupied with this unexpected turn of events. However, I haven't forgotten that I promised you a more comprehensive account of my fellow travellers and the arrival in the city of New York. You shall receive both in my next letter.

Until then I wish I could assemble all the love and tenderness I have for you and our daughter and send it to you on a ray of sunshine, so that you could bathe in its warm and comforting glow.

Yours Faithfully Forever,

C

He carefully folded the papers, put them back in the envelope and laid the envelope on top of the *Januar* envelope to the left of the small stack of envelopes.

What he had just read was incredibly strange and as mystifying as Veronica's fanciful tale of the mind-reading cat that was currently lying on the bed in the adjacent room. However, what he had found the most disturbing was not so much the fact that the cat had talked, as much as the description of the colour of the cat's eyes. It was beyond uncanny and caused him to feel, if not exactly disturbed, at least a bit uneasy.

What were the chances that his predecessor had not only come across a cat that could apparently telecommunicate, but a cat with the same colour eyes as the one that was currently asleep on his bed? Even though he realized that there must be thousands upon thousands of cats with blue eyes, the fact that the author had come across one and written about it in letters that he was now reading, struck him as an almost inconceivable coincidence.

He leant back in the chair, turned his head and looked at the dark mass lying on the bed in the other room. As far as he could tell, it hadn't moved an inch while he had been reading.

As he picked up his cup and got up from the chair, he looked at the cat in the other room. Either it was fast asleep or it was completely oblivious to his presence, because it didn't seem to acknowledge that he was moving around.

He walked over to the fireplace, placed the cup on the shelf while he grabbed the poker, bent down and poked at the burning log.

The glowing mass broke into three separate pieces sending forth a small discharge of miniscule orange particles that danced in the air like an assembly of small shooting stars, rising towards the ceiling.

Holding onto the shelf he reached down and pulled out a split log from the bucket and gently placed it in the center of the bright embers, then he picked up another log and the cup, walked over to the stove, placed the cup on the stove top, picked up the tea towel, turned the handle and opened the cast iron door. He threw the log into the burning belly of the stove, closed the door, poured another cup of tea, replaced the tea towel on the teapot and walked over to the window.

The windowsill was almost entirely covered in snow.

Through the tiny slit at the top, it was impossible to see anything outside but a monochromatic flurry of snow. He thought about opening the door, but decided against it. It wouldn't matter anyway. At some point he would have to dig his way to the outhouse and he was sure he would find out then just how much snow had fallen.

He went back to the table and sat down.

In the other room the cat showed no signs of waking up.

He thought about the letter and how preposterous everything sounded.

A talking ship's cat that for reasons unknown had promised the author the impossible gift of time, the author's outlandish dream and his realization that the cat could read his mind was not only unbelievable, but surely the ravings of a deeply disturbed man. Yet, there was something about the order in which the letters had been written and the honesty of the writer that for some reason or other made the narrative seem less ridiculous.

The author had obviously questioned his own sanity and knew that having a cat silently communicating with him was something that should not be shared with anyone in case they would deem him to be mentally unfit, thereby establishing a certain element of truth to his otherwise insupportable account.

Also, the fact that the letters were apparently written long after the events took place added another plausible element to the narrative.

Why would anyone lie about such a deranged story if they themselves were frightened that they would be labeled certifiable?

He took a sip at the teas and slowly drummed his fingers on the tabletop while humming the opening bars to Brahms' second symphony.

Chapter 9

It was close to dusk when he finally returned to the cottage.

The snow was still coming down like a massive counterpane blanketing the landscape, and it had taken him the good part of an hour to dig a trench to the outhouse following the rope running through the nearly buried sticks in the ground. After having relieved himself in the outhouse, he had dug another trench from the outhouse to the toolshed and finally from the shed to the chicken coop. When he reached the coop he was not surprised to see all the hens inside huddled up against the cold. They looked like a prodigious six-headed feathery monster. He spread a handful of feed by the door and grabbed some snow and put it in the water bowl, and while the birds untangled from each other and had a bit of an almost silent dust up, their cackling drowned in the howling wind, he cleared a large area on the ground and scraped the snow off the walkway before closing the hatch for the night.

He went back to the cottage and cleared a small square on the ground to the left of the door. Then he stomped his feet on the slab of granite, opened the door, stepped into the cottage and quickly closed the door behind him.

The shade of evening was by now covering the interior of the cottage and it took his eyes a while to adjust in the lack of light, but when they finally did, the first thing he noticed was the cat in the center of the table. It was sitting on top of the letters lying underneath the unlit lantern. If he hadn't known it to be alive, he would have assumed the cat was a taxidermied specimen. It sat perfectly still, looking straight ahead, it's light blue eyes gleaming like ice crystals in the gloomy room.

He put the shovel down by the door, took off his cap and gloves, slowly unbuttoned his jacket before removing it and hanging it on the hook on the back of the door.

When he had hung up his jacket, he slowly turned around. The sedentary cat had watched the entire sequence as if it was carefully examining his every move.

The absence of movement engulfed the space and he found that he couldn't meet the cat's cold unblinking stare. He felt as if its penetrating gaze was scrutinizing him, searching for an imperceptible veiled secret that he himself was not aware of, and he suddenly felt extremely exposed, like the animal on the table had the power to somehow make visible what should not be seen.

The sensation lasted for a while and was finally broken when the cat stood up.

It slowly walked across the table and almost silently jumped off the edge. He could feel the vibrations in the soles of his feet as it landed on the floorboards. It stretched its long lean body and dug its front claws in and scratched at the already abraded surface. Then it sauntered across the floor to the food bowl. It sniffed briefly at the jerky, but was apparently displeased, because it passed it by and crouched at the water bowl to lap at the water instead.

He slowly walked across the floor to the pantry, opened the door and searched the shelves, wondering what to cook. In the end he grabbed a piece of salted pork, a small handful of dried apple slices and five small potatoes that he put in a pot and carried over to the sink. He sincerely hoped the pipe hadn't frozen yet and he was relieved to hear the sound of sputtering water. He filled the pot and placed it on the stove top.

The cat had finished drinking and was now sitting by the fireplace cleaning itself. It licked its paw and ran it across its ears and face several times, before changing paws and repeating the action. Its eyes were closed and the sound of its contented purr was the only sound in the room.

He walked over to the fireplace and reached into the bucket, picked up a log and placed it on the smoldering embers in the grate.

The cat refused to acknowledge his presence; it kept its eyes closed and continued to clean itself.

He returned to the stove where the water in the pot had almost come to a boil. He fetched a fork from the cupboard and fished out the fleshy lump of salted pork and put it on the pan, then he cut off a generous piece of butter and scraped it off against the inside of the pan. It immediately slid down the side, towards the pinkish chunk, leaving a greasy trail behind it. After a while the butter began to brown and he sprinkled some salt and pepper on the meat and kept turning it over in the small sputtering pool of grease until it had attained the required colour. He placed the pan at the back of the stove while he strained the potatoes and the now viscous apple slices. He put the ingredients on a plate, poured the remaining browned butter over the pork, filled a glass of water, stuck the Worcestershire sauce under his elbow and carried the ensemble over to the table where he gently deposited it before sliding out the chair and sitting down.

The cat had curled up in front of the fireplace. Its shiny black coat, reflecting in the glowing fire, made it appear as if it was itself a large piece of smoldering coal.

He drizzled a bit of sauce over the pork, put the bottle back on the table, cleared his mind from stories of mind reading blue eyed cats and began to eat.

Slowly and systematically the food disappeared from his plate and the water from his glass. While he chewed, he gazed into the space in front of him, his mind blank like a snowdrift, and his eyes seeing nothing.

After he finished eating, he sat for a while staring into the distance, slowly slipping out of the reverie, allowing the collections of thoughts to gradually percolate through the filters of his mind.

He then put the cutlery on the plate, picked it up and carried it across the room and gently deposited it at the bottom of the sink. He poured a bit of warm water in the teapot, filled the kettle and put it back on the stove. Then he picked up the bottle of sauce from the table, put it back on the shelf in the pantry and grabbed the tea container and placed it on the corner at the back of the stove.

Before making the tea, he bent down and checked the mouse traps standing in the dark corners at the bottom of the pantry.

Peculiarly, there were no rodents in either of the traps and the bait hadn't been touched. Normally at least one of the traps would contain a lifeless victim staring into space with beady emotionless eyes and its broken back firmly affixed to the wooden platform.

He looked at the curled up, sleeping cat at the fireplace and wondered if the rodents were just a lot more careful now that a predator had moved into their domain. He replaced the traps, washed and dried his hands, opened the container of tea and let the tantalizing aroma fill his nostrils. He then prepared the tea, wrapped the teatowel around the teapot, fetched the white porcelain cup from the cupboard, poured a bit of hot water in it and placed it on the stove.

He stood by the stove waiting for the tea to reach its optimal strength, before he poured the pleasant smelling honey coloured tea into the cup and carefully carried it to the table, gently set it down on the edge, pulled out the chair and sat down.

The cat was still asleep when he reached for the next envelope on the top of the pile.

He picked it up and slid the knife into the small opening and calmly ran it across the top. The paper gave way almost silently and he pulled out four small feathery pieces of paper, laid them on the table and gently flattened them with his hand.

The candle in the lantern didn't provide enough light, so he got up from the chair, quietly walked over to the fireplace to pick up the candle holder and the matches. He carried the holder back to the table, struck a match and lit the candle. A candescent glow, like that of a small enervated sun, slowly emanated its sprawling light across the surface of the table. He lifted the cup, took a sip of the hot, slightly bitter but superlative liquid, before replacing the cup near the edge of the table.

He waited until his eyes had adjusted to the light before he leaned forward in the chair and once more began to read.

Dearest E

I miss you more each day that passes. Whenever I think of you and the little one sitting in the flickering sunlight under the willow tree at the edge of the pond, my heart aches like it is in the grip of a vice and the pit of my gut feels like a leadened hollow. My longing for your company is ineffable.

In my uneasy sleep I often see your beautiful face, framed in your soft golden hair and I hear your laughter chime like a small string of bells moving in the subtle flow of a summer's breeze. Alas, when I awake to my parlous state, your features slowly disappear in a nebulous haze and the pleasant sound of your voice is drowned by the endless beating of the waves against the creaking hull. Sometimes, when I absentmindedly walk on the deck or watch the waves, I imagine having a cheerful conversation with our daughter, in which I effortlessly answer her endearing questions about the name of a certain knot or the use of a particular rope aboard the ship. She is always thrilled to hear my answers, although I must admit that some are invented on the spot, as I am not at all knowledgeable when it comes to the anatomy of a ship. I believe she would have found the trip across the sea a most fascinating experience.

The memory of the two of you never leaves me and no matter what happens in the world, you will be part of me for all eternity.

I recall promising you more information about my fellow travelers and my arrival in the city of New York. I swear to you that I shall keep that promise and that I will describe in more detail the acquaintances I have made and the immensity of the greatest city in the world. However, other events have recently dominated my thoughts and I fear that if I don't divulge what happened onboard the ship, I might fail to recall the exact circumstances.

As it had become customary, I was walking up and down on the lower deck of the ship late one evening. This time I was in the company of one of the other passengers.

Brother Thommel, who was journeying in a cabin just across the corridor from my own, was a quiet and somewhat withdrawn man, but since we often happened upon each other entering or exiting our cabins, it was only natural that we began conversing. In the beginning our conversations were merely about the weather, the conditions on the ship and our excited expectations for the New

World, but later they became of an entirely different variety, chiefly concerned with our purpose on this earth.

This particular night the ship was completely enveloped in the thick, almost impenetrable fog and it was near impossible to see more than a couple of feet into the milky soup. The wind had completely died down and the ship had been drifting aimlessly for days, making it appear as if it was trapped inside a dense cloud. In the last three days, not one call of a bird had been heard and not one dolphin or other sea-living creature had been glimpsed around the ship.

The eerie stillness surrounding us was complete and the passengers and crewmen alike grew more and more trepidatious with each passing day. I even heard mutterings of a curse under the breath of some of the older sailors, but, as you well know, I believe myself enlightened enough, not to believe in such irrational rumours.

Thommel was a tall gaunt almost bald Norwegian who was on his way to join his Dominican Brotherhood in Washington D.C. His features were elongated, as is often the case with tall men, but his skin hung like a loosened glove from his skull, giving his face a somewhat macabre appearance that, added to the heavy black rope and hood he wore hanging down his back like a limp pouch, would greatly upset the ship's boy and many of the younger passengers. His heavy lidded watery eyes were light blue and his ears and nose were like large fleshy integrants having been deliberately added to complete the overall flaccid look.

Most of his face was covered in purple blotches, reminiscent of the underside of a spotted piglet and when he talked animatedly about his Brotherhood, waving his large white skeletal hands in the air in front of him, his face would turn quite rosy.

Although I am highly sceptical of the notion of any mystical celestial being, I nevertheless found the Brother an extremely interesting conversationalist and though I mainly listened to him talk, we still passed quite a few nights in deep conversation.

This particular evening, he was talking about one of the main doctrines of the Brotherhood, as he moved like a black clothed phantom through the fog, waving a small lantern back and forth in synchronicity with his steps.

".........Albert the Great said that understanding and wisdom together enhance one's faith in God. According to Albert, wisdom and understanding are

the very tools that God uses to commune with a contemplative. Only the faithful contemplative can know that God truly is, but he does not know what God is. Thus, an eternal contemplation forever produces an imperfect and mystical knowledge of God. Our soul shall surely be exalted surpassing the rest of God's creation but can never see God Himself."

As you are aware, I am by no means a specialist in the area of theology, and don't even count myself among the believers, so my responses to the Brother's monologues were usually vague and unassuming. However, this night I was altogether perplexed by the illogic reasoning.

"How can it be that you can know that something is, and at the same time not know what it is?" I asked, looking at the rather terrifying face of the Brother through the dense fog.

He stopped and held the small lantern up in between us. It illuminated his face emphasising the sagging features of his flesh. The pellucid eyes and ghoulish countenance gave an impression of someone who was genuinely confounded.

"That's a very interesting question," he said pulling at his jowls, revealing a set of large, but relatively strong ivory coloured teeth.

"Albertus Magnus first championed the idea that a true positive knowledge of God is possible, but that the knowledge will be equally obscure. In a sense it is easier to explain what God is not, than to proclaim what God truly is. As a rule, we affirm things of God only relatively, whereas we deny things of God categorically, with reference to what He is in Himself. Taken jointly there is no contradiction between relative affirmation and absolute negation."

"I am not sure I completely understand," I said truthfully, attempting to catch the Brother's crystalline eyes through the fog.

He stopped and thought for a while.

"I am not entirely certain this is the correct analogy to make," he said, "but let us consider the ocean." He made a somewhat superfluous gesture at the surrounding mist.

"For all we know the ocean is all-encompassing and covers most of the earth from pole to pole. We have observed its surface frozen and compact as a sheet of glass and as dark and impenetrable as a pool of ink. We have seen it lying as still and as blank as a mirror and in its most ferocious state, become a

monstrous seething entity. We realize and fear the ocean's almost unfathomable power, and at the same time we choose to sail on it, take bounty from it and constantly put our faith in its ability to support us. Indeed, we now know a fair amount of this particular ocean's magnificent and vast surface, and yet we know hardly anything of what it contains. How many different types of whales, fish, crustaceans and other sea creatures might live beneath its waves? In all honesty we don't know, and no matter how many new species of fish we discover and how much we learn about the ocean's depth and scale, we will never fully comprehend its magnitude. At the end of the day we have to admit, that although we understand and accept the ocean, it will always appear to us as a boundless mystery."

He scratched at his head and nodded to himself repeatedly as if to reaffirm his statement.

"As I said: It might not be the best comparison and certainly not in accordance with the doctrine, but that is the best I can do."

"I found that a very intelligible explanation. It certainly made a lot of sense to someone who doesn't have a deep understanding of the theological precept."

"I am happy you think so," he said. "Although, I am not so sure some of my more stringent Brothers would agree with my rather rudimentary explanation."

"Well," I replied smiling, "it is fortunate that they will never know."

He held up the lantern and gave me a toothy smile back, that in the density of the fog, made him look quite like a frightening ghoul.

"You will have to excuse me," he sighed and lowered the lantern. "I have been feeling quite weary these last couple of days. It is like the unending fog has imposed upon me a deep yearning for my sleep, so I believe it is time for me to retire."

He slowly walked across the deck and descended the stairs, moving like someone whose bones might be giving them discomfort. His dark silhouette and the small cocooned light were finally swallowed by the fog.

"I do hope you have a restful sleep," I called after him. If he ever answered I did not hear it.

Standing alone on the deck in the ever silent, slow moving brume, I was left with my own wandering thoughts. Even the ever present gentle slosh of the water against the hull had subsided and was near impossible to hear. It was as if the fog had had a tremendous subduing effect on the vast ocean and dampened its otherwise breathtaking spirit.

Everything was perfectly still.

Then from somewhere indeterminate came the most beautiful voice I have ever heard.

It is most difficult to explain in writing how it sounded and how it made me feel, but I will do my best.

It seemed as if the indispensable substance and quality of sound had been extracted in its purest form and was now seeping through the fog like a small nucleus that fully saturated everything around me and inside of me. It had no fixed structure but increased and waned mellifluously, consolidating all physical and mental facilities.

I felt like I was being imbued with a sense of undisturbed serenity and instantaneously found myself in the most halcyon place. Although I am not a believer in the afterlife, I still couldn't help myself from wondering if this was what heaven would feel like.

At first I stood affixed on the deck, like I was in a stupor, then I desperately looked around in the surrounding haze seeking the source of the sound.

The alluring voice had captivated me and I was compelled to know where it was coming from. Thus, like a bewildered moth flying towards the candle's flame, I ran to the starboard bulwark and stared unblinkingly into the dense fog until my eyes smarted. There was nothing there, so I ran across the deck, head first into the rigging and knocked myself out.

When I came to, I was lying flat on my back and my head hurt a great deal. I gently ran a searching hand across my forehead and winced when I felt the rather large protuberance. Fortunately, there was no blood on my hand and besides a frightful headache, I seemed to be moderately unscathed. To my utter dismay the sublime voice had departed, leaving me once again alone in an eerie stillness and engulfed in the thick haze. I felt empty to the bottom of my core and my soul was as disconsolate as when I left you behind. I must admit that I speculated that all happiness had somehow been drained from me, since all I was cognisant of was a profound colourless void inside me.

Although my head hurt frightfully and I felt nauseated, I forced myself to *look around and instantly saw a small stationary light glowing in the fog just a couple of feet away. I slowly got up from the deck nursing my throbbing head and carefully walked over to the bulwark where I picked up the small lantern belonging to Brother Thommel.*

I held it in the air and looked at the quite distinctive design.

Besides the basic square construction, two strings of thin copper wire were running across the sheets of glass, dividing the four sides into three equal sections. The top of the lantern was shaped like a square roof with small domed windows on each side and perforated with small symbols that twinkled in the night.

I had a premonition of misadventure and quickly held the lantern away from my face, letting my eyes adjust before I called out into the night: "Brother Thommel......Are you there?" I stopped and listened, straining my ears for any sounds, but all was quiet.

I called out again, this time louder: "Brother Thommel....Can you hear me? Are you there...?"

My desperate shouts in the night were met by an almost deafening stillness. Until that is, a balmy and sangfroid voice broke through the noiseless night.

"I don't believe the Brother will be answering you anytime soon," the cat said, effortlessly jumping up to sit on the railing. Its radiant blue eyes shimmered like a pair of sapphires through the mist.

"As a matter of fact, I believe he might be well on his way to meet his maker."

The cat turned its head and looked into the circumambient mist.

"What happened to him?" I said urgently. "Did he fall overboard? When did it happen?"

"Quite a while ago now."

"Did nobody see or hear anything?" I asked in anguish.

"Nobody heard or saw anything and even if they had, it was apparently in his God's will that he succumbed to the song and drowned in the waves."

"The voice in the night?" I said, suddenly doubting the genuineness of the cat. "You heard the voice as well? Who or what was that? Why did it stop? Is it coming back?"

"You wouldn't believe me if I told you," it said looking straight into my

eyes, "but maybe it will return one day. All you can do is wait not knowing if you are waiting in vain."

The cat stared at me with dispassionate eyes.

"What happened to the Brother when he heard the song?" I asked, somewhat apprehensively.

"He behaved more or less the same as you although with less sprightliness, but very much with the same fieriness and determination. He came back up the stairs, desperately rambling the ship looking for the source of the voice until he decided to continue his search outside the bounds of this earthly vessel."

The cat licked its paw and methodically ran it across the top of its head.

"I do hope the ancient tellurian found what he was looking for in the end."

The cat silently jumped down from the bulwark, ran across the deck and disappeared in the fog leaving me standing on the deck with the late Brother's lantern in my hand. I looked down and as an augury of death the candle inside promptly sputtered and died.

I do not know whom or what it was that caused both me and the dear Brother to behave in this terribly irrational manner. A less enlightened man than myself, might postulate that we were both under a spell and bestowed a dangerous quest with no apparent concern for our own lives. Whatever happened to us that night, it was an anomalous and frightening experience that frankly left me quite shaken. In hindsight I must admit that I count myself fortunate that I ran head first into the rigging and thus escaped with nothing more than a sore head. I dare not think of the alternative.

After the cat left, I immediately notified the First Mate of the Brother's misfortune, but although a couple of sailors and I spent a considerable amount of time calling into the widespread fog, nothing was ever heard of Brother Thommel. In the end I surmised that he failed to resist whatever force had been calling him, and thus made the ultimate sacrifice.

In the early hours of the morning I finally went downstairs and spent a restless night in my bunk, thinking about the implausible event and only returned to the deck when a welcome warm light shone through the bull's-eye. As luck would have it, the fog had lifted. The brilliant sun shone from a clear blue sky and the blessed wind had eventually returned to once more animate the ocean around us, fill the sails to the brim and forcefully push the ship forward through the white tipped waves. Although I readily admit it is far from being logic, I cannot help but wonder if the two events are not linked somehow.

I thenceforth brought the small lantern with me on my nightly wanderings and though it was as futile as spotting a snowflake in a snow slide, I continued the task of scanning the open ocean for any signs of the Brother. Many were the evenings and nights standing by the bulwark staring into the abyss seeing nothing but the limitless space.

I miss you and the little one so much and not a day goes by without me wishing you were by my side. Alas, that is not possible. I can only hope that you somehow receive all the love I have for you and our daughter. Please enfold yourselves in the warmth of my endless and undying affection until we meet again.

Yours Forever,

C

He slowly put down the last page on top of the others, leaned back in his chair and looked at the lantern above him. The candle was flickering in the interior and the small symbols glowed in the semi-dark room, their loose characters creating a soft design on the walls around him. He got up from the chair, unhooked the lantern, held it close to his face and slowly turned it around. As far as he could see there were no initials or any other identifying marks on the surface, yet he was convinced that this was indeed the lantern that had belonged to the Brother, who had tragically perished in the waves.

He grabbed the candleholder from the table, held the lantern up above his head and looked at its base. He had never before thought to look, but he immediately noticed a faded almost disappearing outline of a four pointed star with two large letters covering it: *O P* it said. The star was reminiscent of a compass and he assumed that the *O P* might be the initials of one of the previous owners. Around edge, surrounding the initials somebody had written something that was hard to decipher since most of the letters had been obliterated.: *od akes cer   nds of thou   ble*

He tried to hold the candle at a different angle, but he still couldn't make out the rest of the text, so instead he set the lantern on the table, turned it and looked at the sides one by one. There were no other writings on the wood on the outside, but when he opened the small door to look at the inside frame, he found three small threadlike words camouflaged against the grain. Even though he held the candle as close as he could to the surface the words were difficult to decipher. He put the candleholder on the table and padded across the floor to fetch the small black notebook in his jacket pocket. The boards showed their discontentment by squeaking loudly under his weight and he looked across to the fireplace to see if the noise had disturbed the cat.

It hadn't moved.

He fished out the notebook from his coat pocket and gently stroked the familiar sleek surface as he carried it back to the table. He sat down, opened it to an empty page opposite the notional composition of unfurling ice crystals, looked carefully at the locutions inside the door of the lantern and studiously copied the words at the top of the page. When he had finished writing, he put his pencil down and looked at the three words stretching like a cursive band across the top of the page.

Laudare Benedicere Praedicare

He leaned forward in his chair, picked up the small square pencil, checked the sharpness of the tip with his calloused thumb, turned it over and wrote: *Pray Bless Preach* below the three words. Then he lifted the lantern, attentively examining the base before copying the almost erased sentence below the six words.

od   akes cer   nds of thou   ble

He was staring at the words trying to fill in the blanks, when all of a sudden he caught a movement out of the corner of his eye. He looked up to discover that the cat had moved from the space in front of the fire and was now sitting on the floor only a couple of feet away from the table looking up at him. As soon as its eyes found his, it got up and silently walked towards the door. When it reached the door it sat down and looked back at him.

"Oh," he said, "I suppose I better let you out, if you have to go."

He rose from the chair and walked over to where the cat was sitting.

It didn't look at him but instead kept its eyes firmly on the plank of wood only a couple of inches away from its face as if it had unexpectedly discovered something prodigious hiding in the woodgrain.

He put on his jacket and turned up the collar, then he put on his gloves, pulled down his cap and picked up the shovel. Bracing himself he opened the door.

The snow fell like an assemblage of innumerable silvery curtains carelessly being blown about by the thrashing wind. The falling snow had added to the already substantial drifts pushing up against the cottage, and already covered both the windows. He closed the door, quickly shoveled the snowdrift away from the entrance and once again cleared the square to allow for the cat to do its business.

As soon as he finished, the cat gracefully jumped over the shovel handle and insouciantly squatted in the cleared area. When it had finished it immediately went to sit by the door, leaving behind a beautiful diaphanous flower of pale gold spreading out from the center of the blank canvas.

He tried to capture the image in his mind, before opening and closing the door.

As the cat immediately ran to sit in front of the fireplace, he stomped his feet leaving a small fragmented semicircle of white flakes radiating from the door. They made dark featureless patches on the surface of the planks as they quickly began melting.

He leaned the shovel against the wall, took off his gloves, stuck hem in the jacket pockets, removed his jacket and hung it from the hook, before walking back to the table to pick up his notebook.

He leaned back in his chair, closed his eyes in an attempt to summon up the image of the delicate yellow flower and having completely forgotten the broken sentence on the lantern, he spent the next hour or so drawing.

The flickering light of the candle spilled onto the page creating a series of fluid penumbras that gradually merged with the image, making it impossible for him to distinguish one line from the other. Even though he closed his eyes several times in an attempt to recall the image, the lines on the page inevitably agglutinated, finally becoming a confused overgrown mass.

Somewhat dismayed he closed the notebook, put it down on the table and looked at the cat that was now sitting by the food bowl.

"I think you should have a name," he said out loud.

The cat carried on eating as if nothing had happened.

"I need to call you something," he said, "I suppose I could just call you 'cat', but I think you deserve to have your own name."

The cat got up from the food bowl, walked across the floor and once more sat down in front of the fireplace.

For a while he observed the cat eating and then cleaning itself in the fading light of the glowing embers.

"I believe I have found a name that suits you," he said, looking at the cat. "I think I will call you Loke."

The cat stretched it back and its tail into the air, then it proceeded to walk around itself a few times before curling up on the floor.

For a while the dying embers, reflected in its eyes, made it appear as if they were glowing in the dark.

When they closed they left nothing but blackness behind.

Chapter 10

He was sitting cross legged in the bottom of what very much looked like his uncle's herring drifter, although everything on this boat was white as snow and not permeated with the always pervasive pungent smell of fish, strong tobacco and tar. In fact, when he sniffed the air expecting his senses to be insulted, he found it difficult to detect any smells at all.

He looked around.

The water around the boat stretched as far as the eye could see. It was as motionless as the surface of a pond and flawlessly reflected the stationary fluffy clouds in the clear blue sky overhead, to such an extent that it was close to impossible to differentiate one from the other.

There was no wind to fill the sails, that hung from their masts like a pair of newly emptied flour sacks, and the boat lay perfectly still in its fluid vacuum.

"I wonder what I'm doing here?" It sounded as if he had just spoken into a very large empty space. The words bounded along the uninterrupted surface and dispersed some distance away.

"I brought you here." A cat with piercing blue eyes and fur like that of polished granite had appeared on the bench in front of him.

"Why?" he asked as if the cat had been expected.

"Because I wanted you to meet someone."

The voice was as clear in his mind as if he had conjured up the words himself. The cat stared at him with its crystalline eyes apparently waiting for his reply.

He looked up and down the boat. Apart from himself and the cat he could sense that there was no one else on board.

"Who do you want me to meet?"

"That I am afraid I can't tell you."

"But since there is no one in the boat, why bring me here?"

"This is not where you are going to meet," said the cat, gazing pensively at the vast reflecting surface.

"But where are we expected to meet? There's no wind, the boat is not moving and there's nothing else here."

He looked up at the sky, slowly scooted to the side of the unmoving boat and peeked over the side. It was like looking into an immense exquisite mirror. He turned his head from side to side to see if he could glimpse anything under the surface, but all he could see was his own head moving back and forth against the backdrop of the white clouds in the blue sky above. He watched the unmoving clouds and suddenly had the strangest feeling that they weren't clouds at all, but in fact drawings of very large downy feathers on an immense piece of blue paper.

He was awoken from his musings by a sound of a voice coming from far away.

He strained his ears to listen.

Someone was singing and the music that weaved and furled in the air like a boundless murmuration, sounded as if all the canticles in the world had been condensed into one, bringing forth a complete and unembodied piece that encompassed the entirety of the space in a ceaseless resonating sound.

It was unquestionably the most beautiful thing he had ever encountered. The song was remarkable for the extensive and incredible variation of mood and tonality, and altogether unforgettable because of the way it made him feel.

It effortlessly permeated every part of his body with a sensation of raw unconditional ecstasy that left him short of breath and with a frenzied pyretic mind, like that of horses in a burning barn.

He desperately looked around to locate the source of the voice.

"Over there," the cat said, apparently impervious to the song and to his obvious distress.

He stared in the direction the cat had indicated.

At first he wasn't certain that anything had changed.

The surface of the water was as inert as ever and nothing else seemed to move, but when he scanned the horizon, he finally spotted what looked like a small white hill that inexplicably appeared to advance towards the boat.

As he stood up and looked towards the approaching mass, the song gradually waned until it ultimately dissipated, leaving behind a stifling state of stillness in which the only thing he could feel was the sudden ache of his heart.

As the barren mass smoothly moved along the surface, he noticed a dark smear against the chalky-white background and realized that someone was inhabiting the island.

A tall slender woman with skin the opaque milky colour of marble was standing on the beach not more than ten feet away from him.

Her face was perfectly symmetrical and her large dark eyes, beneath immaculate crescent eyebrows rested on his without fear or trepidation. She parted her full roseate lips, revealing two rows of beautiful pearly teeth, and made a slow welcoming gesture with her long elegant hand.

She was completely nude and her long hair, cascading down her slender elongated neck like a velvet drape, almost hid her well-formed breasts.

She made no attempt to cover herself and he was all of a sudden mindful of the fact that he was staring at the dark alluring area between her soft thighs and had to summon his willpower to lift his eyes to meet her gaze.

As he looked into her obsidian eyes, he unsuccessfully attempted to control the predictable contractions of his member, but it nevertheless began to swell and he blushingly looked down at his notable erection, realizing that he himself was naked.

He considered covering himself, but the woman, apparently unfazed by his predicament, smiled at him and again made a leisurely welcoming gesture with her hand in the air, much like a piece of seaweed in a slow moving current.

He climbed over the side of the boat and carefully lowered himself down to stand on the clear crystal sheet.

It was slightly warm to the touch and when he took a couple of steps towards the woman, it very much felt like he was walking on a large tensile membrane, that somehow anticipated his gait.

Conscious of his problem, he took a few more tentative steps across the flexible surface, walked over to the edge of the small white island where the woman was standing, and stepped off the pliable sheet.

She was the most beautiful creature he had ever encountered, and when he looked at her it was like all forces of nature were flawlessly fused into a single entity. As if she had been expertly created by a magnificent virtuoso at the very pinnacle of his craft.

She was quite simply the epitome of perfection and standing in front of her, looking into her mesmerizing obsidian eyes, he was suddenly conscious of his own being, like that of a nugatory speck in the immensity of space.

She smiled freely and cocked her head slightly.

Her long black hair swayed like an animate substance across her bare chest, when she reached out a long slender arm and took his hand. Her small hand was warm and soft and lay in the palm of his hand like a sentient life form. She curled her long delicate fingers around his hand, turned around and gently pulled him behind her as she began to move steadily to the center of the island. He looked at the impeccable flowing curvilinear forms of her sylphlike body and, walking across a substance not unlike granulated sugar, he felt the well-known contraction in the depth of his loins.

When they reached the center of the slightly raised island she stopped.

They were standing in front of an all too familiar hollow and as he anticipatingly looked down into the void, he noticed a set of steps carved into the side of the pit. The woman looked beguilingly over her shoulder as she slowly began descending the stairs and he followed her willingly into the bed of the cavity.

When they reached the floor and the opening was well above them, she let go of his hand and, as a foreshadow, she slowly turned around to face him.

She placed her long slender arms around his shoulders and gently pushed him down to lie on the snow white ground.

For a while she gazed at him with eyes as dark as the bottom of an inkwell.

Then she placed her legs on either side of him, reached in between them and gently guided him to her. While keeping her obsidian eyes locked on his, she opened her lips and slowly exhaled as she gently pushed herself down.

A delightful tangy smell filled the air.

She leaned forward so that her long black hair encapsulated their heads, folded his hands in hers, pressed them against the ground above his head and ever so slowly began moving her hips up and down.

As he was close to stepping off the precipice to lose himself in the efficacious coital vortex that would suck him to the endless bottom, he heard an innominate voice originating from somewhere near the centre of his mind.

"I wanted you to know that we can share each other's dreams," it said.

He let himself go and was instantaneously lost in the vehement multisensory maelstrom.

Chapter 11

As he woke up, the cat was pushing itself up against him and he felt the potent vibrations of its resonant purring between his legs. His skin felt unpleasantly damp and there was a particular sticky feeling around the area of his groin.

He untangled himself from the sleeping feline, tiptoed over to the sink, removed his nightshirt and quickly doused his face with ice cold water from the sputtering faucet, found an old washcloth, washed under his arms and between his legs before drying himself in an old tattered towel and trotting back to the bedroom to get dressed.

When he returned to the main room, he put a handful of kindling on the embers in the belly of the stove, blew on them until they caught fire, placed a heavy log on top and closed the door, leaving a small gap so that the fire had enough air to rapidly build.

He filled the kettle and put it back on the stove before walking across the floor to pick up his boots. He brought them over to the table, sat down in the chair and stuck his feet in the boots and tied the laces. Then he went back to the door, put on his coat and his cap and fumbled in the jacket pockets for his gloves before opening the door.

The snow was still falling and although it was dark, he could see his breath forming in the freezing air. The drifts were now completely covering the windows at the front of the cottage and had nearly reached the large drifts draping over the edge of the roof like a full head on a glass of a well poured beer.

He stepped back and scraped at the overhanging drift above the doorway. A large mass slid off the roof and almost silently fell onto the snow covered ground, making a cloud like indentation that somewhat resembled a small boat.

He pushed it aside with the shovel and once again cleared a patch for the cat, before he began re-digging the trench to the outhouse.

When he reached it, he leaned the shovel up against the wall, before opening the door and stepping inside. He closed the door, pulled down his breeches, held up his jacket and quickly lowered himself onto the gelid seat.

Sitting in the dingy putrescent room, he wondered about the incredibly bizarre and breathtakingly seductive dream.

He couldn't fathom how it could possibly be, but he was nevertheless certain that the cat who had visited him in the pure white boat and had claimed to have brought him there, was the same cat that was now lying asleep on the bed in the cottage.

Although he accepted the fact that the experience had been a very vivid dream, there was definitely something preternatural about the behaviour of the cat.

The image of the woman or possible succubus he had met on the island was as evocative as anything he had ever encountered, and the sensation of how she silently but forcefully clenched around him at the height of their tryst was still etched in his mind, making his heart pound and his skin perspire.

In fact, the mere thought of her, immediately brought life to his member and he had to concentrate hard to force the image of the woman's seraphic features and heavenly touch from his mind.

Instead he occupied his thoughts with images of white feathers spread on moist soil and dark striated shadows on virgin snow.

He left the stench of the outhouse behind, cleaned his hands in the snow, put on his gloves and dug a narrow trench to the shed and afterwards to the chicken coop. He checked on the sleeping hens cooped up together, before clearing a good sized area, spreading a couple of handfuls of feed on the ground and a small handful inside the coop.

Then he filled the water bowl, fetched a bunch of hay from the bales stacked in the loft of the shed, carried it over to the coop and spread it on the floor.

He gently pushed the birds aside and picked up four eggs that he carefully placed in his pockets. Then he closed the door to the coop and walked back to the cottage.

The cat was sitting on the floor inside and as soon as he opened the door it immediately jumped out, and walked around the small clearing before squatting.

He leaned the shovel against the door, shielded his eyes against the falling flakes, and looked up at the starless sky waiting for the cat to finish.

He didn't have to wait long before the cat got up, turned around and halfheartedly scraped at the snow. However, it quickly changed its mind about covering its traces, returning instead to where he was standing and when he opened the door, the cat immediately jumped over the threshold, ran inside and shook the snow off its paws.

Before he re-entered the cottage, he stared for a while at the collection of small dark trails placed like an incidental symbol in the center of the spreading yellow patch in the white snow. For a moment he thought about pulling out his notebook, but his stomach was growling and he yearned for a cup of tea, so he opened the door and followed the cat inside.

He made eggs and canned ham for breakfast and cut up a couple of slices of ham and put it in the cat's bowl.

The cat had returned to the bed where it sat watching him through the doorway.

He could feel its penetrating chary eyes on his back, and he wondered if it knew of his dream.

When the tea had properly steeped, he carried the plate, cutlery and teacup over to the table.

Then he picked up the sauce and the salt and pepper from the pantry and walked back to the table and sat down.

He pushed all extraneous thoughts from his mind and began his slow and methodical process of masticating each bite meticulously while staring reflexively into space.

When he finished eating, he placed the plate and cutlery in the sink, lit a fire in the fireplace, poured another cup of tea that he carefully carried across the floor and set down on the table.

He felt the soft vibration in the floorboards as the cat jumped down from the bed.

It didn't acknowledge him as it silently crossed the floor to the fireplace where it sat down and began cleaning itself in the glow of the expanding flames.

He lifted the cup and sipped at the edge savouring the understated and delicate smell, before returning the cup to the table.

He reached out and picked up an envelope. He unfolded the pocketknife, pushed the blade in, slid it across, and gently inserted his thumb and forefinger, prying it open. He then removed the five small wispy pieces of paper, unfolded them, put them down on the table and flattened them with the palm of his hand.

He lit the candle, moved it closer and put the smoldering match in the bottom of the holder where it lay sending forth a small ghostlike plume into the air.

He leaned closer to the table and began to read.

Dearest E

It goes without saying that I miss you more each day that passes. The further the waves carry me away from you, the more my heart aches. It seems such a long long time ago that I was lying carefree by the edge of the pond with my head in your lap, looking up at your beautiful face as you stroked my hair with your loving touch. In my fitful and scattered dreams I sometimes feel your gentle fingers playing with my locks, but when I awake, the sensation lamentably passes and I am left with nothing but my weary hand lying heavily across my forehead.

Here the days are long. The sound of the waves hammering against the creaking hull seem to never end.

The incessant beating has yet again become part of everything I do and I had never imagined that I would so crave the stillness that was brought by the fog. Although I still occasionally speak with the other travellers, I tend to spend the majority of my time thinking, reading or writing and have also rediscovered drawing as an excellent device to occupy my time.

The other day I found a dead mouse just outside my cabin door and I had the strangest urge to render it, so I picked it up and placed it on a piece of paper on the small table by the bullseye. I then searched my cabin for a pencil but found nothing but my bottle of ink, so I asked one of my fellow travellers, a young Swedish artist by the name of Bengtsson, to lend me some more adequate drawing materials. He most generously gave me a few sticks of graphite and a stick of chalk and additionally offered to evaluate my work, and though he seemed genuinely interested, I am afraid I am not quite ready to share my dilettante work with a true artist, so for now I have decided to keep my layman drawings to myself.

Although I know that I have made several promises to tell you about my arrival in America and that I have assured you that I would give you more information about my fellow travellers, certain unexpected events have taken precedence and I must confess the need to write them down weighs heavily on my mind.

One clear and windless night, as I was aimlessly strolling back and forth on the main deck staring at the breathtaking cosmic firmament, I suddenly had the strongest feeling that I was being watched. I hadn't heard anyone approach and at first I thought it might be the ship's cat, but imagine my surprise when I turned around to find a young girl sitting on top of a barrel of freshwater no more than ten feet away from where I was standing.

She looked at me with dark penetrating eyes, much like those of a raven.

Her pale face was flawless like that of a doll and her delicate hands lay folded in her lap, like they had been placed by someone arranging a display in a shop window.

Her dominant dark eyes were large and shimmered from the reflections of the infinite stars, and her petite mouth, sitting beneath her perfectly positioned straight nose, very much looked like it had been painted on.

Although it was rather chilly in the night air, she was only wearing a light coloured short sleeved dress and a pair of white socks and shoes that sparkled like pieces of granite when she casually moved her legs. She reached up and absentmindedly played with the end of her long black braid and didn't seem to be paying a lot of attention to me.

Though I have been wandering the ship both day and night and have made many an acquaintance amongst the crew and passengers alike, I had never seen the girl before and must say that I couldn't help speculate on what she was doing alone on the deck in the middle of the night.

I must have been lost in my own thoughts, because a clear voice suddenly broke my reverie.

"Did you know him well?" she asked.

"Who?" I answered, somewhat confounded both by her voice, that was surprisingly bright, and by the most unexpected question.

"The priest who thought he heard someone singing out there and drowned when he went overboard?" She made a small elegant gesture with her hand towards the surrounding sea.

"How do you know about the song?" I asked apprehensively, knowing very well that I hadn't shared any information about that night with anyone else. "Did you hear it too?

"We shall no doubt talk about that later," she said somberly, "but first I would like to know if you knew him well."

"I suppose I knew the Brother as well as you can be expected to know someone you have only just met," I replied. "Which is, truth be told: Not very much at all."

"However, you spent quite a lot of time together, so if you were not talking about anything that gave you a better knowledge of him, what did the two of you talk about?"

"For the most part the Brother talked predominantly about his belief system and the complexities surrounding the existence of his god. I merely listened to his erudite musings and sometimes asked a question, although to his sagacious conjecture, my input was purely academic."

"How can you be so sure?" the girl said, swinging her legs back and forth. *"Isn't it true that you asked him why it is that you can know what something is, and at the same time not know what it is?"*

"How do you know I asked him that question?" I said suspiciously.

"The cat told me," she said cocking her head, looking at me with glinting eyes.

"What do you mean," I said, trying not to sound unsettled.

"You know exactly what I mean and don't you worry, your secret is safe with me."

She smiled and her small teeth glistened like those of a small predator in the dark. *"But please do tell why you were interested in the Brother's ruminations."*

"Well," I said, not exactly sure where to start, *"I believe that's a very difficult question to answer. I am like everyone else interested in knowing why I am here, but unlike the Brother, I don't believe the presence of a deity can satisfactorily answer that question. As a matter of fact, I am often convinced that everything I am experiencing might be an infinite very fanciful dream that merely challenges my perceptual beliefs. Therefore, I have always found it fascinating to hear how others operate within more stringent directives."*

I stopped talking as the girl looked at me shrewdly from her seat on the barrel.

"If you think everything you experience is a perdurable dream, what can you ever believe in?" she asked candidly.

"I don't really know," I replied truthfully. *"I suppose I believe that the knowledge of the content of our mind is more certain and therefore more important than the knowledge outside of our mind. That all we can really trust resides inside the specific element of a person that enables them to be aware of whatever*

surrounds them, and what ultimately makes them think and feel."

I paused for a moment and looked at the girl who was staring back at me with an unfeigned inquisitive look on her face.

"I believe our mind is constantly searching for opportunities to create, store and compartmentalize our collective memories. As soon as we are able to, we record the progress, success and failure of our life and store it away. The infinite amount of images we collate become an extensive depository of amalgamated information, turning our minds into a vast storage space which we then use to systemize and organize our lives. This quickly becomes a daily habit, sometimes even an obsession, and inevitably occupies quite a considerable amount of our time. In doing this I believe we somehow categorize each individual file and deposit it in an already immense system of sounds, visuals and other sensory or intellectual compartments that each become a fragment of our collective whole from which we piece together and interpret our existence."

"That's very interesting, are you perchance including mindreading cats and unexplained ocean singing in this hypothesis?" she asked, laughing lightly, "or do you believe those things are just a few maladjusted figments of your overactive imagination?

"I'm not entirely sure," I answered, looking at the girl, who casually and almost silently jumped down on the deck where she lifted her arms in the air like a pair of pale slender wings and made a slow pirouette. Her sedate movements reminded me of the low branches of a willow tree gently being blown about in a summer's breeze. "However, no matter what I believe them to be, they do become fragments of my entire recollection."

"God or no god, dream or reality, everything you know is real," she said, twirling on the spot making her dress pulsate in the air like a jellyfish. "All you know and everything you will come to know will inevitably become part of your internal fabric. No matter what decisions you make; good, bad or insouciant, they will shape your life much like a river cuts into the landscape. One thought is a fraction of all thoughts and one action is a fraction of all actions. The river broadens and narrows, curves and straightens, flattens and deepens but it's always coming and always going. It deposits and redistributes everything you know and everything you need. The cat with the promise of time, the Brother and the voice in the night, the dreams of your loved ones and the dead mouse rendered on a piece of

paper currently lying on the table in your cabin, all are as real as the ship on the waves and the stars in the sky." She slowly raised her small hand and pointed at the sky above.

"One is nothing without the other."

Following her gaze, I momentarily became lost in the immensity above. When I looked back down there was no sign of her.

I walked across the deck and put my hand on the top of the barrel. It was slightly damp and cold to the touch.

I am not sure why, but I knew it was fruitless to look for the girl, so I went back to my cabin, sat down by the table and lit the Brother's lantern. Looking into the flickering light I thought about what the girl had told me. I don't know how she could have obtained such detailed and surreptitious information without having talked with the cat and while I realize it is not the best defense in proving my own sanity, I am however glad for the knowledge that someone else has shared that experience.

Again I don't know what to tell you about these events, other than I have described them in the way that they occurred. I don't know what they mean or what the girl ultimately wanted me to know. I know it must be difficult for anyone to understand, but I promise you that everything that I write down is occurring exactly as it happened.

I miss you both so much and not an hour goes by without me thinking about you. Someday soon I promise that you shall receive all the affection I have for you and our daughter.

You must wrap yourselves in the warmth of my undying love until we meet again.

Yours Forever,

C

He reached out and turned over the sheet to reveal an additional piece of paper no bigger than the envelope itself.

He carefully picked it up to have a closer look and was instantly mesmerized by the graceful and exquisite rendering.

The mouse, curled up on its side, instantly reminded him of the countless lifeless rodents he had carried outside and removed from the traps.

Its diminutive skeletal hands, with needle like claws pointlessly gripping the air, were drawn up under its body and its long legs with wide, fan shaped feet, were stretched out as if they had been suspended mid jump. Its small mouth was slightly agape exhibiting four tiny elongated serrated yellowing teeth, and the whiskers, spread out from its snout like nearly translucent filaments, almost looked like they were moving.

Below the hind legs the animal's long tail made a beautiful tapered incurve and the fine shadow made it appear as if it was slightly raised above the surface.

Although the artist had perfectly captured the indispensable quality of death, he had nonetheless chosen to embody the animal with an indeterminate impression of life, and looking at the drawing of the lifeless animal with its gleaming unseeing eye, Ambrosius couldn't help thinking about the mouse being alive.

He put the drawing back on the table, got up from the chair and walked into the bedroom where he opened the door to the large wardrobe standing in the corner. He bent down and removed his tattered suitcase, laid it on the bed, flipped open the lid and looked down at the only item contained within. On the bottom against the peeling discoloured brown cardboard lay a small parcel wrapped in a piece of ivory coloured cloth. He hesitated for a moment before reaching into the case to remove the package. He put it down on the bed and took a couple of deep breaths before slowly unfolding the cloth to reveal four small black frames lying face down. He picked up the frame lying on top and loosened the small metal fasteners that held the small piece of backing wood in place, then he removed the back and, mindful not to look at the image, turned it over and put it face down on the piece of wood. Then he wiped the glass with a corner of his sleeve, went back to the table, picked up the drawing of the dead mouse, carried it to the bedroom and put it down on the glass. He then replaced the backing, refastened the small metal pins and turned the frame around.

It was a near perfect fit.

The mouse was now lying in the center of the frame behind the sheet of glass, much like one of the more exotic specimens he had so often observed at the Museum of Natural History in Copenhagen on one of the many excursions he had made there in the company of his aunt.

He carried the frame over to the fireplace, put it down on the shelf, stared at the immured rodent while thinking about the letter he had just read.

Not only was the description of the girl and of her demeanour strikingly similar to that of Veronica, but the conversation the girl had had with the author of the letters, bore quite uncanny similarities to the few talks he himself had had with Veronica in the cemetery. Although he realized that it was preposterous that the two of them could be the same person, he could almost sense the tone of her voice, hear her pearly laughter and imagine the curious but serene look in her dark eyes. The additional fact that she had mentioned talking to a cat only added to his supposition that the events were somehow linked. Yet, he couldn't quite fathom why and how they could be.

He was equally astounded by the author's acute introspection and how closely his musings followed his own. In fact, he was quite certain he himself had had almost identical thoughts on the matter of objective reality and that they had somehow been transmitted, spoken out loud and then recorded by the author.

He rubbed his face in his hands and looked at the sleeping cat lying on the boards next to his feet.

Surely the rational explanation between the eerie resemblances in the encounter, was that they were nothing but extraordinary coincidences.

He walked over to the table, lifted the cup off the surface, carried it over to the sink and carefully set it down. It looked like a small semi-opaque eyeball staring up at him from the relative darkness at the bottom of the sink.

Chapter 12

He once again found himself sitting in the hull of a small boat.

Everything around him was eerily quiet and although he strained his ears, he merely heard his own shallow breathing and the sound of blood rushing like constrained rivers in his ears.

The sky above him, rich with a profusion of stars that illuminated the frozen obsidian plane spread like a vast infinite mirror to either side of him and dissolved in the far distance in a plethora of phosphorescence.

Contrary to the previous boat, this one was black like a piece of newly mined coal and soft as moleskin against his hands, and when he pensively ran his fingers across the shiny velvety surface, he had the unmistakable feeling of a deep vibration coming from somewhere beneath him.

The unexpected stimuli traveled from his backside, up his back like a pulse of electric energy that made the hair on the back of his neck stand up.

He shivered slightly from the unexpected, but not unpleasant feeling, then reticently withdrew his hand and looked for the source of this unexpected phenomenon.

As far as he could see there was nothing visible that could have caused the oscillation, yet the boat clearly produced a palpable rhythmic reverberation, like the cyclic vibration of a small engine.

He waited for something to move, but everything around him was stock-still.

The immobile sable sails hung from the halyards like sculpted flayed skins against the dark masts, that seemed to be dissolving in the void above and if it hadn't been for the slightly unnerving vibration coming from somewhere below, it was like he was sitting in the center of a velvet statue.

He hesitantly shifted to the edge, put his hand on the plushy railing, guardedly looked over the side and was met by his own reflection framed by the immeasurable scores of tiny lights in the immense sky.

Gazing at the sky above him he searched for the familiar star formations and thought it peculiar that the constellations seemed to belong to neither the Northern nor to the Southern Hemisphere. One of the constellations, suspended slightly lopsided just over his head, was reminiscent of a somewhat crooked x and one a little further away to his right looked like a nearly perfect circle comprised of thirteen stars.

He had been preoccupied with searching the sky for recognisable features and very nearly jumped in alarm when suddenly he heard a voice behind him.

"Have you found what you've been looking for?"

He lost his footing on the slippery floor and stumbled when he quickly spun around to face a man standing on the shimmering volcanic sheet no more than five feet away from the boat.

The black cassock he wore created a dark void in the otherwise illuminate space and made the man's head and hands appear as if they were suspended in midair. He slowly raised his left hand to reveal a lantern that had been hidden from view by the folds of his cloak and brought it closer to his face. The flickering yellowish light both brightened his watery eyes and embellished his elongated sagging features, and though he was smiling, revealing his rather large teeth, it nonetheless gave him a pronounced appearance of a gargoyle.

He took a step closer to the boat.

"I know who you are, you're the priest who drowned looking for the voice in the fog. I believe I can recall your name, Thomas? No, Thommel."

The Brother paused a moment before he spoke:

"I am indeed a man who went looking for something that called him in the night, although drowned or breathing, lost or found, dead or alive, dream or reality: nothing is ever what it seems." He spread his arms away from his body indicating the circumambient space.

"While you could certainly imply that I some time ago left an earthly vessel behind, and you wouldn't necessarily be wrong to do so, not everything that happens can be explained in words, and even if I attempted to elucidate for you what I believe occurred between now and then, you would have no source of information to ascertain if I am indeed telling you the truth."

The Brother gave a disconsolate wave of his hand.

"So I will save you the trouble, at least for now."

"Are you alone?" Ambrosius asked, wondering if whatever it was that had lured the Brother to his watery grave was nearby.

"Always in body, but never in spirit," the Brother answered chuckling, taking yet another step towards the boat.

"Do you mind if I join you?" He gestured to the interior of the boat with an attenuated hand, upon which a river system of protuberant bluish veins pressed against the layer of papery skin, threatening to burst through it like a dam after weeks of heavy downpour.

"By all means." Ambrosius reached for the hand that was dry but cold as a sheet of ice, and an image of his contemptuous old priest fleetingly flashed through his mind. However, he didn't let go and watched as the Brother slowly bent his creaking knees and awkwardly lowered himself onto the opposite seat.

"Hmm," the Brother said, placing the lantern on the floor between them, gently running his hand across the seat. For the briefest of moments, it rested on the surface like a fragment of marble against a piece of granite, and Ambrosius had a sudden urge to render it.

He quickly patted his pockets, but when he couldn't find his notebook he instead put his hands on his knees and stared at the Brother's hand, trying his best to memorize it.

"This is a very strange vessel indeed," the Brother said, as he continued to slowly stroke the seat. "Is it me alone or can you also feel the vibrations?"

Ambrosius ceased gazing at the offcut hand and instead looked into the fluttering streaked face suspended in the air in front of him. The impression of a phantom was even more pronounced by the light from the lantern and by the relative closeness between them.

"I can," he said, "although I must admit I have no idea what might cause them."

"I believe there's a fairly simple explanation," the Brother replied, looking around, "but never mind that, let's instead talk about what brought you here."

He disappeared his hands in the folds of his sleeves, and looked across the illuminated gap between them.

"I have no idea what brought me here. I opened my eyes and found myself sitting in this strange soft vessel on the surface of this rigid expanse."

He motioned to the surroundings.

"But surely you are here because you have questions that need to be answered."

"I do?" he asked, somewhat confounded.

"Of course you do, or have you already forgotten?" The Brother reached down and lifted the lantern and held it up in the space between them.

He immediately recognised the easily detectable design of the two strings cutting the panes of glass into three equal sections, and the cutouts of the small symbols under the slightly sloped roof.

"That's indistinguishable from the one that's currently hanging over the table in my cottage," he said, trying to catch the Brother's eye through the scintillating glass.

"That it is," the Brother smiled and slowly turned the lantern. "Now, do you remember what it is that you're looking for and why you came to see me?"

"No, I don't remember and I certainly don't recall wanting to come here. I have only recently read about your peculiar demise in a letter and I never thought it possible that I could one day meet you."

"But you did have a question to ask me. You even wrote it down in your small black notebook."

"How can you possibly know about my notebook? That's preposterous!" Ambrosius was surprised by the loudness of his own voice that rushed through the surrounding space and quickly faded away.

"Relatively speaking I know very little, but one of the things I do know, is that you keep a small notebook that you predominately use for rendering enigmatic quite haunting tableaux. How I know this is really not important, what's important is that I can help you solve the small riddle that you recently wrote down."

The brother lifted the lantern above his head and the shifting shadows fell like a collection of allusive ink blots across his drooping features.

"Look here," he said and pointed with a long thin forefinger to the small lettering at the very edge of the lantern.

"I wrote this down to always remind me of who I am in the eyes of our beneficent creator. You see; it is in fact quite simple:"

Although it was nearly impossible to see the letters in the darkness, the Brother nevertheless moved his long thin finger across the bottom of the lantern, and the sound of the edge of his unblemished ivory nail scraping against the shady underside was remarkably loud in the stillness.

"God makes certain all kinds of thoughts are possible," he read aloud.

"I wrote it down some time ago, when I was still a novice and immensely troubled by the many variations, translations and interpretations of the Holy Book within our denomination. I thought it would provide me with a reasonable amount of clarity knowing that it was God's will that there is an infinite amount of ways to unravel his mysteries."

"Did writing it down provide you with any form of clarity?" Ambrosius asked, not entirely understanding why he wanted to know.

"That depends if you refer only to my apparent freedom from indistinctness and ambiguity? As to perception and understanding: I have come to the conclusion that no thought can ever be completely lucid."

The Brother paused and turned his head to look at the limitless space surrounding them.

"Imagine this surface as a vast lake having never been disturbed by the wind or by any other thing."

He spread his sleeve covered arms gesturing to the immense blank plane, and the image of a raven flashed before Ambrosius' eyes before it discreetly settled on a densely covered branch somewhere in the depth of his subliminal mind.

"When you look into the lake everything beneath the surface is as clear and as vivid as you could possibly imagine. In fact, it appears as if there is no surface at all, and that you are looking deep into an infinite ocean with a complete comprehension of what you are seeing. However, as soon as you begin to contemplate the things you discover, an infinitesimal ripple appears on the surface that ever so slightly obscure what you thought you already knew. So you attempt to concentrate on what recently escaped you, and by doing so you create more ripples, only this time the ripples are slightly larger than the last time and further obscure your view. The more you think, the bigger the ripples become, until the entire surface is in turmoil and you have forever been deprived of what you originally found."

He paused, apparently waiting for a response and when none was forthcoming he continued: "At the end of the day I have to admit to myself that although I understand and accept the concept of lucidity on the very surface of the lake, what I have uncovered when I start contemplating the things I discover beneath the surface, is that they will always appear to me as boundless mysteries. In a manner of speaking I am merely a blind man forever trying to fill a colossal void."

He stroked the seat with the back of his hand and the vibrations underneath them became more pronounced.

He lifted the lantern from the bottom of the boat, and slowly turned it in the space between them staring intently at the small cutouts as if he was examining them for the first time. Then he brought it close to his face, opened the small door and blew out the candle.

"Look," he said, as the lights in the sky ceased to shine and they were cast into impenetrable darkness, "everything is illuminated."

Chapter 13

He slowly prised open his eyes and looked at the blurry rafters above the bed and waited until they slowly came into focus and sharpened in the muted light.

The fur of the cat felt soft beneath his hand and the recurring vibrations made the palm of his hand and his fingers tingle.

He pulled out the watch from his pocket and checked the time. He had settled in for a light snooze after lunch, and hadn't expected to spend more than an hour in the arms of Morpheus, so he was quite surprised to discover that it was already late in the afternoon. He sat up, and without disturbing the sleeping cat, he swung his legs over the edge of the bed and slowly stood up.

He rubbed his shoulders then stretched his arms over his head and yawned. The uninhibited sound broke the stillness in the cottage like that of the roar of a bear in its cave and the cat briefly lifted its head and looked at him with a penetrating glare. When it realized that there was no immediate danger, it replaced its head on its paws and went back to sleep.

Ruffling his hair, he shuffled over to the window and looked at how the amalgamated flakes of snow had combined to create a nearly uniform structure that now completely covered the pane of glass. Hardly any light was penetrating the surface and against the glass, the compressed snow looked a great deal like a layer of whitish ash.

He slowly walked across the creaking floor to the fireplace, bent down to put another log on the fire and counted the remaining pieces of wood in the bucket, then he grabbed another piece and carried it over to the stove, opened the door, threw it on the small glowing fire and watched as the newcomer was welcomed with gentle licks from the multi-tongued resident.

Soon he would have to bring the bucket out back to replenish the firewood, but for now he picked up the kettle, filled it under the sputtering faucet by the sink and put it on the stove top. Then he walked over to the cupboard, picked up the mustard coloured box, flipped open the lid and let the aroma of the contents beguile him.

While preparing the tea he chewed on a piece of stale bread and thought about the dream.

As far as he could recall; his dreams of the past had never been particularly vivid. They were generally a lot more nebulous and never the sort of dreams he had had the last couple of days. Furthermore, there was something extremely outlandish about the level of clarity with which he could recollect both the images and the conversation, that left him with an unsettling but unambiguous feeling that what he had experienced was somehow real.

He looked across the space at the sleeping cat and wondered if it was by some inexplicable means responsible for these bizarre aberrant incidences.

Unexpectedly, as if it knew what he was thinking, the cat raised its head and gazed at him with unblinking eyes that glinted like drops of ink suspended in the murky space.

He avoided its gaze and instead turned around to involve himself in the making of the tea. He lifted the teapot, made a couple of slow rotations with his hand and waited until the liquid settled. Then he poured the tea in the cup, put the pot back on the stove, covered it with the towel, and carefully carried the cup and its steaming content across the floor and delicately deposited it on the table top.

He pulled the chair closer, sat down, picked up his notebook and flipped through the pages until he found the page he was looking for, placed the book on the table, reached for the matchbox, struck a match on the side of the box and lit the candle in the holder on the table. When the flame had taken proper hold of the wick, he blew on the match and cherished the sulfuric smell of burnt wood before depositing the burnt spillikin in the tray where it sluggishly smoldered.

For a while he just stared at the page in the book.

' od   akes cer   nds of thou   ble '

Then he picked up the pencil, sharpened the rather dull tip with his pocketknife, bent over the book and meticulously filled in the missing letters.

When he finished he sat back up, leaned his back against the chair, lifted the book and looked at the completed sentence.

He let his hand drop on his lap and gazed with blank eyes across the room as the book lay like a dusky white winged moth against the darkness of his trousers.

The finished sentence was exactly as had been prognosticated by the Brother and it didn't matter that he wasn't sympathizing with either the Brother's statement or his general beliefs. It was still an incredibly uncanny elucidation and one that made him feel both uneasy and decidedly curious.

He could not fathom how these events could possibly be connected, and yet lying in his lap was an unequivocal demonstration that he was somehow associated to the letters and even more disturbing, to the actions within them.

He put the book back on the table, rubbed his head in his hands and pressed his palms into his eyes until a multitude of tiny lights zipped across the inside of his eyelids, like a collection of miniscule disorderly shooting stars.

He removed his hands, blinked a couple of times to alleviate the bombardment and picked up the cup and sipped from the edge.

He briefly closed his eyes to savour the taste of the mellow hot liquid before replacing the cup and reaching out for the envelope at the top of the small pile.

He opened it and carefully removed the seven pieces of almost weightless paper within, unfolded them, placed them on the table and smoothed them against the surface.

Dearest E

I miss you with every fibre of my soul and whenever I think of you a shiver runs down my spine. It feels so like the fine sand in an hourglass, finally settling as an internal mound near my core. I count the days until I can wrap my arms around you, hold you tight and bury my head in your beautifully soft neck and immerse myself in your alluring scent. Please believe me when I tell you that we are destined to meet again and that no matter how long we are apart, it will merely prepare me to better express how much I love you.

The snow has yet to stop falling and is entirely covering the cottage in a thick impenetrable blanket. I haven't seen another soul for the longest time and when I am too tired to write, read or draw, I spend most of my hours preoccupied with the memories of you. I am sorry, but often I do not quite remember what I have already written to you, so please forgive me if I am repeating myself. It feels to me like time itself is standing still and I often wake up in the middle of the night imagining the sounds of the waves hammering against the creaking hull. The sound has become an assertive and unabating companion barraging me with its unsolicited company that has seeped into my being like an infection and invaded my mind in such a way that it is now an intrinsic part of everything I do.

Even in the deadening blanket of snow that has otherwise muted all other sounds, I hear the incessant waves. I had never imagined that I would so crave utter silence.

Lying on my back in long grass looking into the blue sky with no other sounds then the gentle whisper of your voice, has lately become my fragile fabricated escape.

I am completely aware that the things I have already told you seem utterly preposterous, and I can assure you that everything I have experienced is still extremely perplexing to me.

Nevertheless, I have decided to share all of my adventures with you, because I trust that you will believe me when I tell you that I am not merely fantasizing. I promise you once more that I have not been drinking too much wine or any other liquor, and that whatever I write down is indeed a truthful account of my experiences. I understand that it must be very difficult for you to accept the stories as I tell them, and that some might even frighten or disturb you, but please let me assure you that I am not in any way trying to hurt you. My only hope is that you can find it in your merciful heart to forgive my transgressions.

There are still some events that haunt my dreams. Indeed, I still spend many of my hours awake thinking about them and wonder what might be happening to me. I still occasionally wandered about the ship and conversed with the other travellers, but during the day, when there was too much commotion, I devoted an increasing amount of time to my cabin where I spent the majority of my time thinking, writing or, as I have already told you, drawing. I made quite the assemblage of acquiescent subjects and occupied a great deal of time studying their physical deterioration to the chargrin of a few of the crew members who found my fascination with dead rodents somewhat disturbing. Others must have thought differently however, because occasionally I would find that a new subject had been placed by my cabin door as a small but very much appreciated benefaction.

I studied them like I would any other nature morte and devoted a considerable amount of time deciding the best angle from which to represent the lifeless creatures. I must admit that this became a rather time consuming undertaking and that many hours passed where my mind was completely lost in the endeavour. The walls in my bunk quickly crowded with drawings and I had to borrow additional drawing materials, sheets of paper and a notebook from the Swedish artist, who was quite intrigued by my newfound obsession and often, but to his dismay, fruitlessly attempted to engage me in a conversation about my work.

One night, trying to stave off my insomnia and keep my mind busy, I was once more traversing about the deck lifting tar stained, salt encrusted ends of rope, searching for new subjects to draw. At the bottom of coils, I would sometimes find discarded victims of the ship's cat's nightly escapades that I would quite gladly scoop up, encase in my kerchief and put in my pocket so that I could later render them in my cabin.

This was an extraordinarily clear and quiet night with a multitude of stars casting their bright gleam on the surface of the ocean as if to admire their shining countenance. They made the fluctuating surface sparkle like an infinite amount of pearls had been spilt and were silently rolling to and fro between the points of the ever moving waves.

There was no one about to disturb me and I was rather engrossed in my task when I suddenly heard a voice. It seemed to be emerging from quite a distance away, and at first I thought that the wind must have been playing a trick on me, but then I heard it again, this time appearing much closer: 'Day after day, day after day, you are stuck, with no wind nor motion. As still as a painted ship on a painted ocean'. A clear, elated, almost euphoric voice, not unlike that of a young girl cut through the stillness of the night like a sneeze in a classroom. The rhyme, although loosely interpreted, was of course terribly familiar.

I quickly spun around expecting someone with a twisted sense of humour to be standing behind me smiling at their literary witticism.

There was nobody there.

Apart from the usual nautical equipment, the deck was completely uninhabited.

I looked around searching for the source of the voice when I spotted a large narrow shadow in the air some way away from the ship.

It was the colour of darkened ash and effortlessly moved in the night, silently flowing back and forth behind the ship's stern, much like that of a wide tapered kite suspended from an invisible string.

The albatross turned its slender neck and looked at me with a large black eye that, reflected in the starlit ocean, made it appear as if it was itself made of liquid. Even from a distance I had the strangest sensation that I was looking into an infinite inkwell, from which could be extracted an inestimable amount of knowledge.

I stared at the solemnly gliding bird in utter disbelief and somewhat circumspect of its intentions.

"Where are you heading when nothing is moving and time is still?" the bird asked gleefully, turning its head in synchronicity with its drifting.

"What is that supposed to mean?" I answered, somewhat perturbed.

"Where are you heading when nothing is moving and time is but still?"

Although it was difficult to determine if it had changed its expression, the bird was undeniably amused by its own question.

"Am I to understand it as a riddle?" I asked.

"Understand it as you wish," the bird replied joyfully, "it won't make the slightest bit of difference."

"Have we met before?" I asked, "I believe I recognize your voice."

"Water, water everywhere and not a drop to drink," the bird sang

poetically in a voice extraordinary similar to that of a young girl.

"Why do you keep referencing that poem?" I asked, somewhat vexed by the bird's joviality and it's calculated deflections. "Am I to be amused or concerned by your recitation? Because I have a difficult time deciding if your casual recital is meant as an introspective caricature or an ineptly veiled warning."

The bird glided silently from side to side behind the ship, slowly turning its head always keeping an obsidian eye locked on mine.

"Where are you heading when nothing is moving and time is but still?" it asked again.

I was somewhat baffled by the incongruous question.

"I don't know," I finally said, curious to know where this conversation was heading, "nowhere I suppose."

"Aha," said the bird, repeatedly clacking its long hollow beak.

The clamorous series of sharp sounds reminiscent of castanets ripped into the silence like a cat's claws in the soft underbelly of an unsuspecting mouse, before drifting away, dissipating in the wind and the waves.

"Where is nowhere?" the bird then asked cheerfully.

I was now convinced that it was intentionally toying with me, and I carefully contemplated the question before I proffered my answer.

"That depends of course on where you are in the first place," I said. "Nowhere is always somewhere, and somewhere could be anywhere, and anywhere could be everywhere, so if nowhere is also everywhere that's where I'm heading."

There was a somewhat extended pause where the bird silently passed from side to side in the starlit expanse.

"Clever," it finally said, "I should have known you have played this game before, and therefore knew the answer." It sounded quite disgruntled.

"I haven't played this game before, it's just something that from a logistical viewpoint makes sense. It is in actual fact merely a matter of perspective."

"Hmmm," said the bird, obviously still upset by my dismantling of its riddle.

Then it made a tiny adjustment with its wings such that the horizontal arch instantly widened and the bird drifted further and further away from the ship.

Every time it made a pass behind the stern it decreased in size until it was just a tiny elongated greyish fleck in the horizon.

"Why were you reciting the poem?" I called out.

My voice was quickly absorbed in the immensity.

I listened for an answer, straining my ears for any sound. But all I heard was the gentle caress of the waves slapping against the hull.

Then precisely when I thought that no answer would be forthcoming, I heard an almost imperceptible fugacious whisper, like that of someone trapped at the bottom of the sea compelling their last breath or air to break through the surface.

"You will learn soon enough," it said, before instantly melting into the cool night air.

Hearing the nearly inaudible murmur emanate from across the waves, I must admit I shuddered involuntarily and quickly pulled my collar close around my neck to ward off the suddenly bracing air, before leaving the deck, escaping to the relative warmth of my cabin.

I shut the door behind me, leaned against it and swiftly surveyed the closed quarters of the cabin. The light from the Brother's lantern cast a muted fluttering light across the rather macabre assemblage of rodents in variant stages of decay that covered the wall in my bunk.

That night, after having spent a great amount of time fervently twisting and turning in my insomniatic state, so as to bring a complete disarray to my bed coverings, I must have finally drifted into a troubled sleep, because I had the most peculiar dream.

I dreamt that I was flying, or perhaps gliding is an apposite description, through a vacuous space in between two seemingly separated planes embellished with a profusion of coruscating lights. I didn't have a sensation of moving towards anything in any particular way and it appeared as if the landscape, if you can even call it that, was entirely without contours. In fact, it felt like I was suspended in the air between two immense sheets of glass that were slowly being repositioned by some unseen force. I found that I could turn around in the space with no gravitational pull and thus my incomprehension of what was up and what was down completely unbalanced me.

For a while I was drifting along in this seemingly endless space wondering what had brought me there, when I spotted a small black fleck on the surface beneath or above me some distance away. When I got closer I realized that the fleck had the outline of a small boat. It was as black as ink and its surface shone like that of polished silver, illuminated as it was by the multitude of surrounding stars. It was sitting upon the surface as if affixed and although nothing hinted at the mass pushing against the crystalline plane, it nevertheless seemed to be moving. As I silently drifted closer, I spotted two sedentary figures in the center of the boat.

A young girl was sitting on the seat facing towards me.

She was, I reckoned, about twelve years old and her prepossessing face was dominated by a pair of large dark eyes over which sat two perfectly formed tapered eyebrows. Her skin was so pale it seemed almost translucent and her raven-black hair made it look as though she was somehow affiliated with the vessel in which she was sitting.

She was dressed all in black and against the dark background, it appeared as if her head and her hands were suspended in midair. The unhurried languorous gestures she made with her hands were reminiscent of large leafed seaweed choreographed by a slow moving current, and I was reminded of something indeterminate, that no matter how hard I tried to bring it into focus, remained but a tiny speck in the periphery of my consciousness.

I instead turned my attention to the other passenger.

Judging from the rather large black coat covering the quite powerful looking shoulders, my presumption was that it was a man, although to be honest it was rather difficult to tell as his face was completely shaded by a tattered black cap.

His elbows were resting on his knees and his hands were concealed under his chin as he leaned forward, evidently attentive to what the girl was saying.

I effortlessly glided closer to the boat and silently hovered above it.

There was an elongated shadow in the plane suspended above me. I first assumed it was a mirroring of the boat below, but when I looked closer I wasn't able to detect either of the two passenger's reflections in the surface. I was forced to reach a provisional conclusion that something else must be creating the shadow, although I had at that point no indication of what that could possibly be as there were no other visible objects around.

"........so you see, the cat has already told me how you occupy your days."

The crystalline voice of the girl was clear and bright. The varying tones ricocheted across the planes interflowing like a multitude of instruments in a speculative artistic creation, before finally dispersing leaving a palpable silence behind.

She cupped her hands and rested them in her lap.

The lack of movement that ensued made her appear somewhat constrained, rather like a small figurine or marionette waiting for someone to pick up her strings.

"You do think about where you are, don't you?" She then asked solemnly.

I couldn't hear if she received a reply to her question, but it was clear from her expression that her companion had in some way communicated his answer.

"Good," she said, "but beware of all that closes from behind and all that hangs in the space above." She pointed with one of her long attenuated fingers to the exact point I was suspended, while surreptitiously producing two small white objects that she, with a languid flick of her narrow wrist, rolled across the bottom of the boat.

The man slowly turned his head towards me, and as the objects bounced silently on the velvety interior before coming to rest in the space between them, I realized with a jolt of horror, that I was gazing at my own careworn countenance.

I must have screamed in fear, because I woke up in my bunk both terrified and confused.

The sound of my howl was still clasping the air like a glutinous substance and my nightshirt was clinging to my body like a supplemental layer of skin.

I don't know what to tell you about the events or indeed the dreams of mine, other than I have described them to you exactly as I recall them.

Besides; I couldn't possibly explain what the dream means or what the girl in the boat was trying to tell me. Although I of course understand that it could be read by some as some kind of omen, I do however, with my rational mind, refuse to believe what I am observing in my sleep is more than just a series of evocative illusory figments brought forth by a combination of utter exhaustion and an already overzealous mind. I will pay a visit to the ship's doctor to ask if I can be administered something that will help induce sleep.

I ache for you in the deepest recesses of my heart and not an hour goes by without me dreaming about the day when we can again be together. I promise that everything you have been waiting for will be bestowed upon you. Until then you must rest assured that my love for you is everlasting and all encompassing.

    Yours Forevermore,

    C

He put down the sheet on top of the other papers to the left, leaned forward in his chair, rested his chin on his hands, and stared at the small intricate drawing lying on the surface in front of him.

The mouse was lying on its back with its front paws pulled up under its chin and its hind legs spread out from its body. Its tiny serrated front teeth were visible under the pointed snout and its long dark tapered tail curled like a fishing hook to the left of its body.

The rendering was exquisite.

The artist had expertly utilized the light soft haired belly of the rodent and perfectly integrated it with the colour of the paper, making it appear as if the animal was somehow merging with the material. The lack of shadow beneath it and the slight indication of wispy fur around the edge of the animal gave him the strangest feeling that the mouse had been deliberately depicted as being suspended in space.

He wondered if the artist perhaps subconsciously had been trying to portray his own experiences.

He got up from the seat and, grabbing hold of his hands, stretched his arms above his head and bent his upper body first to the left and then to the right, listening to the muffled grinding sound of his aching joints.

Then he walked into the bedroom, picked up the old torn suitcase from the bottom of the wardrobe and put it on the bed next to the sleeping cat. For a moment he stared at the small package, then he reached into the suitcase, unwrapped the paper and, careful not to look at the drawings, picked up one of the frames.

He gently pried open the back of the frame and removed one of the drawings.

He positioned it face down on top of the remaining frames, then replaced them at the bottom of the suitcase and closed the lid, encasing them in darkness.

He carried the frame into the next room, picked up the piece of paper with the deceased rodent, carefully positioned it face down on the sheet of glass, replaced the brown backing board and turned the frame around.

The rodent was now suspended behind a sheet of glass, framed on all sides by a dark rigid boundary.

He walked over to the fireplace and put the frame down next to the other effervescent rendering and while looking from one to the other he admired the skill with which the artist had brought forth such an extraordinarily aliveness in his insentient subjects.

It was as if the artist had sketched the rodents while they were asleep and that he somehow expected them to spring back to life as soon as he had concluded his rendering.

Ambrosius continued to study the drawings leaning up against the sooty stone wall, as he pondered the dream recounted in the recent letter.

It didn't make a difference that the girl in the boat had been dressed in black and that her demeanor had been less than cheerful, he nonetheless had an unequivocal feeling of who she was. What she was doing there and how she could be such an affecting presence in another person's dreams, he really couldn't tell.

He failed to recall exactly what she had said, so he went back to the table, turned over the paper, slid the candleholder closer, grabbed the edge of the table and bent down to better search the page.

He was however thwarted in his plans by the cat, which had silently jumped down from the bed, run across the floor and now stood on its hind legs digging its front claws into his upper leg vying for his attention.

He looked into its eyes.

The flickering illumination from the candle trailed across the azure spherules like thin streaks of reddish yellow clouds on an evening sky in late summer.

As soon as the cat realized it had his attention, it extracted its claws and inaudibly made its way to the door where it sat down, turned its head and looked back at him.

"I suppose we might as well both go," he said, walking across the creaking planks to where the cat now sat absentmindedly licking its paw and washing its face.

He slid his arms into the sleeves of his jacket and pulled it on, then he fished out the gloves from the pockets, put on the old cap and pulled it down on his head, grabbed the shovel, reached for the handle and opened the door.

The door had left an intrinsic and delicate embossed imprint on the snowdrift that was nearly halfway covering the opening.

Though the wind was howling and the snow kept falling from a monotone colourless sky, he still felt compelled to bend down to look at the grainy motif that ran like a varied composition of static rivers through the cold fabric.

He inserting the shovel, making a deep horizontal gash in the center of the fluid but fixed markings, wondering how he could somehow replicate the self-executing drawing without losing its inherent veracity.

For a brief moment he thought about fetching his notebook, but the notion of the cat beside him made him reconsider and he instead began moving the snowdrift in front of them.

When he had cleared enough space, the cat ran outside and squatted in the center of the fresh clearing, its tail moving like an adder behind it.

When it had finished, it quickly returned to the cottage and he closed the door behind it.

He put the shovel down and looked around.

The snow now covered everything in the surrounding landscape, and although he strained his ears for any sounds, all he heard was a heavy silence.

As if the sound of death had wrapped the world in an impenetrable blanket.

He was wondering if the sounds that he made, the wheezing in his chest, the blood flowing in his ears, and the words he spoke were the only things that proved he was still alive.

He cleared his throat and the noise lingered like a small infelicitous postlude, before dissipating in the cold exanimate landscape.

Chapter 14

It was rather late in the day when he finally returned

The colour of the sky had changed from a light downy white to an ominous tenebrous grey and the snow, showing no sign of abating, was still falling steadily, nonsensically whisked about by the ever present wind, rapidly creating new drifts on the paths he had already cleared.

He had spent a good couple of hours digging the trench between the outhouse, the shed and the chicken coup, thinking mostly about the letter he had recently read.

He had immediately recognized the albatross evocative of the bird in *The Ancient Mariner* and now he puzzled over its ominous arrival and, though it wasn't exactly sibylline, the curious riddle. Also, the bird's last foreboding statement was certainly a matter of conjecture.

The appearance of the innominate faceless character in the boat had him equally flummoxed. He wondered if the letter writer, perhaps cognitively debilitated by his severe insomnia, was more susceptible to night terrors, although that seemed somehow unlikely judging from his earlier correspondence. Even though some of the events had been difficult to explain logically, the letters themselves seemed to have been constructed from a place of reasoning.

He reached the coop and cleared a space on the ground, wiped the snow off the walkway and made sure the hens, quietly foregathered in their berths, were fed and watered, before he walked back to the shed, and picked up an armful of chopped firewood that he carried back to the cottage and deposited in the bucket by the fireplace, dragging a trail of snow across the floor.

He bent down and scooped up most of the compressed pieces and threw them in the sink, leaving behind a series of small dark marks, like the prints of a mystical creature, temporarily imbedded in the planks of wood.

He took off his jacket, hung it from the hook on the back of the door and removed his cap, ran his stiff aching fingers through his damp

139

bristled hair, reached into his jacket pockets and picked out five eggs the colour of milky coffee.

He carried them over to the stove and put them in the small pot where they rolled around against the hard edges of the darkened metal, producing a sequence of small hollowed taps in the otherwise quiet room.

He picked up a couple of logs from the bucket and placed one in the fireplace, opened the door to the stove and threw the other one into the hot chamber, where it landed in the glowing embers sending a cascade of fiery particles into the air.

He pushed the door shut and washed his hands by the sink, walked over to the cupboard, picked up the hump of bread, the butter and a can of beans and brought them over to the stove. He put a lump of butter in the pan, cracked three of the eggs and watched them float around like small clear glutinous islands on the glistening pond.

While he waited for the viscous substance to coagulate, he cut a couple of slices of bread, opened the can of beans, filled the black kettle with water and put it on the stove.

Then he cut up some ham and put it in the bowl on the floor.

When his dinner was ready he carried it over to the table, sat down on the chair, pushed all thoughts to the outer periphery of his mind and began to eat.

When he finished eating, he placed the plate and the cutlery at the bottom of the sink, walked over to the cupboard, picked up the mustard yellow can and began his customary tea making routine.

In a way that was influenced by the part of the mind that was not fully aware, his mind and body obeyed an established pattern of habitual measured movements, following a sequence of steps and gestures that made it appear as if he was moving to a silent rhythm.

He poured the amber liquid into the white porcelain cup, carefully carried it across the floor and set it down on the table. A small amount of tea spilled over the edge, ran down the side and circled the bottom of the cup. He lifted the cup off the table and wiped at the spilled liquid with his shirt sleeve, and stared at the beautiful aqueous ideogram on the tabletop while cautiously sipping at the edge of the cup, careful not to burn his lips on the hot liquid. Then he replaced the cup a little further away, sat down on the chair, picked up another envelope, removed the eight nearly transpicuous sheets and placed them on the table next to the small celestial drawing.

My Dearest E

Whenever I think of your beautiful eyes resting on mine and of your soft pale arms around my neck enclosing me in your loving embrace, I am in an abrupt emotional turmoil. Like a hermit in the desert desperate to quench his thirst, my body and soul yearn for your company. You are as always in the forefront of my mind and I have viewed the image I carry of you so many times that I fear I somehow excoriate your features from the surface of the paper.

I once again tell you truthfully that I am not inventing or exaggerating the sometimes inexplicable events that continue to happen to me. Although part of the narrative will be near impossible for you to accept, I am merely attempting to give you a full and truthful account of my experiences, and while I understand that the circumstances onboard the ship might have had quite a significant impact on my increased insomnia, it cannot fully explain the mysterious encounters I continue to have during the hours of darkness.

When I recount the events of my journey, I am at times at a total loss as to the order in which they occurred. Often they strike me as having happened at the same time but in different places, or perhaps in the same place but at different times. You will have to excuse me if I am recounting things that I have already written down, but there are peradventure too many comparable incidences in my mind, that sometimes makes it difficult to keep the images and events apart. Although it is absolutely quiet here, the incessant hammering of the waves against the groaning hull are the only sounds keeping me company throughout the night and I wonder if their intermingled hydrous duet will forever dwell in my ears.

Lately I have found myself more steadily occupied with rendering the deceased rodents. It is now rare that I read or even write anything but my letters to you. I have also found it gradually more troublesome to partake in any other activities aboard the ship and I therefore tend to keep my distance from the other passengers, whom I often find too distracting with their unabating vociferous prattle. My days are for the most part spent in fitful rest in my darkened cabin and my nights by wandering the ship or drawing by the glowing light of the lantern.

On one of my nightly excursions traversing the main deck, I was most unexpectedly joined by the Captain of the ship.

G E Sharon was a rather tall man of medium build. His most distinguishing feature, besides the mane of unruly hair that fell, like a tenebrous waterfall across his broad forehead, were his large penetrating eyes that were so dark as to appear like two black pearls having been artificially inserted deep in their owner's interior.

Like the eyes of a taxidermied animal, they revealed nothing but a reflection of what was currently in front of them, and though he was looking directly at you it was impossible to know what he was thinking.

He was mainly preoccupied with the conditions of the ship, the crew and the weather and not known to involve himself with trivial chit-chat. As a matter of fact, we had never spoken directly and this was the first time I had the opportunity to properly make his acquaintance.

He came down the companionway, measuredly walked across the deck with a sway in his steps that betrayed a deeply ingrained familiarity with the continued rolling of the ship, loudly humming what I believed was The High Mass in B Minor by J. S. Bach, a quite evocative piece of music that brought some haunting images to mind.

I don't believe he expected anyone to be around at that hour, but when he noticed me standing by the bulwark, he immediately stopped humming, walked across the deck, stood beside me, laid both his long fingered hands on the railing and looked out at the unceasing circumambient white tipped waves. The straight tall pipe in the corner of his mouth gave out a sweetened plume of tobacco smoke that entwined itself around him like a ghostly mist.

It was an overcast, quite chilly night and as I had left the lantern behind in my cabin, it was difficult to make out the Captain's features in the darkness. His dark eyes, black hair and quite notable sideburns, that inimitably framed his square jaw, gave him quite the devilish look, and I believe I caught a facinorous glint in his dark eyes when he slowly turned his head and looked my way before turning his eyes back on the ocean.

"Do you believe it is possible to imagine how large it is?" he said, removing his pipe.

The question, spoken in a rich baritone, briefly hung in the air between us.

"I have spent a lifetime on the ocean and I'm still confounded by the

enormity of it. Its mass seems so utterly incomprehensible that it boggles my mind."

He returned the pipe to his mouth and turned around and stared at me with his golem like eyes as if studying my face through the darkness.

"Does the incomprehensibility of the external world trouble you as well?" he asked.

I was completely taken aback by the gravity of his question and it took a good while for me to consider his question.

"External in what way?" I said finally, looking at his darkened somewhat brooding silhouette. "With regards to how we comprehend it in the mind, there is really nothing in the world that is literally external. Of course out there," I gestured to the surrounding darkness, "objects and places can be variously situated, to the left or to the right, up or down, in front and behind, but no such organization is possible for things that only transpire in the mind. In here," I said, pointing to my temple, "everything is entirely metaphorical and can therefore be positioned in any configuration and scale. We have an innate ability to make everything we think about infinitesimally small or immensely large, thus the understanding of what we deem our external world is really dependent on how we internalize it."

The captain evidently considered his reply, because he was silent for quite some time.

"Still, that doesn't eliminate the obvious evidence of the seas physical immensity," he replied through his teeth, his voice slightly gruff.

"Of course not," I replied, "it's all just a matter of how we observe and understand things. I am in no way arguing about the immensity of the ocean in its reality in front of us, I am merely stating that when you asked if I had trouble conceiving the immeasurability of the external world, I was merely wondering about how we frame the parameters. The idea of the ocean or indeed the world is in essence dictated by our own physical relationship. However, as soon as that relationship is allowed to be dictated by our mind instead, the physical borders or means of measurement become theoretical only. It's a bit like asking: 'how big is the world?' Do we measure it according to our own physicality? Or do we look at it as a small crust covered rock in relation to the immensity of the universe? Both can be a veracious account depending on the circumstances."

The captain removed the pipe, bend his head back and laughed.

The hollowed raspy sound came from a place deep within him and the sudden unexpected outburst bounced across the waves like a shoal of frightened flying fish safely re-entering the sea someway in the distance.

"You sound very much like someone I once knew who followed me wherever I went and always questioned my ability to find the quickest route across the immense sea," he said when he had stopped laughing.

"Who was that?" I asked, curious who would have been brave or foolish enough to question this rather redoubtable character.

"I think you might already know," came his cryptic reply. "However, if you are indeed suggesting that the ocean around us can be as small as we want it to be," he said, quietly chuckling to himself, "will you promise to come and notify me, when you've discovered a more expeditious route across it? It would most certainly help for me to know, especially considering where we are going."

Then he jovially slapped me on my back, replaced his pipe, bid me adieu, walked across the deck to the companionway and disappeared up the steps once more humming loudly to himself, leaving me to my own thoughts in the enveloping darkness.

A while afterwards I returned to my cabin and although I was feeling enervated, I was not yet ready to sleep. I instead decided to continue one of my studies and sat down at the small desk and began to draw in the limited light from the lantern.

I was thus engaged when, in the middle of the night, I heard a soft knocking at the door.

At first I must have disregarded it on account of the usual noises of the creaking wood and thumping waves, but the knocking occurred again several times in the same manner.

I looked hastily around my cabin. With the amount of crumbled pieces of paper and items of clothing strewn across the floor, I wondered if it was more appropriate to pretend that I was asleep, as the room was in such disarray and I was not dressed to receive a visitor. However, the knocking continued with only a slight interspace, so I finally decided to put on my jacket and before answering the caller, I quickly grabbed as many of the pieces of paper and items of clothes as I could and threw it in my berth before closing the curtain. Then I walked across the floor pushed down the handle and peered out of the half opened door.

I don't believe I have ever had a more astonishing experience in my entire life than when I saw you stand before me in the darkened corridor. Your beautiful face, lit merely by the feeble gleam of the lantern, was as usual framed by your comely golden curls that flowed like a honeyed waterfall around your long soft neck and cascaded down your narrow shoulders.

You were barefoot and wearing the white summer dress that you usually wore when picking flowers between the tall grass in the meadow near the pond. In fact, I believe you effused the fragrance of flowers into the briny air and I breathed in as heavily as I could to fill my lungs with the scent.

I was completely dumbstruck and couldn't even respond when you placed your delicate cool hand on my chest and gently pushed me into the interior of the cabin.

Benumbed as I was by your unbelievable presence, I looked into your deep blue eyes that glinted like sapphires in the faint light, and thought that I must be dreaming.

However, you continued to push at my chest so that I stumbled backwards into the chair and awkwardly knocked it against the table when I sat down.

The sound was muted by the ceaseless battering of the waves against the groaning hull.

You never uttered a word, but merely cocked your head, smiled your mischievous smile and looked at me with narrowed eyes before slowly moving closer, lifting your dress with your delicate fingers to reveal your long slender legs. When you reached me, you placed a leg on either side of the chair and lowered yourself onto my lap keeping your eyes locked on mine. Then you leaned forward and extinguished the candle in the lantern.

When your soft honeyed locks brushed against my face it was like the licks of a thousand tiny flames had suddenly set me alight and although I was totally transfixed in my seat, I nevertheless felt an arousal that I cannot possibly express in words.

I began perspiring profusely, my breath intensified and my body shook uncontrollably like I was in a feverish delirium soundlessly screaming for fulfilment.

When you noticed my obvious distress, you reached between our legs to swiftly unbutton my trousers and free me from my constraints. You then slowly lowered yourself upon me until I was completely absorbed in your warmth.

While keeping the rest of your body completely still you pressed your hands against my chest and leaned forward to gaze into my eyes as a small vibration began from somewhere deep within your body. It gradually gathered in strength, taking a firm hold and you began moving your hips in a smooth wave-like motion, undulating to the rhythm of the rise and fall of the surging reverberations. As you began to move faster and your breathing intensified, I put my hands on the top of your uncommonly smooth legs, and gazed intently into your eyes that, virtually concealed by the shadows, were now less than a couple of inches from my own.

Your quickened breaths became increasingly shallow, and as you were nearing the apex and your enraptured body clenched around me, your fingers dug into my chest as if attempting to usher the very heart out of me.

In the same exact moment, a wan stream of moonlight slipped through the density of the clouds, briefly illuminating the cabin, and as I released myself I saw the reflection of my own stupefied face in the elongated feline pupils in the dark blue eyes that were nearly covered by the long sable like hair falling across the features of an altogether unfamiliar face.

I instantly recoiled, closed my eyes and quickly removed my hands from the unnaturally sleek body while feeling myself diminish.

The pressure on my lap gradually lifted and I instantly felt a coolness envelope me as if I had been swathed in several layers of damp cold blankets. I shivered in the chilly air and waited a good while before opening my eyes. When I finally had the courage to do so, I saw that I was alone.

Whatever it was that had visited me had disappeared and except for the quite pungent briny smell, that was rather more pronounced than usual, the cabin was as before.

With shaking hands, worried what I might find, I felt around my waist in the darkness.

The buttons in my trousers were undone and there was an unpleasant dampness in my groin that proved my speculation was warranted.

Thoroughly distraught by the events of the night I fell into my berth and surrounded by crumpled pieces of paper containing the nugatory renderings of dead rodents and the pungent mixed smell of discarded clothing and brine I fell into an oppressive delirious sleep.

I was standing in a white boat with two masts from which a couple of large soft sails the colour of snow were suspended, like a pair of pendulous wedding dresses permanently waiting for their brides.

The boat was sitting on, what I can best describe as an absolutely immense sheet of glass, although when I carefully moved to the bulwark and tentatively looked over the side, the surface was as colourless as the sky above and I could see nothing move beneath the sub fusc plane.

There was no wind to fill the snow-white sails and everything around me was eerily quiet.

The boat lay absolutely still, like it was forever frozen on the opaque sheet, and the light that brightened everything around me, placing an ivory monochrome hue on the surroundings, must have come from an unknown source, because there was no sun in sight.

I was wondering what I was doing in this desolate landscape, when I noticed a shadow moving in the distance.

It was coming from a place beyond the outlying whiteness and at first I couldn't decipher what it was. It mostly looked like a fly against a piece of frozen glass, but as it got closer it appeared as if a large black elongated kite was floating silently towards me.

When it finally got close enough and circled the vessel hovering above me like a dark foreboding harbinger, I realized that it wasn't a kite after all but a large pitch black albatross.

It continued to silently circumnavigate the boat while slowly turning its head, inspecting me with its black shiny eyes.

Flashing through my mind was an image of an overflowing inkwell the contents of which spilled like dark river systems onto two pristine pieces of paper. However, as soon as the ink had created the obscure images it was immediately absorbed into the fabric, leaving the pages unspoilt once again, much like a version of the current landscape.

I stared at the bird gliding past me. It's unfathomably long pointed wings were the colour of gunmetal and glistened in the air like a pair of expertly made sabers cutting through the windless air. Although, when truth be told the wings hardly moved, making it appear as if the bird, instead of flying, was held up by an undisclosed impelling force.

It continued to silently circle the vessel.

"Who are you?" I called out.

The bird made another pass and turned its head.

"I'm an ancient mariner," it answered.

Obviously amused by its own hilarity, the bird then made a series of swift clacking sounds.

The paroxysm of noise bounced off the semi opaque milky surface and generated a swarm of echoes that spread like a wave in the otherwise quiet space.

"Is that intended to amuse me?" I said, looking at the passing bird. "Or is that a comment that is only meant to amuse you?"

"That depends on whether or not you find it humorous?" The bird's voice was like that of a jubilant child who had just found a long lost favorite toy.

"What am I doing here?" I asked, ignoring the bird's question, focusing instead on its dark gleaming eyes.

"That is indeed a very good question," it answered, turning its head as it glided pass the bow, "a very good question indeed. What exactly are you doing here?"

"I don't know. That's the reason why I asked you, because I thought you might know why I'm here."

"I do know where you are, but not why you are here."

"So where am I?" I asked somewhat exasperated, running my hand through my hair that felt strangely unfamiliar; it was short and stiff like the bristles on a hog.

"That depends on what you see," the bird said enigmatically, continuing its airy curvilinear flight. "What do you see?"

"What do you mean, what do I see? I suppose I see the same as you; A white boat with flaccid sails sitting on an opaque glassy plane in a colourless void. Is there anything else to see?"

"There is," said the bird convivially, "there is you and there is me."

"Of course," I exclaimed, somewhat annoyed by my oversight, "I merely *forgot those factors."*

"How could you forget yourself?" the bird asked cocking its head slightly.

"I didn't forget about myself, I merely forgot to include myself and you in what was contained within these parameters."

"How is that even possible when there's apparently so little else to see?"

"I don't know. I simply forgot to mention it."

"Hmmm, do you reckon there are other things in this place that you've seen but have forgotten to mention," the albatross continued, "or could it be that you have not been looking hard enough?"

"I am not certain I understand," I said, staring at the bird circling the vessel, "I'm positive I haven't seen anything else but the things I have already told you."

"Look at the space in front of you, and tell me what you see."

Bewildered by the bird's command I looked down and was startled by the appearance of a small square table standing in the center of the white boat.

I was absolutely convinced it hadn't been there when I arrived and I was perplexed as to its unexpected materialization. On the tabletop sat what looked like two small bundles of white envelopes and next to the envelopes sat a small white teacup that had left a blurry outline of a circle in the wood.

The objects seemed somehow familiar and yet I hesitated for a brief moment before I took a step forward.

However, as soon as I reached out a hand, the table immediately receded from view and I was left staring at the white planks that themselves slowly dematerialized leaving me afloat in an empty colourless void, listening to an almost reproving voice.

"What did you see?" it said, "What did you see?"

I woke up in my bunk late the next morning utterly confused by my latest apparition.

I cannot imagine you would understand any more than I do what is happening in my sleep. I am describing the events or the visions of mine exactly as I recall them and though I promise you that I am not losing my sense of reality, I do however entirely accept that my tales must sound like the delusions of a crazed person.

I find it most difficult to write about and explain the visit of the succubus, who must have sensed my profound deprivation. Her presence felt so frightfully real and as I am writing this, I am afraid of how you must now look upon my wretched and pusillanimous soul. I can merely hope you can find in your most generous heart an ability to forgive this most reprehensible behaviour.

I of course understand that the presence of the black albatross could be read as yet another woeful omen, but I am still refusing to believe that what I experience in my sleep is but a series of unusually imaginative and fanciful dreams, that mean nothing more than what they are.

When I saw you standing in the soft flickering light in the doorway to my cabin, I thought my heart must have stopped beating and I was seeing your beautiful countenance in the afterlife.

I miss you like my heart is about to burst and whenever I think of you it brings a flood of unstoppable tears to my eyes. I wish for nothing more than for us to be together and nothing on this earth would be sweeter than to once more enfold you in a loving embrace.

With all my heart and soul, I am forever yours,

C

Chapter 15

With trembling fingers, he put the piece of paper down on the top of the other sheets, carefully folded the pages of the letter and inserted them into the envelope that he placed on top of the bigger of the two small piles.

Then he slowly got up from the chair, put his hands on his lower back and pressed forward, listening to the muted crunch in his vertebrae as he stared at the sleeping cat in the dim light of the fast approaching evening.

The window panes were now like sheets of murky dense fog that were letting through just a suggestion of leadened light into the increasingly tenebrous interior.

He picked up the candleholder, walked over to the fireplace, lit the candle with some difficulty and put another log on the embers before leaning against the shelf while staring pensively at the suspended rodents in their black frames.

His hands were still vibrating uncontrollably and although he stared at them willing them to stop, they kept shaking in small rhythmic intervals, until he grabbed onto the wooden shelf and pushed forward as if trying to sink the shelf deeper into the stone.

After a while the shaking stopped and he let go of the shelf and rubbed his sore hands against each other.

There was no denying he was disturbed by the accounts he had just read.

Although he knew it was an improbability, he had the most unnerving feeling that the table in the dream was the exact same as the one standing on the floor behind him.

Wary of what he might find, he slowly turned around to face the softly lit tableau in the center of the room.

Though the wet circle from the tea cup had now almost dried out, the image he was looking at was nearly identical to the one described in the letter.

He very much wanted to disbelieve what he saw and began rubbing his face with his hands while making a series of humming guttural noises, as if he could somehow physically obliterate the vision already knowing that it wouldn't make any difference.

When he removed his hands from his face and refocused his eyes, the table, the letters and the teacup were as before, stock-still in the space exactly where the author of the letters had placed them, except from the fact that they were not situated on the narrower planks in a white boat in another man's dream, but standing five feet away on the rugged floorboards in a small stone cottage.

He looked across the room at the cat lying on the bed and like a premonition it slowly lifted its black head and looked at him. He quickly averted his gaze and instead walked over to the door and put on his jacket, gloves and cap. Before opening the door, he glanced back at the cat, but it showed no interest in joining him, instead putting its head down on its paws, ostensibly to sleep once more.

He grabbed the shovel, pushed open the door and stepped outside.

It had finally stopped snowing and the thick clouds had disappeared leaving a dark starlit sky overhead. The temperature had dropped significantly and he was met with a gust of frozen wind that tore into his face like a ferocious animal with thousands of miniscule pointed teeth.

When he took a surprised breath it hurt like a small amount of gunpowder had been ignited inside his nose, so he covered his face with his glove and rapidly made his way to the outhouse clearing a path by ramming the shovel into the powdery snow and driving it in front of him.

After he stood in the freezing dark of the outhouse emptying his bladder, he quickly went over to check that all was well in the coop, before collecting a single egg and closing the hatch for the night.

Then he picked up the shovel, hurried back along the cleared path, quickly opened the door and fell into the warmth of the cottage as a log of wood eagerly welcomes the warm silky caresses of the multi-fingered flames.

He stood the shovel up against the wall, removed his jacket, gloves and cap and deposited them on the hook, walked across the floor to the stove, picked up the kettle and turned the handle on the faucet.

A long compressed squeaking followed by a couple of muted banging noises emitted from the pipe before a slender stream of water began flowing from the tap.

He held the kettle underneath the slim waterfall and waited patiently as it filled. When the kettle was full he placed it on the stovetop and grabbed the larger pot from the hook and put it in the sink under the thin strip of slow flowing water.

If the temperature kept dropping there was no doubt he would have to clear a path around the house to get to the water barrel in the back. As he turned the handle on the faucet and the weak stream of water stopped running, he made a mental note to remember to bring the small pickaxe back from the shed.

He poured a bit of hot water into the teapot and swirled it around creating a small dark vortex in the enclosed chamber, placed it on the stove and watched as the miniscule bubbles in the whirlpool rose to the surface and slowed down until they barely moved. Then he fetched the tea from the pantry, poured out the slightly discolored water in the sink, added a couple of generous pinches of tea to the pot and waited until the water in the kettle started boiling before grabbing the dishtowel, lifting the kettle and pouring the steaming water into the warm dark belly of the pot.

He let the leaves stew until the tea reached an adequate colour, then he poured the hot amber liquid into the white cup and carefully carried it across the floor and gently set it down on the table.

With the sleeve of his jumper he wiped the warm moisture off the top of his hand, picked up the candleholder from the top of the fireplace and placed it on the table next to the envelopes, sat down in the chair, lifted the cup and sipped at the burning contents before replacing it near the edge of the table.

He reached out and picked up another envelope from the slightly smaller pile, carefully opened it with his pocket knife and slid out nine small threadbare pieces that he unfolded and flattened against the table top.

He leaned forward in his chair, that groaned in disapproval under his shifting weight, and started reading.

My Beloved E,

I can't seem to stop myself from looking at the rendering of you that I now carry around in my coat pocket, so that I can gaze at your beautiful face whenever the need comes over me. I must have stared at your countenance so intensely and for so long that whole days have gone by without me realising. My body and soul cry out for your company like an abandoned wolf cub lost in the impenetrable wilderness, hoping against hope that it may one day be found.

The dark cold days are infinitely longer than the nights and the nights pass slowly and tediously as if there is an actual retardation of time. I can't entirely remember what I have told you of my accommodation, but no matter the glow of the fireplace and the warmth of the stove, my days continue to be cold, dark and lonesome. I haven't seen another living soul for the longest time and I cannot recall when I last had a conversation with another person. I sometimes find myself speaking out loud, just to hear the sound of a voice and to break the ever present silence.

Mostly my days are consumed by drawing my faithful subjects and by dreaming of the reunion of the three of us. In my scattered dreams I often feel your soft playful fingers tenderly stroking my face, but when I awake, it is nothing but a small feather poking through the fabric of my pillow or a lock of my own hair falling across my face. Although I so wish for it to not be true, the reality is that you are never truly there.

One night I was walking back and forth on the main deck looking out at the sea at the back of the ship while drifting in and out of thoughts of home. I imagined you standing at the sink in the kitchen, bathed in sunlight. Then I was briefly sitting in the field surrounded by the smell of grass and flowers and the sounds of songbirds and you and the little one feeding the ducks in the pond, laughing delightfully when the ducklings frantically circled around each other in their pursuit of a piece of bread. I awoke from my reverie to disparagingly discover that I was standing with my feet solidly planted on the seemingly sempiternal deck. It seems like such a long time ago that I left you that I can hardly believe it. The further I am removed from you the more intense my need becomes.

I began walking up and down the deck, oblivious to what was happening around me, which frankly wasn't much as I hadn't encountered any other passengers or crew members. In fact, when I come to think of it, I can't actually recall when I last saw another person aboard the ship. The last person I spoke to was the Captain and if I remember correctly that was quite a while back, although when truth be told I can't tell exactly how long ago that was. During the day I stay in my cabin trying desperately to get some rest and I rarely venture out when I can hear the commotion of other people, which has strangely abated the longer the vessel has been at sea.

Because of my now severe insomnia time has a tendency to play tricks with my mind and I'm often finding myself incapable of telling what time of day it is or even what day of the week it is. One day effortlessly slides into the next and then into the next and into the next until they're all the same. I am often wondering if that is what the cat meant when it said that it would grant me more time, which I of course know is an improbability. However, it does seem very much like the ship is somehow lying stationary on the waves, because whenever I look at the stars overhead, they are always locked in the same position.

This particular evening there were no stars in the sky, and I had unnecessarily brought the Brother's lantern with me because the night was uncommonly light. Even though it was well past midnight, there was hardly any wind and a strange green hue lay over the nearly immobile waves, bestowing on the ship a quite ghostly appearance.

I stood by the bulwark looking into the distance when I noticed a mass of dark clouds quickly assembling, like a flock of mountain sized slate gray sheep being forced together by an eager sheepdog. The sight felt especially ominous so I looked around to see if there was anyone I could alert to the atmospheric change and when there was nobody to be found on the main deck, I walked over to the companionway, walked up the stairs to the quarter deck and attempted to hail the sailor posted at the helm, whom I first assumed was the first mate but on closer inspection realized was the captain. He was standing completely still with a hand on either side of the large wheel, his face turned towards the oncoming storm. I was confounded to see that he was alone and looked around to see if I could spot any other members of the crew busying themselves with hauling in the sails, securing the water barrels or any of the other equipment, but to my dismay there was not a single soul to be seen.

I feared the storm would entirely take the ship by surprise and although I shouted the name of Captain Sharon as loud as I could, he didn't seem to notice, but kept looking straight ahead at the rapidly approaching clouds that were now less than half a mile away. They were accompanied by an immense display of lightning that transmitted a bright violent flash through the clouds and caused an enormous thunderclap that rippled across the waves.

So colossal was the impact of the expansive forces, that it sounded like Thor had brought down his hammer on a mountain and cracked it in two.

I have never in my life heard anything quite like it and I fruitlessly attempted to draw the attention of the captain, although this time less vigorously as I honestly didn't know of what I might inform him.

At that point it was clear to me that he understood that the ship would soon be engulfed in the ferocity of the thunderstorm and before I found myself caught in its mauling center, I decided to make a hasty retreat to my cabin. I thus ran across the deck, down the stairs, through the darkened corridor and pulled open the cabin door, shut it behind me and sat on my berth gasping for breath.

Holding onto the edge of the berth, sending furtive glances at the bullseye I waited for the onslaught.

My body was as tight as a string on a bow, prepared as I was for the barrage of thunder, and I quite literally leapt in the air as I heard a soft knocking on the door.

I hadn't seen a living soul for many days and as I moved guardedly towards the door, opened it and hesitantly peered out, I wondered who in their right mind would be visiting in the midst of a colossal thunderstorm.

In the murky light in the corridor stood a young girl.

Her long raven black hair was held back by a broad white hair band revealing a face that was as flawless and expressionless as a Venetian mask. So meticulously placed were the dark symmetrical eyebrows over her large dark eyes that it looked as if they had been artificially constructed. Her small straight nose sat over her full lips, that even in the faint light gleamed like they had been recently painted.

There was a slight iridescent glow to her pale, slightly translucent skin that made me think about sculptural works in marble and I was suddenly curious if she might also be cool to the touch.

Her white summer dress and her small white shoes made it look as if she had merely stopped by my door on her way to a picnic. She held her hands behind her back and turned back and forth as if she was on the verge of asking me a question, which she finally did:

"Are you not going to invite me in?" She looked up at me with her obsidian eyes and cocked her head slightly making her long dark hair move like a black velvet flag in an evening breeze.

"I don't believe it's comme il faut for a young lady to be visiting a gentleman in his cabin so late in the evening," I answered, not knowing if the implication had registered.

"Don't worry," she said matter of factly, "what nobody sees doesn't actually occur."

"You know that's not true," I answered, immediately flustered, "that's merely a theoretical postulation. I know that you're here and you know that you're here, so if I invite you to enter my cabin, and if you do, that is a definite action."

"Only to the two people present," she said smiling, "to everyone else there's no difference between the occurrence and the nonoccurrence, ergo the occurrence might as well happen as not happen."

"This is not like playing a game of secrets," I said, lowering my voice, "I can't possibly invite a young lady into my cabin without the potential for unintended consequences. What would your parents say if they knew that you were visiting a man in his private cabin?"

"Like I said: to everyone else there is no occurrence, therefore the interest and affect of this matter is entirely left to you and me. I am only here because you say I am, and you are only here because I say you are. It's that simple." She laughed, briefly showing her small white teeth, that shone like mother of pearl in the murky corridor.

"Nothing is ever that simple," I said, "also, that statement doesn't explain anything. It's entirely based on your own observation or experience, not taking into account other people's actions, theories or generalities. It is deeply flawed to think that we can trust a wholly heuristic process. What if somebody saw you enter my cabin and you didn't see them, would you still say there was no occurrence?"

She paused for a moment, apparently considering the question, but then shrugged her shoulders dismissively.

"Let's not concern ourselves with that notion, as there are no other individuals around to observe what might or might not transpire in or outside your cabin."

With lightness of action she pushed on the door, ducked under my arm and entered the disarray within.

I anxiously looked in either direction of the dark corridor to check that we were indeed unseen, before I closed the door and turned to look at the girl who was already standing at the table studying one of my drawings.

"Why have you come here?" I asked, still standing by the door, as she rather haphazardly rifled through my drawings.

"These are interesting studies," she said, "tell me: why are you so fascinated by rodents? It seems to be quite the obsession." She gestured with a long slender hand to the walls of my bunk.

Her movements were unhurried and strangely sedate as if she operated only at low speed, slowly passing through a separate space with a slightly different ether.

"I don't really know," I answered truthfully, "I suppose the main reason for rendering them is that it fascinates me that they can still appear alive even though I realise they're dead."

"I suppose that is quite a curious, or should I say paradoxical concept?" She held out her delicate hand in front of her face pretending to gaze at something in the hollow of her hand.

"To be or not to be, that is the question?"

She looked at me and laughed, clearly amused by her own literary wit.

The sound, reminiscent of a string of small silver bells, flowed like tea from the edge of an overfilled cup and trickled into the space where it was quickly absorbed.

"Please tell me why you're here," I asked, when the sound of her laughter had dissipated and the room was silent once more.

Too silent I suddenly thought, having completely forgotten about the upcoming storm.

I quickly walked past the surprised girl and looked out through the bullseye.

There were no massive gray clouds gathering on the horizon, no thunder or greenish hue lying over the sea, in fact there was absolutely no sign of a storm. The only things visible were the eternal starlit sky and the white tipped waves.

I was completely nonplussed by the changes in atmosphere and once again looked through the glass to make certain that I hadn't been mistaken, but everything was as before. The seemingly endless ocean lay like a giant liquid blanket in undisturbed tranquility and the ship oscillated gently to and fro accompanied by the sound of slapping waves and creaking wood.

"I am here to recite a poem," the girl said, bringing me back from my reverie.

"To do what?" I said, not sure that I had understood her words correctly.

"You heard me," she said, "I am here to recite a poem. It's rather long and somewhat convoluted so I would very much appreciate if you were paying attention, so that I don't have to repeat myself."

"I cannot fathom why you would want to recite a poem to a stranger in the middle of the night?" I exclaimed, slightly bemused by the direction this visit had taken.

"Firstly: As we have already conversed, you are strictly speaking not a stranger, and secondly: the large bird asked me to memorise the poem so I could recite it for you."

"Which large bird?" I asked, further flummoxed by the strangeness of the conversation.

"The albatross," she said, as if I should already know this, "the large bird that often circles the ship? The one you've talked to?" She looked at me suspiciously.

"I don't know to what you are referring. Talking to a bird is something that I think I would very much remember, and I don't recall having ever had a conversation with a bird. Also, you said that we have met before? When exactly did that take place? I don't remember having ever laid eyes on you or indeed spoken with you before. As far as I know I met you for the first time just a moment ago when I opened the door and you were standing in the corridor."

She cocked her head and stared at me as if she was searching for something imperceptible, like the solidity of a small black pearl sitting at the bottom of an inkwell.

"Is that so?" she said, somewhat skeptically. "Well, I better try to forget about that for a moment so that I can concentrate on the message I was meant to give you. Could you please sit down and pay attention, as I've already said, I would not like to repeat myself."

She then stepped into the middle of the room, flattened her dress, tucked a couple of strands of loose hair behind her ears, folded her hands and waited until I was seated on the edge of my berth. The lantern on the table emitted a faint glow that made the scenario strangely theatrical, as if I was about to watch a bizarre performance.

"Actually, before I begin you might want to get a pen and a piece of paper, so you can take down the words," she said, pointing at my drawing materials on the table, "I would rather not waste any time going back and forth."

I got up from the berth, moved to the table and picked up a sheet with a half-finished sketch of the head of a mouse suspended in the upper corner of the page, sat down on the chair and picked up a quill and dipped it in the inkwell.

When she was satisfied that I was giving her my full attention, the girl looked straight at me, slowly nodded her head and began her recital.

Her clear elated voice rang out in the closed quarters. She spoke slowly and perspicuously making certain to pause between the stanzas so that I was able to follow her.

Day after day, after day after day
We are stuck, with no wind no motion
We lie as still as a painted ship
On the waves of a painted ocean.

Sky and water, everywhere
The whole world seems to shrink
Sky and water, everywhere,
But not where you might think.

The very deep lies rotten
How could it ever be

You make the creatures wait for you
Beneath the slimy sea.

Most of your dreams have been
Of spirits that plagued you so
Seven foot deep they'll follow you
To the land of mist and snow.

Good day it is to you my friend
I heard from old and young
Instead of death the Albatross
Did chant a different song

The girl finished the recital and the cabin fell silent once more, like it had suddenly been enveloped in a heavy downy blanket. She waited until I had finished writing, before she slowly spread her arms and opened the palms of her hands, apparently inviting me to respond.

I didn't exactly know what to say, so I remained on my chair staring at her in disbelief.

It was clear that the recital had been a strangely condensed reinterpretation of S.T. Coleridge's most famous poem, and that it was directed at me, but for whatever reason I could not comprehend.

"Why did the albatross send you to recite the poem?"

It was the only thing I could think to ask.

She pushed her long black hair over her shoulder, tilted her head slightly and gave me a most endearing smile.

"I was wondering about that as well," she said, "but it told me that although it would love to have been able to be present, it was unfortunately destined to visit someone else. Also, it wanted you to hear it immediately and seemed to think that you might enjoy my recital."

"It was correct, I very much enjoyed your recital," I replied truthfully.

"When did you learn the poem?"

"Yesterday evening," she answered, and added when she noticed my look of bewilderment: "I am very good at remembering things."

"You surely must be," I said, barely able to hide my amazement.

"What is the meaning of it?" she asked candidly, "of course I understand most of the words, but what does it signify? Why do you think the albatross wanted you to hear this rendition?"

I thought about it for a moment. I had not the slightest idea why a sea bird would want me to listen to a young girl recite a reinterpreted curtailed version of a famous seafaring poem.

"I don't know," I answered, "I really don't know."

I leaned forward on the edge of the chair and rubbed my face in my hands, feeling the stubble on my chin and face scrape against my palms like a piece of pumice.

"Hmmm, that's mysterious," the girl's voice seemed to be coming from a place far away, like she had suddenly been displaced and when I looked up, the spot in the center of the cabin where she had been standing a moment ago was empty.

I quickly turned around to survey the empty room, and even bent down to look under the table, but the girl wasn't anywhere to be found. I hadn't heard the sound of footsteps or the creaking of the door, and although I realize the preposterousness of the statement: it was as if she had all of a sudden dematerialized leaving behind only the slightest obscuration in the air.

I walked across the groaning floor, opened the door and looked up and down the deserted corridor before I went back to the table, sat down and read the poem once more.

When I finished I still couldn't think of a single reason why an albatross would have wanted me to hear this echoic imitation from the mouth of a young girl.

The candle in the lantern flickered and died. The bluish grey smoke from the smoldering wick filled the interior like a genie in a bottle and as I reached across the table to release it, the sooty waxy smell caused a multitude of images to flash through my mind. Snippets of home, of you, our daughter, my uncle's library, the painting of the forest above the fireplace, the sleeping cat on the red chair, the snowy fields and many other images converged to create a whirling kaleidoscopic picture plane in which I attempted to immerse myself, but which quickly faded leaving me stranded with nothing but a doleful tenebrosity. I sat in my chair and listened to the waves' gentle caress, wondering how I could have possibly encountered the girl or conversed with an albatross as neither event seemed to have registered in my memory.

That night I had yet another lucid dream. I dreamed that I was trekking across a snowy field surrounded by clusters of silver birch trees, whose naked fingerlike branches cast a web of dark interwoven shadows on the pristine glittering surface.

I didn't know where I was going and every so often I would change direction as if I was walking according to a predetermined plan. I soon discovered that I was following the shadows of the trees and that my footsteps were tracing the already laid pattern in the snow, so I continued to walk around in the snow until I had traced all the shadows. I was sweating and breathing heavily when I finally finished and trudged up a small hill adjacent to the field, shaded my eyes and looked down.

Beneath me in the snow was a large drawing of what I can best describe as a large two masted ship. It wasn't an exact replica, more like looking at a cloud formation and seeing something that you think is recognisable. Nevertheless, it was unambiguously a vessel and one that somehow seemed familiar, but that I couldn't quite place.

I removed my cap and ran a hand across the top of my head that felt stubbly and strangely alien.

"That's an interesting drawing," someone said, although no one was standing next to me.

When I looked down, a large black cat was sitting in the snow by my feet. Its voice was devoid of intonation or of sentiment. It was as if it had merely made a non-committal statement to an uninteresting question. Its fur glinted in the sunlight like polished granite and its large blue eyes focused on mine as if it recognized what was buried in my soul.

"Is it?" I answered. "I'm not sure what it's supposed to be."

"It's clearly a ship," the cat said.

"But I was merely following the shadows?" I said, "Why would the branches of the trees depict a ship?"

"That's a good question," said the cat, "a very good question indeed, for which I have no answer."

We were both quiet for a while, staring at the drawing below that seemed to be gently rocking back and forth.

"What am I supposed to do now?"

"I don't know," the cat answered. Then it got up, turned around and walked down the other side of the hill towards a small cottage far off in the distance.

I shaded my eyes and followed the cat until it was a mere speck against the whiteness.

When I turned around there was nothing there but a colourless void.

I realize that the events I am describing must sound to you somewhat fantastical and that you might be suspicious of their validity. While I completely understand your skepticism I do however rely on the fact that you are the only one with whom I can share these bizarre events without prejudice or hysteria, and that you know that I wouldn't invent such an outrageous narrative. Believe me when I tell you that the events are as incredulous to me as they are to you. While I readily admit that my lack of sleep could very well have affected my facilities and my rational competence, I still do not know why these strange activities and phenomena are happening to me. However, I am beginning to feel that I am somehow becoming engaged in actions of which I have little or no command. Like I am an unwilling participant in a ludicrous and aberrant theatrical performance with ambiguous symbolism and hidden meaning.

You must trust me when I say that I miss you with all my heart and that I can hardly wait until we meet again. My soul aches for you like a fish on land yearns for the ocean.

Love

C

In the upper corner of the last piece of paper a small delicate drawing of a rodent's head floated in space like a small disconnected celestial body orbiting in space. Its large gleaming eye reminded him of the tension in the surface of an overfilled inkwell, and its half open mouth, exposing its slightly bowed serrated teeth, seemed rather fruitlessly to be ready to bite down on the papery void between them. He turned over the sheet and read the five verses that were neatly inscribed down the center of the page. Although he was relatively familiar with the original poem, the author of this adulterated version had allowed for quite a few creative liberties to deliver the enigmatic and somewhat dark message. Although he thought he understood the centrality of the theme, mainly because it wasn't too far removed from the original, he didn't quite know what to make of it. Although it was obvious from the letter that it had been delivered as a personal missive and read to the recipient as such, there was something about the last couple of verses, an almost preternatural feeling, that caused him to believe the poem was somehow aimed at him as well.

He carefully folded the sheets, inserted them in the envelope, put the envelope down on the top of the bigger pile, leaned back in the chair and stared into the glowing embers of the fireplace.

The cat jumped down from the bed, walked across the floor and sat down by the door looking back at him. The small cutouts from the lantern cast their familiar pattern on the ceiling and walls. As he stood and walked towards the cat, the candle inside the lantern flickered and died filling the compartment with a thick waxy smoke that soon spread from the small openings and emitted an unmistakable smell in the room.

Faint and rather nebulous images of his youth floated past him, like a quilt made up of many small sections that was difficult to focus on. They seemed to quickly blend into one mass of smaller fractions, like that of a broken mirror each depicting a section of a blurred equivocal image.

He put on his jacket, gloves and cap and as he opened the door he looked back at the candle in the candleholder that fluttered in the cool breeze, but held onto the wick as he closed the door behind him.

It was dark out and the stars glittered like precious stones carelessly spread on a piece of indigo velvet. He cleared the spot by the door and the cat jumped over the handle of the shovel and quickly squatted and created a small misty cloud that made it seem as if it had set itself in fire. When it had finished doing its business, he opened the door a smidgen and the cat disappeared inside. He then shut the door and walked down to the outhouse covering his mouth and nose with his glove against the freeze.

Sitting on the freeing wood in the cold dark room he thought about the poem.

There was something curiously eerie about the words in the fourth verse that he couldn't help repeating in his mind:

Most of your dreams have been
Of spirits that plagued you so
Seven foot deep they'll follow you
To the land of mist and snow.

Chapter 16

He was sitting on a seat in the substructure of a white boat.

Although the sky above him was the colour of ink, the countless twinkling stars illuminated the darkness, casting a brilliant luminescence on the surrounding motionless surface that looked like a massive sheet of obsidian ice or perhaps like a dark impenetrable mirror found in an ancient fairytale.

The white sails hanging limp from the rigging of the two masts sparkled like crystals, as indeed did the rest of the vessel. He instinctively ran a hand across the seat beside him and was surprised by its cool marble like smoothness.

He gazed at the firmament above wondering why it seemed so strange until he realised that several of the celestial constellations were disparate from the ones found in the Northern Hemisphere with which he was accustomed.

One of them directly above his head looked like a three pointed crown and one of the others, a little further away in the horizon, appeared to be two large semicircles connected by a row of stars. Although they seemed familiar, it was as if they were faint echoes of something buried deep in his mind, and though he closed his eyes trying to remember he couldn't quite place them. It was like reaching for an item on the top shelf of a wardrobe, but inadvertently pushing it further into the darkened corner with the very tips of his outstretched fingers.

When he again opened his eyes there was a large white cat sitting on the seat across from him. It's sizeable blue eyes appeared almost luminous in the starlit night and its long tail, curling around its lower body, completely covering its paws, made it seem as if it was physically connected to the vessel.

The cat watched him with unblinking eyes and he felt like he was being carefully examined, as if it was trying to extract something imperceptible, deep from within his mind.

Although he tried to push most of his thoughts to the periphery of his brain, the slightly unsettled idea that the feline was somehow able to read his innermost thoughts kept surfacing in his mind, making him wonder if the cat thought that he was paranoid.

However, when it finally spoke, it didn't seem to be bothered by his distress.

"You read the poem," it said in a tone of voice that belied a question.

"I did?" he purposely called his answer into question and for a brief moment the cat's whiskers moved gently up and down as if it was smiling.

"What did you think?" it asked, keeping its azure eyes locked on his.

"What did I think?" he slowly repeated, although he somehow questioned if that was indeed the cat's exact words.

"Yes," it replied, "what did you think?"

"To be honest I didn't really know what to think. Somehow I find the whole concept of an albatross writing a richly modified adaptation of Coleridge absurd to say the least."

"I suppose there's an undisputable irony in that," answered the cat jovially.

"Also, I wonder if you can answer this question? Why did the bird not recite the poem itself if it believed it was that important?"

The cat paused, turned its head and looked into the distance.

"Because it had to be somewhere else," it said.

"Do you know where it had to be?"

He followed the gaze of the cat and noticed a dark shadow, like a small moving crevice in the air some distance away from the stern.

It moved like a large elongated kite gliding effortlessly from side to side in wide sweeping motions.

"Yes," the cat answered, "It had to be here."

"I don't understand," he said, "how can it possibly be here?"

"It can be anywhere it chooses to be, whenever it chooses to be there," the cat replied elliptically.

"Hmmm," he said, thinking that the cat knew far more than it was revealing.

For a while he stared at the serene, quite mesmerizing flight pattern of the approaching bird. It was soundlessly slicing through the air like a large horizontal pendulum, whose invisible rope seemed to be anchored to the boat.

He followed the bird as it moved closer. It continued to move swiftly and smoothly behind the stern, until it was close enough that he could look into its eyes that glimmered like a pair of highly polished black pearls. The rest of the remarkable creature was black like a raven and its feathers, illuminated by thousands of stars, shone like satin in the night.

It didn't utter a word, but continued its silent sweeping movements behind the stern.

He was about to ask the cat a question and turned around, but the place it had been sitting just a moment ago was now empty. He leaned forward, reached out and laid the palm of his hand on the very same spot, but found no variation of heat.

The seat was as smooth and cool to the touch as a marble grave marker standing in the shade of a large oak tree late in an autumn evening.

He got up from his seat and looked around to see if he could glimpse the cat anywhere, but it had disappeared from view, so he instead focused his eyes on the albatross circling the air behind the ship.

He waited for the bird to engage him in conversation, but it continued to inaudibly traverse the space, remaining strangely quiet.

"What do you want from me?" he said, finally breaking the silence.

Although he believed it was unintentional there was nonetheless an undeniable demand in the tone of his voice.

"What do you mean by that?" the albatross answered equably in a voice that divulged nothing of its origin.

"What do you mean, what do I mean by that?" he answered, "I would like to know what it is you want from me."

"I don't think that's entirely correct," the bird gave him a long penetrating stare, "you came to see me did you not? Therefore, you have to ask yourself this question: what that is you think I want from you?"

He looked at the bird trying to discern the level of gravity of the last statement.

"Is this some kind of trick?" he asked, confused by the direction the conversation had taken.

"You tell me," the bird made another silent sweep through the air.

"How can I possibly tell you if you're playing a trick on me?" he said, "that simply doesn't make sense. Also, what's the point of this elliptical exchange? And don't tell me that that's another question I have to answer myself."

"But isn't everything?" the albatross replied shifting its head, looking at him with a small impenetrable obsidian dome.

"Bah," he answered, waving his hand dismissively, "that's merely a sophistic statement deliberately used to deflect my original question. You're intentionally attempting to make this conversation go around in circles."

"Am I now?" There was a marginal intonation in the bird's answer that made him think that it was finding the entire conversation quite humorous.

"You know you are," he replied loudly, vexed by the bird's abstruse esoteric behaviour.

"Can I ask you a question?" the albatross said after a while, plainly ignoring his latest outburst, "what is it you're hoping to accomplish here?"

He gazed at the surrounding inhospitable scenery in a despondent hope that it would somehow provide him with an answer.

"I don't know," he answered finally, "I honestly don't know."

"Do you mind if I show you something?" the bird asked amiably.

"Not at all."

"Good," it said, "perhaps you should bring the lantern."

He looked down to find a strange looking lantern standing between his feet.

It was reminiscent of something unspecified, something that he couldn't quite recall but that nonetheless seemed familiar. He hooked a finger through the ring at the top and picked it up. It was much heavier than expected and the weight of it pained his finger as he lifted it to his face to look inside. However, the glass was black as ink and completely impenetrable, giving off only a tenebrous reflection of his distorted face, that appeared somewhat alien in the dark vacuous surface.

As he lowered the lantern and moved over to the bulwark, he wondered why the albatross wanted him to bring such an unusable item, but he nevertheless leaned over the edge, placed the lantern on the smooth blank surface before swinging his legs over the railing and lowering himself down onto the massive sheet.

The surface felt strangely supple beneath his feet, bending easily and flexibly with each of his steps, as if it was anticipating where he would next put his foot down well before he did, deliberately impelling him forward.

He followed the bird across the apparently immutable pliable surface until he was nearly breathless and his arms and fingers were aching from carrying the heavy dark lantern.

"Hold on a minute," he uttered breathlessly. He stopped, put the lantern down on the surface beside him, turned around and looked in the direction from which they had come. He had expected to see the white boat in the distance and was thoroughly confounded by the sight with which he was confronted.

Not fifty yards away stood a small white cottage with two square windows placed about three feet apart on either side of a rather heavy looking door. It appeared not unlike his own and yet there was something about it that caused him to pause. The black defunct rigid window panes looked like a pair of limitless wells from which not an iota of light was reflected or released.

He turned around and attempted to locate the bird, but although he scanned the horizon it was nowhere to be found.

The surface around the cottage suddenly began to glow like it was being lit from below by an unknown source. First he assumed it was just a trick of the light from the abundance of stars, but the glow gathered in strength and intensified until the entire plane upon which he was standing turned a milky opaque white.

The stars in the sky above slowly dissolved in the whiteness leaving a monochrome colorless void in its place.

He shaded his eyes with his hand and looked towards the cottage whose black windows appeared like a pair of dark glasses suspended in the all-encompassing whiteness.

From the corner of his eye, next to his feet he suddenly noticed what appeared to be a small dark shadow flowing across the white surface towards the cottage.

He looked up to check if the bird had come back, but when he couldn't see anything moving in the space above his head, he bent down to look closer at the slow moving dark patch and realized that what he had assumed was a shadow was in fact a semi viscous black liquid that flowed like a small stream from the small gap at the bottom of the lantern. As he watched the liquid making its way across the plane, he suddenly heard a sound like that of a rushing river coming from the cottage.

A thick mass of discharged black liquid oozed from the aperture onto the pristine ice like sheet and collated like a giant pool of ink on the chalky-white surface.

The small amount of displaced liquid from the lantern flowed across the plane like a flat elongated single celled organism, extending its fingerlike projections in the direction of the cottage until it touched the very edge of the now substantial pool getting immediately soaked up.

He stared in amazement as the cottage, now simply an empty shell like a fine filmy substance consisting of cobwebs spun by thousands of small spiders, collapsed onto itself.

Within minutes it was reduced to a translucent membranous sheet that spread onto the white surface like a deflated silk air-balloon, before it completely dissolved and was absorbed into the ground, until all that remained in its place was a colourless plane.

In front of the place the cottage had only moments earlier stood, a large nearly perfect rectangular black mass had formed. There seemed to be a peculiar tensity to its marginally curved edges that rose about half an inch from the plane.

He picked up the empty lantern and wondered if the black viscous surface, shining like a flawless sheet of volcanic glass in some way presaged a threat, but before he could discern if he was in danger, he unexpectedly started moving towards the Stygian rectangular pool as if he was subconsciously drawn to it, not knowing or expecting what would happen when he reached it, much like a small moth transfixed by the flame inside a lantern.

He carefully moved forward, stepped onto the black glutinous surface suspecting his feet to be immediately submerged and was surprised by the substance's capacity to hold his weight. His boots made peculiar sucking noises against the tenacious surface and he felt like he was walking on a large sheet of stickum as he cautiously moved to the center of the pool where he stopped, looked around at the vacant landscape and waited.

At first nothing happened, but then the surface suddenly gave and his feet began a slow descent into the tarry mass. For reasons unbeknownst to him he wasn't panicking, he merely watched as the black mass enveloped the upper parts of his legs, then slipped around his torso steadily making its way up to his chest.

While it was difficult to discern exactly what he had expected, the semi liquid mass didn't feel at all constricted or foreboding. As a matter of fact, the substance was remarkably soft and pliable and the sensation he had when sinking into it was comparable to being wrapped in a cosy warm blanket.

He deliberately immersed his hands and arms into the black viscous mass and when it finally reached his neck he took a long deep breath and fully submerged himself.

He was still, keeping his eyes closed and holding his breath when he heard a clear convivial voice speaking in the darkness.

"I thought you would never make it," it said.

He opened his eyes and looked directly into the crystal blue eyes of the black cat sitting on the opposite side of the bed.

"What did you say?" his gruff voice sounded rather loud in the otherwise quiet room.

For a while the cat gazed at him with its large unblinking eyes, before it casually began licking its paws and cleaning its face.

"You know I heard you speak just now?" he said, "you said you thought I would never make it. Why did you say that?"

The cat didn't answer.

Instead it jumped down from the bed and walked across the floor to the water bowl where it sat down and appeared to be gazing mesmerized at the blank surface of the water.

Then it stood up, leapt into the bowl and disappeared.

He woke up with a jolt and looked around the room in an incomprehensible swivet not exactly recognizing where he was.

Not three feet away the dark eyes of the cat glinted in the darkness.

Chapter 17

The collective glare of the countless stars almost cancelled out the darkness of the early morning when he opened the door to let the cat out. The freezing air washed across the floorboards like a fast moving fog, expertly penetrating the multifarious crevices rapidly expelling the gathering warmth.

He closed the door against the gale and while he waited for the cat to return, he thought about the somewhat unnerving dream.

The latest dream was so vivid that he had been convinced that the cat had talked to him and then disappeared into the water bowl. So vivid that he had gotten out of bed, walked across the cold floorboards and bent down to stare into the blank surface. After a while he had ruptured the plane sticking his hand into the bowl and when the tip of his finger immediately and expectedly touched the bottom, he pulled out his hand and wiped it on the sleeve of his shirt.

He opened the door when he heard the cat scratching. It ran back inside and he quickly shut the door behind it to rebuff the advancing frost. Then he picked up a towel from the small cupboard, wrapped it around his head so it covered his ears, secured it with the cap and put on his jacket and the gloves, grabbed the shovel handle and ventured outside.

The freezing wind continuously hurled thousands of miniscule pins at the exposed parts of his face and although he tried his best to cover his nose and mouth with his gloved hands as he made his way through the trench to the outhouse, it was as if the delicate folds around his eyes were being rubbed with sandpaper.

When he reached the outhouse and closed the door against the howling tempest, he removed his gloves and rubbed some warmth back into his face, before he loosened his belt, dropped his trousers and lowered his buttocks gently onto the icy board.

He leaned forward in the darkness, closed his eyes and tried to recall the poem that the girl had recited in the letter, but no matter how hard he tried he found that he could only remember a couple of lines from the last verse: 'Seven foot deep, they'll follow you to the land of mist and snow.'

In his estimation there was a perspicuous and exclusive message in those words. A message that awoke something obscure and indefinite in the deepest sequestered well of his being and though he pressed his fingers against his temples in an attempt to remember, he was unable to bring anything of value back to his mind.

When he returned to the outside the brilliant whitish rays of the sun sweeping across the wintery landscape momentarily blinded him. He shut his eyes, turned around, and sightless, he closed the door to the outhouse. Then he rinsed his hands in the freezing powdery snow, rubbed his hands against his trouser leg and with his head down, avoiding the dominant glare of the rising sun he made his way to the shed to pick up the chickenfeed.

Then he walked over to the chicken coop, to feed and water the hens making sure that the birds were doing as well as could be expected in the forbidding conditions. He gently pushed his hand underneath the warm slightly protesting cackling birds and picked up five eggs that he carefully placed in outside pockets of his jacket, before he backed out of the coop, closed the hatch behind him and walked back to the cottage.

He put the eggs in the small pot, removed his jacket, gloves and cap and hung the towel from the hook on the cupboard door, put a new log on the dying embers in the fireplace and another log in the belly of the stove, before he began preparations for breakfast.

The kettle was a little more than half full, but when he carried it over to the sink and turned the handle on the faucet nothing happened. It had just been a matter of time before the pipe froze so he wasn't particularly surprised, he was merely annoyed that he had to get dressed and go back outside to collect water from the barrel at the back of the cottage.

For now, he put the kettle down on the stovetop, picked up the container from the pantry and prepared the tea.

While he waited for the water to boil he buttered the pan, cracked three eggs, cut up a chunk of cured ham and the last of the desiccated hardened hunk of bread. He put a portion of the ham in the cat's bowl on the floor and sprinkled the remainder on top of the eggs frying in the pan.

When the smell of fried eggs permeated the cottage, he deposited the eggs on the plate and carried it across the room and put it down on the table, then picked up the small salt and pepper shakers and the small bottle of Worcestershire sauce from the pantry, placed them on the tabletop, and sat down on the chair that groaned slightly beneath his weight.

He reached for the shakers and sprinkled a bit of salt and pepper over the yellowish white gelatinous mass, then he shook the bottle and slathered a generous amount of the dark glutinous sauce on top, put the bottle down, gazed into the space in front of him, cleared his mind and began to eat. He chewed his food methodically and only paused to sip at the remainder of the now lukewarm water that he had poured into the glass from the kettle.

When he finished eating, he carried the plate, cutlery and glass over to the sink and cautiously placed it at the bottom. Then he turned around, lifted the teapot off the stove, swirled the hot liquid inside, put it back down and waited until the leaves settled before pouring the dark amber liquid into the small porcelain cup. He inserted his index finger and thumb in the small earlike handle, picked up the cup and carefully carried it across the floorboards to deposit it at the edge of the tabletop away from the letters.

The cat was curled up in front of the fireplace and the glowing flames reflected in its sable coat made it appear as if the feline was internally permeated by heat, much like a small dragon lying at the mouth of its lair.

He lifted the cup to sip at the hot liquid, then he gently replaced the cup, reached out his hand to pick up the penultimate letter, inserted the pocket knife in the tiny crevice and ran it across the top, creating a small serrated opening from which he withdrew nine delicate pieces of paper, that he carefully flattened against the table with the palm of his hand.

Then he leaned forward in the chair and began to read.

Dearest E

My heart is saturated with undying love for you and the unimaginable amount of elucidatory words in the world are profoundly insufficient when it comes to describing my eternal longing for you. I feel as if my soul is being torn to threads when I think of the time we have already been apart, and when I realize that it will be some time before I will once again hold you in my arms, I feel as if my weakened heart could quite literally burst.

In my significantly sleep deprived and feeble mind I have found it impossible to let go of you and I spend more and more of my time awake gazing endlessly at the rendering of you that I now carry around with me everywhere I go. My yearning for you is endless and vast like an altogether infinite abyss and I live in hope that I shall one day be able to wrap you and the little one in my arms.

Due to my tremorous emotional state I have increasingly sought refuge in my dark and crammed cabin that I now seldom leave, dedicating myself instead to the study of your portrait and of the deceased rodents whose renderings now fill all available wall space. I have not met another living soul for what might be days or weeks, and I often feel that it's impossible to tell how the days are separated. In fact, I find it steadily more difficult to tell just how much time has passed if indeed any time has passed at all. I am as always in the company of the everlasting all encompassing waves that carry on their tireless and ceaseless sloshing against the creaking hull day and night.

One evening or perhaps it was already night, I was sitting by the table drawing a tiny rodent in the glowing light of the lantern when there was a rather loud knock on my door. As I wasn't expecting any visitors and my cabin was in a state of disarray my first inclination was to ignore the disturbance, but the person in the corridor was apparently quite adamant in their attempt to rouse me because they continued their loud hammering on the door, compelling me to walk across the floor kicking aside pieces of crumpled paper and items of clothing to open the door a smidgen. It took a bit of time for my eyes to adjust to the gloom before I could make out the recognizable features of the captain. His penetrating dark eyes, impressive sideburns and long black locks falling across his broad forehead emphasized his commanding attire.

He didn't say anything but merely flicked his wrist instructing me to follow him as he turned and walked down the corridor towards the stairs.

He had almost disappeared from sight as I hastily grabbed my coat from the hook on the back of the door and hurried down the corridor wondering what it could be that was so important that the captain wanted to share it, and perhaps more importantly; why he thought it necessary to share with me.

I was breathing quite heavily when I finally made my way up the stairs and joined the captain on the otherwise deserted lower deck.

He was standing by the bulwark staring into the quiet night, and although the ship was rolling gently from side to side, he seemed to be strangely stationary in space following the sway of the ocean with an almost uncanny natural ability.

I followed his gaze and I was nearly lost for words by the extraordinary beautiful sight surrounding us. The celestial bodies spread their brilliant luminescence onto the ocean making it appear as if the ship was resting on an enormous gently moving blanket inhabited by millions of tiny glowing creatures.

The captain slowly turned his head and looked at me with glistering black eyes that were like a miniature embodiment of the surrounding ocean and without uttering a word he once again beckoned me to follow him. He walked across the deck to the companionway and slowly ascended the stairs. I followed behind still wondering what it was he wanted to show me.

We didn't meet another soul as we made our way across the main deck and walked up the few steps that led to the forecastle. When I joined him at the top of the stairs I stopped and looked towards the helm, and was extremely surprised to discover that it was unmanned. In lieu of the first mate a heavy piece of rope had been tied around two of the wheel handles and fastened to the tiller ropes, thus preventing the ship from changing course. I was confounded by this unexpected circumstance and began looking around the ship not knowing exactly what I was searching for.

At first I couldn't discern that anything was out of the ordinary, but all of a sudden I realized that though the night was as still as the air in a church, the untended dilapidated sails, hanging like wilting yellowish leaves from the riggings, had been set as if the ship was expecting a considerable breeze and yet not one man was present to guard them.

I have to confess that the surrounding spectacle unnerved me deeply and that I couldn't help thinking that I was having yet another vivid dream and that I had somehow been transported onto the legendary ghost ship doomed to sail the oceans forever, never being able to make port. Indeed, when I again searched the ship, everything onboard seemed to have aged considerably within a matter of minutes.

The dirty, rotting deck planks were splintered and cracked, the ropes and riggings were covered in blackened seaweed, fistfuls of large barnacles decorated the decrepit railing of the perforated bulwark and the pungent smell of brine and decaying lumber permeated the air.

I turned to the captain to see if he had noticed my obvious distress, but he was standing by the railing looking into the distance through a spyglass. Although I shaded my eyes with my hand and followed the direction of his gaze, the illuminated sea completely intermingled with the sky and I couldn't make out what he was looking at.

After a while the captain silently handed me the spyglass, lifted a long elegant hand and pointed at something undetectable in front of the vessel. I lifted the heavy spyglass, steadied my arm, shut my left eye and looked through the glass in the specified direction.

The brilliant liquid ocean and the effulgent sky intermixed in such a way that everything seemed to become a replica of everything else, and though I tried to focus my search in the given direction, I couldn't quite fathom what I was meant to be looking at. I looked fixedly into the glimmering space for the longest time, and I had almost given up hope of finding anything, when I suddenly saw something move.

At first I thought the disruption must have been the tiniest shimmer of a star, but when I focused the spyglass on the spot in the horizon, I realized that the disturbance hadn't come from a celestial body.

Two large sea birds, one black and one white, were circling what appeared to be a large dark spot on the surface beneath them. The unexplainable and eerie darkness below gave the impression that the birds were hovering above a massive well from which no light could escape.

After spending some time watching the birds gliding in large circles above the apparent abyss, I lowered the spyglass in trepidation and turned to look at the captain, who seemed to have accepted the perturbing situation with exceptional *equanimity.*

"What awaits us out there?"

I must have anticipated the answer for when it came, I was not in the least surprised.

"The maelstrom," he answered soberly.

"Is it to be avoided?" I asked, looking at the decrepit sails hanging like decaying flayed hides from the crumbling worm-eaten masts.

"Not likely." He accepted the spyglass, collapsed it and deposited it in his pocket. "It would seem there's no escape from the inescapable. The course of our destiny has been laid and now we must abide by its concomitant conclusion."

"Where will it take us?"

"Down," he answered with not a hint of sarcasm.

"What do you expect will meet us there?"

He looked at me with something in his eyes that in any other circumstance could have been mistaken for pity.

"I believe we will finally have an opportunity to discover what's on the other side," he said.

"You mean to say that we are destined to perish at the bottom of the ocean and that there's nothing we can do to prevent this from happening?"

"That's pretty much the crux of the matter," he answered making a sweeping gesture with his arms.

"I refuse to believe that there's nothing we can do to avoid the maelstrom," I said, looking somewhat desperately around the ship, "surely there must be a way for us to steer the ship away from danger?"

"I am afraid it's already too late to change course," he replied, looking towards the circling birds that were now visible with the naked eye.

I gazed as the antithetical slender shapes effortlessly cut through the air like a pair of sharpened blades above the dark foreboding mass on the horizon.

"How long do we have?" I asked apprehensively.

"I don't know," the captain said, staring into the horizon, "much less time than we can hope for I suppose."

I suddenly felt a sense of urgency, like an area of my mind had surreptitiously cleared and I could think clearly without any intervening time or space. I looked around at the decaying vessel as if seeing it for the very first time, but only now realizing what exactly I was looking at.

"There's something I need to do."

I hurriedly crossed the forecastle, descended the rotting steps and made my way back across the slimy ill-smelling main deck. I caught a sight of the helm and was utterly unprepared for the ludicrousness that met my unbelieving eyes. I stopped dead in my tracks and stared in shock at the bizarre tableau in front of me.

Two large cats, one white and one black, were sitting on either side of the helm. The ropes that tied the wheel to the tiller were missing and although the cats were sitting with their backs turned to the wheel, it was obvious that they were somehow in control of the vessel. They both gazed unseeingly into the space in front of them with their large sapphire blue eyes, and the Sphinx's question to Oedipus flashed through my mind.

"This is not the appropriate time to celebrate the answer to an already solved riddle."

The combined voices of the unmoving cats abruptly awoke me from my stupor and sent me in a headlong inelegant dash across the deck, down the stairs towards my cabin, frantically wondering whatever motive the cats could have for steering the ship towards the abyss.

When I opened the door to my cabin I had yet another surprise that left me standing in the doorway with my benumbed hand resting on the door handle.

A young girl with a beautiful, almost unnaturally flawless face was sitting at the table. She was dressed entirely in white and her long raven black hair, held back with a broad white hairband, glistened like a raven's wing in the glowing light from the lantern.

She held a small white feather in her delicate hand and was leaning over a piece of paper lying on the table top as if she was writing something. She was apparently lost in her own thoughts, humming what appeared to be one of Bach's cello suites, slowly moving her head to and fro in harmony with the tune.

At first she didn't seem to realize that she was being watched, but soon the murmuration ceased and with slow languid movements she laid the feather on the table top next to the paper. Then she straightened her back and folded her hands in her lap before turning in the chair to look at me.

"It's a lot more difficult than it looks," she said, gesturing with a slender

arm to the drawings, "bringing life to the departed I mean."

The sound of her voice filled the cabin like the chime of silver bells and I was reminded of something in the outer periphery of my mind, like the very last reverberation of a familiar melody that I couldn't quite bring into focus.

She picked up the small piece of paper by the edge.

For a moment It casually dangled between her thumb and index finger, like a rectangular yellowish leaf from a pair of pale fleshy twigs, before being discarded and slowly spiralling to the floor.

I looked down at the paper at my feet and even in the gloomy light of the cabin, I could tell it was the most exquisite drawing I have ever laid eyes on. The intricate details of the rendering were so implausible that I felt as if the rodent's black sentient eyes were surveying me. It appeared as if the drawing itself had been executed by the hand of one of the old masters and I wanted nothing more than to pick it up to closer study the particular aspects, but I suddenly remembered why I was there.

"The ship is sinking," I said in alarm, looking up at the girl who didn't exhibit any distress and showed no signs of moving from her seat.

"I thought you would never return," the girl said, apparently unaware of my agitated state.

"What do you mean?" I said, desperately looking around the room trying to remember where I had last seen the box.

"Why wouldn't I return? It's my cabin," I said, bending down to pick up the drawing on the floor. I dropped it on the table on my way towards the berth, where I commenced my search by hoisting the pillow and blanket off the mattress.

I found nothing,

"That's not what I meant," she replied smiling, "I was just surprised to see that you came back."

"Back from where?" I asked, confused both by her lack of distress and the queer conversation.

"You know," she said knowingly, tilting her head, making her long black hair cascade like an inky waterfall over her shoulder coming to an abrupt stop at her upper arm.

"I can assure you, I have absolutely no idea to what you are referring," I

said, continuing my search in the narrow space under the berth.

"I find that somewhat hard to believe," she said, "surely you must know where you have been and how you have been spending your time?"

"I've been spending my time here on this ship in this cabin, making all of these," I said exasperatedly, throwing out my hands to summarize the surrounding drawings, "that's all I've been doing."

"That's not the only thing you've been doing now is it?"

Her enigmatic voice and impassive facial expression were impossible to read.

"What's that supposed to mean?" I asked, frenziedly searching for the box under an assembly of malodorous smelling clothes in the corner.

"Do you fail to remember the fascinating things you have seen, the intriguing conversations you've had and the remarkable places you've visited on your voyage?" she said. "Certainly they must be incorporated as part of your most essential experiences."

I stopped for a moment to look at the girl.

She smiled back at me from across the room as if it was the most natural occurrence to be engaged in informal conversation in time of impending doom.

"How do you know about my conversations?" I asked, knowing that I didn't really have time to hear the answer as time was rapidly running out and I had yet to find what I was looking for.

"The cats kept me informed, but never mind that," she said, lifting a small metal box from the seat behind her and set it on the table next to the lantern, "I believe this is what you've been looking for."

I rushed across the room and grabbed the box off the table, opened the lid and checked the content and let out a sigh of relief when I saw that the four small picture frames and the whitish ash grey envelopes were still lying unscathed at the bottom.

I put her drawing of the rodent on top of the envelopes, closed the lid of the box and tucked it under my arm.

"We need to go," I said, lifting the lantern off the table.

The golden light flowing across the unmoving girl's beautiful features made it appear as if she was a character in a Pre-Raphaelite painting.

I quickly searched the cabin, but I could not find anything else that was *necessary to bring with me on the journey.*

"We need to go," I repeated, heading for the door.

"Why do we need to go when it makes no difference how we get there?"
There was absolutely no defiance or sarcasm in her voice. It merely sounded as if
she was commenting on the easiest route to the local market. In my haste to leave I
was already halfway across the floor, but her soft rational voice made me stop and
look back at her.

She sat in the chair in the same position as before; slightly turned in her
seat with her hands neatly folded in her lap and her dark impenetrable eyes focused
on mine. She showed not the slightest inclination to move and if I had harboured
any thoughts that she might be joining me I was sadly mistaken.

"I realize you have to go and make yourself acquainted with whatever it
is you think is on the other side," she said, "and whatever you find you can rest
assured it will be nothing in comparison to what is already here. You open a door
and step outside, but while you think that nothing changes, everything on the inside
has already shifted. Like a mouse gnawing on the lid of a breadbin, time is
continuously leaving its tiny needle sharp claw marks at the edges of our existence,
assiduously and studiously tearing at the fabric that holds us together, until it falls
apart and we finally fall down. Yet some live with the indefatigable belief that
they can somehow change the inevitable outcome, that they can control or stop the
gnawing, but of course they can't. Everything ends in the end."

She paused, tilted her head and smiled at me in the semi darkness.

"I can already tell that you will not remember having ever met me before,
but I will undoubtedly meet you again."

Then she lifted her hand and seemingly immersed in thought, waved me
out of the cabin.

I stood on the threshold looking back at her, pondering her cryptic
statement, but her unseeing dreamy eyes already seemed to be focused on something
absent in the space.

I turned and awkwardly ascended the stairs at the end of the corridor
holding onto the box and the lantern that was hitting the rail with each step,
making repetitive hollow clanging noises against the wood.

I made my way back across the rotting ship, passed the stationary cats by
the helm and joined the captain on the forecastle. Although it seemed like he

hadn't moved from his position, he had lit his pipe and the bittersweet aroma of burning tobacco encased him in a silvery greyish smoke, that made him look like a big dark animal giving off heat on a cool winter morning.

I silently stood beside him following his gaze.

Ahead of the ship, less than half a nautical mile away, what appeared to be a massive black hole was awaiting us. Apart from the circumventing birds the dark surface beneath lay absolutely still, like a drop of ink on a new piece of paper, and I watched in trepidation as the ship slowly made its way across the waves to the ominous site.

Although the looming abyss frightened me more than ever and my body was uncontrollably shaking in terror, I still couldn't take my eyes off the blackness. It was as if I had been mesmerized, and that the chasmic depths of darkness were calling the most profound parts of my being. I finally tore my eyes away and looked instead at the captain beside me. He showed no sign of fear, but kept his bottomless black eyes focused on the two birds gliding over the upcoming abyss.

"Are they here to guide us?" I asked, gesturing at the circling birds.

"I am the captain," he answered stoically, "perhaps they misunderstand their mission, but I have accepted the responsibility of my burden and do not require a shepherd."

He dismissively waved a hand, but the birds uninterruptedly kept circling, apparently unaware of their redundancy.

When we were no more than twenty feet from the edge, I held the lantern over the railing to see if I could discern what might be awaiting us. However, it was impossible to see anything at all. An absolute darkness spread across the ocean like a huge velvet blanket absorbing any light that might have fallen on its surface. There was no indication of where it ended and it was impossible to see where it began. It was like I was looking into an enormous black void.

I turned my head to cast my eyes at the captain beside me. Without turning around to meet my gaze, he slowly nodded his head and put both his hands on the decaying railing, leaning forward as if in consent to whatever would meet us in the impenetrable darkness.

The bow slowly progressed, soon touching the edge of the darkness and shortly the entire ship began to list as if it had unbalanced cargo. With the box secured under my arm and the lantern between my feet I sat down with my back against the bulwark. Although the ship was now heeling over quite dramatically there was no sound of slapping waves or groaning timber.

In fact, I suddenly realized that it was utterly soundless, like the entire event was somehow taking place inside a massive vacuous space from which not the tiniest of sound could escape.

I looked up to see if I could locate the birds, but they must have finally left us, because all I could see in between the rotting rigging and the dead lingering sails was the immense starlit sky that spread like a coruscating ocean above.

As the ship finally keeled over and slowly descended into the prodigious tenebrous well, I attempted to recall an image of you and the little one sitting in the long grass, below the willow tree by the pond, but all I managed to conjure up in my mind was an unnavigable dense darkness that seemed to go on forever.

I cannot tell you how exactly this occurred, but when I again opened my eyes I was sitting on a rickety chair at a small square table in the center of a room in a stone cottage. The fire in the fireplace across the room illuminated a large black cat lying asleep on the broad rough floorboards.

The flickering flames reflected in its fur made it appear as if the cat was glowing like a piece of coal and I was reminded of another similar image I had recently seen somewhere else. The unlit lantern was placed near the center of the table and the small metal box stood beside it. I opened the box and removed a blank piece of paper and a writing tool and immediately began writing this letter so that I can as accurately as possible inform you of the latest's events.

To tell you the truth, I no longer seem to understand if I am dreaming or if everything I have experienced is indeed real. Sometimes I'm afraid that I might be losing my faculties and that my fatigued insomniatic mind might be playing some cruel tricks on me. Perhaps even sitting here at this table is all part of an elaborate dream and I will once again wake up in my berth on the ship, surrounded once again by the hundreds of dead rodents staring at me from the walls, while the eternal waves smack against the creaking hull.

However, one thing that is more definite than ever is the fact that I know that I miss you with all my heart and that I cannot wait until we are reunited.

You are the everlasting love of my life and I am forlornly counting the

days until we meet again.
Yours Forever
C

He put the small semi translucent piece of paper down on the pile and stared, deeply in awe at the ink drawing lying on the table top.

The assured and serene master craftsmanship was like nothing he had ever seen before, and the rodent positioned on its side appeared to be lying on the paper still conveying its surroundings with its gleaming black eyes. The virtuosity of the artist was nothing less than astounding, and the eloquence with which the subject had been conveyed made the hair on the back of his neck stand up.

The more he looked at the drawing, the more unambiguous it became that he was looking at an astonishing rendering created by a bona fide genius. The drawing of the mouse was executed so extraordinarily well that it appeared it was still alive and the longer he gazed at it the more convinced that the wispy hairs on the creature's belly moved up and down in synchronicity with his own breathing.

After a while he put the drawing back on the table, collected the pile of papers, carefully folded them and reinserted them in the envelope. Then he slowly got up from the chair, walked across the creaking floor into the bedroom and opened the suitcase.

He picked up the penultimate frame, removed the backing, turned over the small piece of paper and inserted the drawing of the mouse, closed the frame and carried it over to the fireplace and set it on the shelf leaning up against the stone wall, careful not to step on the sleeping cat.

He stood back and looked at the triptych.

The drawing in the center made the other two renderings appear as if they had been drawn by a capable enthusiast and he again marveled at the absolute artistry with which the center piece had been executed.

He was interrupted in his reverie by the cat who had gotten up from the spot in front of the fireplace and was now stretching its legs out, spreading its paws and sticking its long front claws into the floorboards. When it pulled its claws back it made a series of thin lines in the old timber that reminded him of the deep dark furrows in a newly plowed field. The cat stopped scratching and silently moved to the water bowl where it sat and lapped at the clear surface with its long pink tongue.

He walked over to the door, put on his jacket, gloves and cap and looked back at the cat that had taken up position in front of the fireplace.

Dark clouds must have moved in, completely covering the sky because when he closed the door behind him he was enveloped by a nearly impenetrable darkness.

For a while he stood on the granite platform waiting for his eyes to readjust before he fumbled blindly for the rope and slowly made his way to the outhouse, as the freeze tore into his exposed skin and left him breathless.

He closed the door, removed his gloves, opened his jacket, pulled down his trousers and leaned over the black spot in the darkness.

While he relieved himself he thought about the recent letter.

There was no doubt in his mind that the author had been describing the exact same arrangements of objects currently present in the cottage and he couldn't help thinking about the vicissitude of the man who had been sitting at the small square table disconsolately writing letter after letter to a loved one, who would never receive them.

The thought of it made him feel terribly sad and when he trotted back to the cottage a couple of tears almost froze his eyelashes shut, but that could equally be because of the intense cold.

When he reached the cottage he stomped his feet on the granite slab before quickly opening and shutting the door.

He removed his jacket, gloves and cap, and walked across the floor boards to warm himself in front of the fire.

When his hands began prickling, he picked up a log from the bucket and considered putting it on the fire, but instead he walked over to the stove, covered his hand with his sleeve, opened the door and deposited the log on the embers.

A flurry of escaping particles flew through the opening and whirled in the air, euphorically celebrating their newfound freedom before quickly extinguishing in the darkness above.

He closed the door, walked over to the table, picked up the lantern and went into the bedroom casting an eye at the sleeping cat by the fireplace. It slowly raised its head and looked in his direction. The gleam of its eyes in the murky shadows gave him the impression that it knew what he was thinking.

"Goodnight Loke." His voice hung in the stale air like a small cloud of smoke before slowly dispersing.

The cat looked at him from across the room, and just as he thought it was about to reply, it put its head down on its paws and closed its eyes, leaving him to wonder if it had understood what he said.

Chapter 18

He was standing on what appeared to be an immense colourless plane that stretched endlessly into the distance.

His bare feet pressed against the pliable somewhat tepid surface and he was somehow reminded of his daughter's implausible laughter as the small water skating beetles, on their long outstretched legs, glided effortlessly across the shimmering surface of the pond.

He leaned back his head and looked above.

There was nothing at all.

It was like looking at an infinite piece of unblemished paper and though he understood the futility of his thoughts, he nevertheless wondered who would get to draw on it, what the subject matter would be and what material they would use.

Rather irrationally he searched his pockets but quickly realized the futility as he was dressed in a pocket-less white nightshirt.

Also, the sudden realisation that if he did manage to find a pen, there was no possible way for him to reach that surface immediately made him stop searching. Instead he pulled on the long flowy sleeves of the shirt that nearly covered his hands and turned around on the spot.

There was nothing to see.

Everything in the space was the same exact hue and if it wasn't for the slightly flexible surface beneath the soles of his feet, he would have thought that it was like being in a perfect void.

"Hello," he called out, not because he was expecting an answer, but because he was intrigued to hear what would happen to his voice in a place with no apparent vertical boundaries. Like an elongated note his voice drifted into the empty space like a small ship on a vast ocean and was absorbed by the void without a hint of an echo.

Then from a place a great distance away another voice answered him.

"Hello," it said.

At first he thought he had mistaken the rushing of blood in his ears, but then the barely audible voice added: "Is someone there?"

"Yes," he called out, not exactly knowing how to explain where he was, "I'm here."

"Where?" the rather sonorous voice of a man asked.

"Over here," he answered, immediately accepting the irony of the statement.

"Don't you think that's quite the ludicrous declaration considering the given circumstances?" The voice sounded like it was getting closer.

"I suppose so," he called out, "truthfully: I was thinking more or less the same thing as soon as I said it."

"Keep talking," the man said, "I think I might know where I'm going."

"Alright, what do you want me to talk about?"

"I don't think it really matters. You can just say a string of arbitrary words that enters your mind, or you can ask me a question or perhaps even sing me a song. Come to think of it; it's been quite a while since somebody sang me a song."

"Where are we?"

"That's a good question," the man replied, "a very good question indeed. It would seem we're in some sort of equilibrious space. Although, why that is, I cannot possibly tell you, if that was indeed going to be your next question."

"Yes, I suppose it might have been," Ambrosius said, turning around, shading his eyes with his hand staring into the surrounding nothingness.

At last he noticed a small dot appearing in the distance.

"Over here," he shouted, waving his arms back and forth over his head, "over here."

Against the colourless void the black spot reminded him of a tiny fly crawling across a vast window pane in an inefficacious attempt to escape.

Ambrosius kept shouting and the black speck steadily grew in contemporaneousness with his voice.

It turned from a speck to a smear and from a smear to a mass until he recognized the black robe hanging like a dark sail from the body of the Brother.

His hands were hidden in the folds of his robe and he moved with the measured rhythm of someone who'd been walking for quite a while.

"I know who you are," Ambrosius called out, "you're the Brother who followed the voice into the sea."

He couldn't quite recall from where he had this information, but the image was as clear in his mind as if he had created it himself.

He waited until the Brother was close enough that he could make out his rheumatic eyes and pinkish fleshy features before he asked:

"Did you ever find what you were looking for?"

The Brother slowly shook his head making the drooping flesh below his chin wobble like the wattle on a turkey.

"No, I'm afraid I did not." He removed his hands from his robes, lifted a long attenuated index finger and wagged it back and forth in front of his face a couple of times before re-inserting his hands in the long sleeves. They reminded Ambrosius of elongated hairless animals disappearing into a dark hole in the ground.

"Though it's very difficult to explain an irrational behavior in retrospect, I have to inform you that although it was a compulsion like one I have never felt before that caused me to go overboard in the first place, the truth is that I never fully understood or expected what I might find when I did as commanded."

"So what did happen when you went overboard?" Ambrosius asked.

"That's another excellent question, to which I have no appropriate response" the Brother said, looking around as if the answer might be flowing somewhere in the space around him.

"I suppose this best answer I can give you is that this happened," he made a sweeping gesture to the surrounding void.

"How is that possible?" Ambrosius said, rubbing his head feeling the short rough bristles sticking into the palms of his hands, "you must have gone overboard decades ago."

"That is of no importance here," the Brother said, "by all accounts it would seem that the reality of now is being continually added as time passes, thus making all events past, present and future. In effect making my excursion into the sea happen at precisely this moment in time."

"I don't understand," Ambrosius said, "are you telling me we are trapped in a distortion of space in relation to time whereby we can move between one part of time to another?"

"I'm not certain that we can actually move anywhere at all, but that we are nonetheless moving everywhere at the same time."

"That statement doesn't make sense," Ambrosius said, looking around at the colourless space, "it's a physical impossibility to be still and moving at the same time. It simply goes against the laws of physics."

"That all depends on how you understand the element of time." The Brother unfolded his hands and spread them like he was welcoming an embrace.

"All you need to do is suspend your belief in the present as a sequence that moves between the past and the future," he said, staring at Ambrosius with his watery blue eyes. "If you focus on this moment as the only acceptable reality, you will consequently prevent the effect of time."

"Please don't give me that codology," Ambrosius shook his head, "it makes absolutely no sense whatsoever. No matter how much you think about the present as the only acceptable reality, there is no possible way of stopping time."

"If that is indeed true, how do you explain the presence of the cat and the visit from the girl at the cemetery?"

"How do you know about the cemetery?" Ambrosius asked staring suspiciously at the Brother, who held his gaze and cheerfully replied:

"The girl told me. She said that she had visited you a couple of times while you were busy digging and that she left her cat to look after you until it was time for her next visit.

"She told you it was her cat?" Ambrosius asked, a bit taken aback.

"That's what she said. Is something wrong?"

The Brother must have noticed the slight concern on his face.

"No, no everything's fine, I'm just a bit surprised to hear that the cat belongs to Veronica. I was under the impression that it was its own master."

"I am pretty certain she said 'my cat', although it's always a possibility that I misheard her. My ears are no longer what they used to be."

To emphasize the last statement, he grabbed his rather substantial earlobes with his thumb and forefinger and tugged at them.

"Now that you mention it; the young lady never gave me her name, so it might have been a completely different person telling me about you."

"I find that very hard to believe," Ambrosius said, "also, she's the only person I have encountered in the cemetery, who was in the company of a large black cat."

"Ah," said the Brother, slowly shaking his head and pursing his large fleshy lips, "well that settles it I suppose."

"What was she doing here?"

"Speaking with me."

"No, I mean; why does she come here?"

"Like I said: to speak with me."

He looked at Ambrosius with placating eyes.

"What do you speak about?"

"Oh, this and that. Although I must admit our conversations tend to be mostly about the creative disciplines and philosophy. She is an incredibly erudite conversationalist and her wealth of knowledge is astounding. It is like she's a living breathing library that has accumulated several decades or even centuries of information on its limitless shelves. Although I have tried to the best of my ability, I have yet to find a theme or discourse, no matter how obscure, with which she is not familiar. I sometimes have the feeling she even knows what I am about to say."

"Does she come here often?"

"That's an impossible question to answer," the Brother shook his head and closed his eyes, "as you recall, I already informed you that time has no effect in this place, so it's futile to ask if she comes here often, when she's already here."

"But if that's the case where is she?" Ambrosius turned around and gazed into the space.

"Theoretically she could be anywhere," the Brother made a sweeping gesture with his hands, "perhaps she's sitting in the boat talking to someone, or walking across the plane lost in her own thoughts. There's really no way of telling."

"A boat you said? What boat?"

"I don't believe it's of any real significance, but there's a black boat sailing around this plane. Although, the word sailing should perhaps be used in the loosest possible sense, as the boat appears to be more like an effigy of a vessel that doesn't seem to travel anywhere. It's really a lot more like a sculptural piece than an actual boat."

"Where is it right now?"

"Your guess is as good as mine," the Brother said, "but like everything else in this place, it's never far away."

"I don't understand? What am I supposed to do here?"

"It's difficult to say whether you are supposed to do anything at all or if you are already doing it. For all I know you might be here merely to conduct this conversation. Perhaps everything else has been leading up to this point."

"That's a well-worn and rather platitudinous statement," Ambrosius said, "but let's pretend for a moment that it's true, what is this meeting expected to accomplish?"

"That's another impossible question to answer," said the Brother, shaking his head looking at the ground. "It could be that we're supposed to find a way of answering that question ourselves. Perhaps the meaning of this meeting can be reduced to our intention of inducing a belief that the meeting matters by way of recognizing its significance."

What difference does that make? If there's no one else to verify the meeting took place or document its outcome, how do we understand its importance?" Ambrosius replied rather abruptly.

"Hmmm," the Brother ran a hand across the top of his balding head, "do you believe it matters to a deaf man if a tree falling in the forest makes a sound?"

He didn't wait for a reply.

"You see, what I believe is the importance of the deaf man's understanding of the condition of the tree both before and after the fact. Whatever happens in the middle, what we consider a philosophical conundrum, has no apparent influence on his ability to reason. The tree stands until it falls. Perhaps what we're really doing here is making the sounds of a tree falling to the ears of a deaf man."

There was a glint in the Brother's eyes and he revealed his large yellowing horse like teeth as he guffawed.

The hoarse guttural sound bounced off the surface like a large hispid animal before getting absorbed in the void.

Ambrosius smiled.

"I appreciate the analogy, although it doesn't exactly explain the core point of the theoretical problem."

"I never claimed it would," the Brother said still smiling. "I never claimed it would."

Ambrosius shielded his eyes with his hand and gazed into the apparently endless surrounding space.

"Do you think I should attempt to find the boat or the girl?" he asked after a while.

"Perhaps you should wait for the girl to find you. Last we talked, she told me there's something she very much would like to share with you."

"Really? Do you know what that might be?"

He waited for a reply.

When none came he looked over his shoulder to face his companion, but there was no trace of the Brother anywhere, and when Ambrosius turned around to look for him all he saw was nothing.

For what seemed a significant amount of time he couldn't seem to figure out exactly what he was looking at.

A couple of images of preternatural pilose creatures hanging from the ceiling in the depth of a cave flashed through his mind. It was a most disconcerting feeling and one that didn't completely disappear even after he recognized what he was looking at.

The young girl was standing by his head.

She was leaning over and her dark eyes were nearly obscured by the long black hair framing her face and although he didn't know exactly where he was, the immense starlit sky surrounding them was enough to give it away.

He located the small circle of stars and the crooked formation of an X when he unhurriedly searched the sky above him.

Then he moved his head and looked to the side.

A large greyish white boat was sitting on the surface twenty or so feet away.

Its unfilled sails hung purposeless from its masts like the shirtsleeves from an armless man and its hull glistened in the starlight like white granite, sending a small echoing swarm of glittering sparks into the night.

"How's the cat?" the girl asked before he got to his feet rubbing his face.

"What?" he replied, still trying to wake up.

"How's the cat?" she repeated the question as if she hadn't already asked him.

"The cat's fine," he replied, "right at this moment he's probably asleep in front of the fireplace." He yawned, scratching at his shoulders and back.

"Did you name him?"

He turned his head to look at the girl.

Her eyes were huge and lambent in her otherwise imperturbable face.

"As a matter of fact I did. You never told me what to call him and I believed he deserved a name if we were going to spend a long time together."

"What may I ask did you name him?"

"I named him Loke," he said, "I thought that was an appropriate name for him. Although, I'm not so sure he's lived up to his Scandinavian namesake as he's been spending most of his time asleep."

"I wouldn't worry too much about that," she answered jocularly, "I am positive he's somehow made sure. In my limited experience, he rarely misses an opportunity to manifest himself."

With a languorous movement of her hand she brushed her hair away from her face, and for a moment the strands flowed in the air as though they were thin fluid lines drawn with ink before they slowly resettled like a black symmetrical curtain around her marble white neck.

"No matter his current name, it will soon be time for him to move on," she added matter of factly.

"Why?"

"Everything always comes to an end one way or another," she said, cocking her head.

"I understand that," he replied, "but the cat has just arrived and I thought you said that I had to take care of him. I assumed that you meant for me to look after him during winter."

"I did," she replied, "but when all the days have gone, there's nothing more for you to do. The cat fully understands and accepts the situation and has already taken the necessary measures to prevent something inconvenient from happening."

"What's that supposed to mean?" he asked, confused by the girl's latest statement.

"It's preparing for the final chapter," she answered casually, apparently ignoring his question.

"I don't understand," he said, "the final chapter of what?"

"Of the story of course," she turned around and walked towards the white boat.

She easily climbed over the railing and sat down.

On the seat across from her he thought he could make out the faint silhouette of a white cat, but it could conceivably have been a trick of the light.

He thought about something to say but remained quiet.

The girl was humming a tune that he couldn't quite recall, but that he thought he had heard quite recently. Then the surface under his feet began vibrating making his entire body shake. He held his arms away from his body and concentrated on keeping his balance.

He looked over at the girl as she raised a slim relaxed arm and slowly waved it back and forth like a tubiform caught in a slow moving current.

He watched in awe as the white boat slowly sank into the obsidian surface and disappeared like a white pearl submerged in an inkwell, leaving nothing but a blank surface behind on which the profusion of stars above cast their abundant luminescence.

He swung his legs over the side of the bed and let his toes explore the surface of the floorboards before he took a deep breath, planted his feet, stood up and pulled on his trousers and socks.

It was freezing in the cottage and his breath made small eruptive clouds in front of his face as he put on his boots. He grabbed his sweater, pulled it over his head and rubbing his hands together he walked over to the fire place and bent down.

When he slowly waved his hand over the ashes, he could hardly feel the heat from the embers buried beneath, so he moved a couple of logs to grab a handful of kindling from the bucket to build a small conical structure on top of the dying embers.

Then he lifted an old yellowing folded newspaper from the bottom of the bucket, ripped out a page, crumbled it into a small ball, put it inside the structure, knelt down and carefully blew on the embers.

The paper soon began smoldering, releasing a fairly thick grey smoke, before a handful of bright orange flames enveloped the crumbled newspaper, overruled the smoke and quickly set the small structure on fire.

He watched as the fire quickly ate into the thin pieces of kindling, that contorted in the heat like deformed blackened fingers desperately reaching for something just beyond their grasp.

When he was satisfied that the fire wouldn't be smothered, he added a split log that crushed the now brittle limbs, sending a conglomeration of sparkling particles into the chimney, where they immediately got swallowed by the darkness.

He picked up another log and carried it over to the stove, opened the door and threw it on the remains of the half eaten log that was still pulsating in the dark like a recently blown off limb.

He shut the door and opened the vent, picked up the kettle and made his way to the door to put on his coat, gloves and cap.

The cat was lying curled up at the end of the bed and made no attempt at getting up. It didn't even lift its head when he opened the door and stepped outside.

Although the wind had died down, the frost of the clear morning was still piercing and mercilessly bit into the exposed parts of his face like a tiny multi-fanged ravenous creature.

He put the kettle down on the slab, before he walked down the path to the outhouse, opened the door and stepped inside. The stench had almost been completely stifled by the frost and for the first time in a long while he was able to breathe through his nose there. He closed the door, loosened his trouser belt, lifted up his jacket and gently lowered himself onto the freezing surface.

He thought about the dreams.

Although they were supposedly just imaginative fantasies built on an already established narrative, there was something about the encounters that made him increasingly uncomfortable. He couldn't quite rid himself of the feeling that the many connections between himself and the author of the letters was more than a coincidence. Furthermore, the similarities between them seemed to grow the more letters he read and the more dreams he had. Sometimes he even had the feeling that he knew some of the other people appearing in the dreams from somewhere other than the letters, but even though he had spent quite a while ransacking his brain, he couldn't quite recall where that could have been.

He got up, pulled up his trousers, opened the door, stepped out and crouched down to grab a handful of snow to wash his hands. The powdery crystalline particles turned the skin on the back of his hands bright red and he kept rubbing them together until the prickling sensation in the tips of his fingers subsided.

Then he trudged over to the shed, picked up a small pick ax and some chicken feed and proceeded to the coop where he checked on the huddled up hens.

He spread some feed on the ground, put a handful of snow in the water bowl and picked up four still warm eggs, before he closed the hatch and slowly made his way back to the cottage.

Before he reached the granite slab, he stopped, turned around and looked up at the bright blue sky stretching endlessly above him.

Although he strained his ears, the only sound that broke the quietude of the surrounding snow covered landscape was his own laboured breathing.

There was something moving in the sky above him and he shielded his eyes with his hands making a small three sided fleshy box.

A small sliver, like a thin piece of paper or a tiny petal from a white flower slowly floated across the sky. He was relatively certain it was a sea bird, but it was too far away to tell what kind it was. It kept rising higher and higher, gliding in large sweeping motions across the bright blue plane, until it finally disappeared from view.

He would have to break the ice and get some water from the barrel at the back of the house later on, but for now he bent down, took off the lid and packed the kettle with snow.

It squeaked against his glove covered hand as he pushed the white mass into the dark rotund belly until the surface became as hard as a rock and his hands began smarting. Then he replaced the lid, picked up the kettle by the handle and opened the door.

He was startled by the cat that unexpectedly jumped over his foot and quickly ran over to the small clearing to squat.

He closed the door and waited until the cat had finished and ran back inside, before he took a couple of steps closer to look at the newly made mark.

The center of the still steaming blot was a rich colour from which a series of much lighter diluted petal-like strands merged with the pristine snow.

The image was quite beautiful and although he couldn't remember having ever seen anything similar, the small yellow flower like drawing still reminded him of something suspended in the filmy periphery of his mind.

For a moment he deliberated over fetching his drawing materials to make a sketch of the mark, but the cold was too intense and the tip of his fingers were already getting numb, so he decided against it.

Instead he went back to the cottage, stomped his feet on the granite, opened the door and stepped inside.

He walked over to the stove and put the kettle down, then he took off his jacket, stuck the gloves in the pockets, hung the jacket on the hook on the back of the door and placed his cap on top.

He walked back across the groaning floorboards and began preparing breakfast.

He picked up and cracked the four eggs that he'd just collected and while they sputtered in the buttered pan he grabbed the box from the pantry and got everything set for making tea.

The kettle was beginning to warm and when he lifted the lid to look inside all that was left of the snow was a small opaque malformed gloog, hanging motionless in the clear water.

When the eggs were ready he cut up a handful into small squares and put them in the cat's food bowl. He didn't know if cats ate cooked eggs, but he reckoned he would find out soon enough.

He put the rest of the food on a plate, grabbed the cutlery and the salt and pepper and carried everything over to the table and set it down on the tabletop.

He stared into space, pushed all thoughts to the outer ambit of his mind, and slowly began to eat.

When he finished eating he brought the plate and utensils to the sink and put the salt and pepper back on the shelf in the pantry, then he poured a small amount of warm water in the teapot to rinse it and waited for the water to boil before making tea.

He brought the box to his nose and inhaled the tangy fragrance, subtly suffused with overtones of flowers and sweet tobacco, before adding a couple of pinches to the pot.

Then he lifted the kettle off the stove and poured the hot water into the teapot and watched as the leaves spun around in the vortex. They slowly became saturated and began their sedated descent to the bottom of the pot where they came to rest like autumn leaves in a pond.

He poured a bit of hot water into the white porcelain cup and swirled it around waiting until he thought the leaves had stewed long enough, then he emptied the cup in the sink and poured in the steaming amber colored liquid, picked up the cup and carried it to the table.

Halfway across the floor a small amount of tea spilled over the edge and splashed onto the worn out floorboards making an unusual pattern.

He stopped and turned his head sideways to look at the damp mark, that very much looked like the profile of a rodent lying on its side. He stared at the drawing as it slowly absorbed into the wood and transformed to something nonrepresentational. Then he shook his head and walked the last couple of steps to the table, pulled out the chair and sat down. He held the cup to his mouth, gently blew across the surface of the hot liquid, creating a small ripple that rebounded from the edge of the cup, before he carefully took a sip and placed the cup at the edge of the table.

He reached out and picked up the last envelope marked *Slutningen*, slid the pocketknife into the small opening at the top and ran it across, splitting the two sides open. Then he inserted his thumb and forefinger and picked out the last eight fine pieces of paper, unfolded them and spread them on the table top.

He leaned forward in chair, rested his chin on his hands and began to read.

Dearest E

I think about you every hour of every day. When I'm not drifting in and out of an apparent hallucinatory fantasy, I dream about your beautiful eyes resting on mine and of your soft pale arms enclosing me in a loving embrace. When I wake up from one of these entrancing dreams my emotional state is like that of a ship endlessly being thrashed by the frenzied ocean. My body and soul yearn for your company like fish flapping around on the bank yearn to be back in the pond and I often clutch the image I carry of you and stare at it in fear that if I do not, I will somehow forget your entire personae.

As I have already told you: I am at times at a total loss as to the order in which the events occurred. They often strike me as having happened to someone else entirely, but at a completely different time, which of course sounds preposterous.

You will also have to excuse me if I am recounting things that I have already written down, but there are too many incidences in my mind that are so alike that it sometimes makes it difficult to keep the images apart. Lately I have come to believe that I have been dreaming the same dream over and over, but each time with slight variations, as if my insomniatic nights have become an endless fugue. To tell you the truth I feel increasingly that my dreams are interfering with my reality and sometimes I find it incredibly difficult to separate the two.

It is so absolutely quiet here.

The snow is now covering the entire cottage in a giant white blanket, making any outside sounds impossible to hear. However, I have yet to escape the never ending slapping of the waves against the groaning hull and those eternal sounds forever keep me company throughout the night. Sometimes I do ponder if this watery motif will ever fully leave me.

I have recently been in a terribly splenetic mood, mostly due to the fact that I now sleep less than a couple of restless hours at a time, but also because I believe the imposing solitude has finally ensnared me. To be perfectly honest, I cannot seem to remember the last time I had a conversation with a person not in a dream or hallucination, although I find it more and more difficult to separate the two, and even more difficult to know whether or not these conversations have actually taken place.

Sometimes in a rational moment, I believe that everything that has happened and is happening is as real as everything else, and that it makes no difference whether or not anything has actually occurred. How can anything I see and experience in my dreams really be any different than any other event verifiable by observation or tangible experience. Whatever it is that I am experiencing is to me completely heuristic and enables me to discover and learn something for myself. What that knowledge is for however, I cannot possibly tell you, as I am no closer to figuring out why these bizarre events continue to happen.

You must believe me when I say that I would have never in my wildest dreams thought that I would write to you about sentient animals talking to me or reading me poems, or of meeting with apparently deceased people in places with no distinguishing features or of a young girl with an extraordinarily astonishing mind visiting me over a span of many years. Frankly I do not understand how any of this is possible, and I have no logical explanation to offer you or anyone else for that matter. The more time I spend trying to figure out why this is happening to me the further it appears I get to understanding it.

The factuality is that I am beginning to feel that I am truly lost.

One night some time ago now, when I was sitting at the table drawing the dried out skeletal remains of a rodent with hollowed out eye sockets and papery skin, there was a knock on my cabin door. I didn't know what time it was but as it was dark outside the bullseye, I reckoned that it must have been sometime late in the night. I didn't expect any visitors at that hour, so for a while I remained seated and continued drawing. However, whoever it was outside in the corridor was rather persistent and kept wrapping on the wood with quick motions like a small woodpecker until I got up from my chair, collected my robe around me, walked across the floor and opened the door.

The young girl with the raven black hair was standing in the corridor. Her small dainty hand was raised in readiness to knock and her elegant slim arm glowed ghostly in the gloom. She looked up, smiled and walked right past me into the cabin, where she made herself comfortable on the edge of my berth. I was quite embarrassed by the disarray of papers and items of clothes strewn on the floor and suddenly, having had a sniff at the air in the corridor, I noticed how strong the odour was in the cabin. The pungent smell of sour unwashed clothing and old food scraps permeated the stale air, but if the girl had noticed she didn't let it be known, instead she looked at me with her large obsidian eyes and tilted her head slightly from side to side as you tend to do when you're attempting to measure something from a distance. I kept standing with my back to the cabin door, wondering what this strange girl wanted to speak with me about at this late hour.

"Have you ever wondered how things are happening to you and not to someone else," she asked quite joyfully, "I mean: how can you ever know that you're the only person that a particular thing is happening to? What if thousands of people are experiencing the exact same thing as you at exactly the same time? Do you believe your experience will still be unique?"

I was completely taken aback by her inordinately complex question, and rubbed my face in my hands as I've found I often do when confronted with difficult situations.

"That's a difficult question to answer," I replied, after having given some thought to the question. I looked at the girl sitting on the edge of the berth, with her hands folded in her lap and her attentive eyes glinting in the shadows.

"In many ways a man or woman is truly no different from that of any other living creature", I began slowly, gathering speed as I talked, "they live, they procreate and they die. However, I believe a person is not simply a living being. It is my belief that a person with identity, who can reason and reflect upon themselves as themselves and have the ability to imagine themselves in different places at different times will always experience whatever is happening to them as unique, and thus be able to differentiate their experience from everyone else."

The girl nodded her head in approval and lifted her still folded hands up to her chin.

"But what if, hypothetically speaking, you're experiencing the same thing as the same person in the same place, but that time itself is irrelevant, thus making it impossible for you to know how many of you there are and if there's even a before and after the event? Will that experience make it less unique for the individual?"

"I don't know if I even understand the question," I said truthfully. "First and foremost time cannot ever be irrelevant, it goes against the natural physical laws, so even if an action is repeated, nothing can actually happen more than once at any given time. Also, if time is irrelevant, nothing could actually be happening at all and everything in the universe would be suspended in perfect *equilibrium. Or rather: nothing would have ever happened in the first place."*

The girl covered her mouth and giggled a little. The sound trickled like a snapped string of pearls and bounced off the sparse furniture, before rolling across the floorboards, coming to rest in the dark crevices along the walls.

I was surprised by her sudden outburst and she must have sensed my confusion, because she stopped laughing and shot me a teasing look.

"'Nothing would have happened in the first place', that's quite an amusing statement don't you think? In the context of our conversation it's an interesting misnomer, I mean how can there even be an 'in the first place' when there is no 'in the first place'?"

She parted her lips and laughed. Her perfectly formed teeth shone like mother of pearl in the sparse light of the lantern and her pink tongue quivered like a small moistened creature from behind the enamel gates. The girl stopped laughing, closed her mouth and gave me a knowing smile, as if she knew what I had been thinking.

Although I hadn't had any imprudent thoughts, her gaze nonetheless made me uncomfortable and I didn't know how to respond to her gaze other than returning a somewhat strained smile. For what seemed like quite a long moment we sat looking at each other across the room, while listening to the liquid sound of the ever present waves gently caressing the hull.

I had assumed the girl would continue the conversation on time, but when she finally spoke, it was on a different topic entirely. She repositioned her hands in her lap and looked at me with equanimity. Her voice has changed as well, it was now half an octave lower and she spoke with a level of serenity I had not previously heard.

"Clemens, I know what happened to them," she kept her eyes locked on mine, making sure that I was listening, and supposedly to see how I would react. When she was certain that she had my full attention she continued: "I know that they were gravely ill and that they both succumbed to the fever while you were away on your mission to save them. I know that when you finally returned with the doctor, you encountered some terrible terrible things. Images of such horror that, no matter how many other images are currently found in the superimposed layers, they cannot be unseen. I know because I have seen them too."

The girl stopped talking, but kept her dark eyes trained on mine, presumably waiting for me to respond. I was however stupefied by the direction the conversation had unexpectedly taken and simply stared at her unseeingly; my brain was at an utter standstill.

Little by little the images slowly began to emerge, like they were drifting to the surface from a bottomless well. Black scaly claws digging into white decaying skin, long curved beaks, the colour of gunmetal, picking at crusty hollowed out eye sockets, terrifying silent screams originating from lipless skeletal mouths, nightgowns stained with a mixture of congealed blood and bird droppings and the relentless odour of putrescent flesh permeating the air like a tangible entity. I began to rub my eyes in terror attempting to remove the offending images from my retinae, but to no avail; the images, smells and sounds kept assaulting my senses with renewed intensity: Two grinning masks of death staring at me from the bed across the room, smells like those of hell itself smiting my nostrils and the squawking black crows flapping their wings around my head in victorious celebration mixed with an earsplitting howl of despair that I too late recognized as my own.

I was lying in the middle of the floor surrounded by discarded papers and sour smelling clothes when I felt a small hand resting on my shoulder. My soul was racked with anguish and shame, and I could feel my body desperately gasping for breath between the loud sobs. The strong arms of the evocative nightmare were still firmly wrapped around me.

"You realise it doesn't have to be like this," the girl whispered close to my ear, "you can be free if you let me help you."

"How could one ever be free?" I answered sobbing uncontrollably, the vivid vision still penetrating the recesses of my very soul. "Tell me how someone could ever truly be free from the horrors that only makes them dream of a swift and merciful death? How could someone be free when all they see when they close their eyes are the images of their loved ones, pure of heart and soul, being brutally torn apart and devoured by hellish creatures? How could a man be free if his heart is forever broken?"

"Trust me," the girl said quietly, "I can make it stop. I can make all of it appear as if it never happened, but you have to trust me."

She somewhat awkwardly helped me up from the floor to sit in the chair and waited until I had calmed down and my breathing had normalised before she produced a small soft handkerchief from a pocket in her dress and carefully dried my eyes. She bent down, took my hands in hers and looked at me with great sympathy. Her hands were warm and soft and although they were a lot smaller than my own they were supple and strong.

"Everything will be as it should," she said, holding a firm grip on my hands, "but you have to do exactly as I say. Do you understand?"

I looked into her beautiful inky eyes and slowly nodded.

"Good," she said, "first I would like you to close your eyes and concentrate on clearing your mind of all thoughts, exactly like you do before you start eating."

How she could possibly know about that was beyond the pale and I must have looked at her in disbelief, because she waved her hand dismissively, as if she was slightly annoyed by the distraction.

"Don't think about that," she continued, "think about making the center of your mind into a vacuous space. When everything else has been pushed into the periphery and you have obtained a level of mental stasis, I would like you to move towards the center and listen for someone knocking on a door. There will be three knocks in quick succession and after the third knock you will open your eyes and all shall be revealed."

She pushed a loose strand of her long jet black hair behind her left ear and looked at me with earnestness.

"Do you understand what I am asking you to do?"

I nodded my head consenting to whatever might happen, and she gave me a most charming smile.

"Good," she let go of my hands and took a step backwards. "Please close your eyes and concentrate on emptying your mind."

Although I feared what I might see in the darkness, I did was I was told and concentrated on clearing my mind. At first the terrifying images returned, but somehow I managed to banish a large proportion of them, leaving only a few obscure fragments that fluttered past me like disoriented moths and rather quickly vanished in the opaque mist. When I was finally suspended in an absolute imageless and soundless space, wondering how I could possibly tell where the center of the void would be, I suddenly heard three loud knocks on something that sounded very much like a heavy wooden door.

I awoke from the dream, opened my eyes, blinked a couple of times to adjust to the dim light and found myself sitting on a rickety chair at a square wooden table in the center of a small stone cottage. A small white porcelain tea cup with thin reddish rings on the inside stood in the center of the table. I had an intense urge to count the rings, but decided against it afraid of what I might discover. The dying fire in the fireplace cast an orange glow across a large black cat lying on the floorboards and the candle burning in the unique lantern flickered above the table.

On the shelf above the fireplace three rodents in black frames, each proffered an uncomfortable animated stare that somehow seemed all too familiar.

My hand was holding a white quill and the inkwell was situated just a smidgen above the right hand corner of the thin piece of paper, as is my custom when I write.

I am waiting to hear the sound again, now that I know where it is coming from.

He jumped in his chair when the sound shattered the stillness.

At first he thought that he had been so engrossed in the narrative of the letter that his mind had played a trick on him, but he was now convinced that there had been three loud knocks on the cottage door.

He looked apprehensively towards the heavy oak door, then he placed his hands on his knees, and stood, pushing the chair away from under him.

Roused by the commotion the cat sat up, turned its head and followed his movements with its large blue eyes.

When he returned its gaze he had the distinct impression it somehow knew what he was thinking.

He tried not to think about it as he walked across the broad groaning floorboards and put his hand on the door handle.

He left his hand on the cold metal, took a couple of deep breaths and braced himself.

Then he pressed down on the handle and slowly let the door swing into the cottage.

The monotone milky white light outside the cottage made him squint and he automatically raised his hand to shield his eyes.

The girl standing outside was dressed in a light flowy summer dress, white socks and shoes and her long raven black hair was held in place by a wide white hairband.

She had her hands behind her back and as she swayed back and forth, she looked up at him with expectant eyes, as if she was preparing to play a game or engage him in conversation.

He was however preoccupied with the surroundings.

Where everything should have been, there was nothing but a vacuous colourless space that stretched far into the distance.

For a while he stared searchingly into the surrounding void, but when he couldn't discern any difference between the ground and the sky, he instead redirected his gaze and looked at the girl.

"Hello Moerk," she said, presenting him with a most endearing smile. "Nice to see you again. How have you been? I hope both you and the cat have been well and that you've enjoyed each other's company."

He was too surprised by her presence to respond, so for a short time he just stared at her beaming face.

"What are you doing here?" he asked somewhat unsettled, unsure at first if she was another apparition.

"Can I come in?" She didn't wait for his reply but walked straight past him and disappeared into the cottage.

He stood for a moment gazing into the unpigmented space, before he turned around, followed the girl inside and closed the door.

She was crouching on the floor by the fireplace in front of the cat.

For an extended period of time, the two of them stared into each other's unblinking eyes, and though he still wasn't exactly sure that he believed what he saw, it very much looked like they were having a silent conversation.

After a while the girl nodded her head and stood up.

She casually brushed the grey flakes of ashes off her dress and turned to face him.

"The cat tells me you named him Loke," she said unceremoniously, "that's an interesting choice, don't you think?"

He was surprised by the directness of her inquiry and it took a while for him to answer. "Well, I thought that it would be appropriate for him to have a name since we were going to live under the same roof, and Loke seemed somehow to fit his general demeanor."

"He would like me to tell you that he appreciates the name and that he believes you chose well."

"I'm happy to hear that," he said and looked at the cat licking its paw in the orange glow from the fireplace.

Then he looked back at the girl and repeated the question that had been on his mind since he opened the door:

"What are you doing here?"

"I am here to make sure that everything is as it should be," she said.

"What does that mean?" he asked, mystified by her statement.

"It means that I am here to assist you."

"Assist me how? I'm not in need of an assistant. I can still perform my duties well enough without any help." He subconsciously flexed his arms under his shirt.

"That's not exactly why I'm here."

"So if you're not here to assist me, why are you here?"

She paused and looked up at him with her large dark eyes.

It was like looking into a bottomless inkwell and he recognised his own careworn reflection deep within the glossy surface.

He almost got lost in his own inconsequential thoughts when her low whispering voice broke his reverie.

"I now know why you never use your middle name."

He straightened his back and gazed at her with an expression of disbelief on his face.

She fixed him with an unwavering stare and for a long while neither of them spoke.

"She was the only one who ever used it," she continued, "to everyone else you've always been Ambrosius, but to her you will only ever be Clemens."

"How do you know?" he said quietly, focusing on something indistinct in the space in between them.

"Remember I once told you that the cat tells me everything that it picks up and that I translate what I supposedly need to know? That's how."

"So was that the reason you asked me to look after the cat? So that it could keep me under surveillance?"

He shook his head in bewilderment.

"Don't be upset Moerk, I needed to know your entire story, so that I can properly help you finalize it." She reached out and wrapped her small warm fingers around his large calloused hand.

"You have to trust that I have always had your best interest at heart," she said, holding on to his hand. "Now, if you would like to come with me, I have something very important that I would like to share with you."

She optimistically pulled on his hand and he took a couple of tentative steps in her direction and followed her as she walked across the floor, out through the door and into the colourless space.

The biting cold had been replaced with a mild windless atmosphere that enveloped him in a comforting embrace that strangely seemed to support his body, gently moving it forward through space.

When they had walked for only a couple of minutes, he let go of the girl's hand, stopped and looked back at the cottage.

Although they had just departed, it was as if he was seeing it from far away through a slightly clouded lens.

It looked different than he remembered it. More decrepit somehow, like it hadn't been looked after in years.

A few of the windowpanes had numerous cracks running through them, like a spider had etched immutable divergent webs into their surfaces.

There were no traces of anything around the cottage and he wondered exactly where they were and where everything else had disappeared to.

"Are we going to return?" he asked, "some of my possessions are quite precious to me."

"Don't worry," the girl said reassuringly, "you are always going to return."

Her mellifluous voice floated in the air like a small cluster of dandelion seeds carried away on an autumn breeze.

"What about the cat?" he said, "will he be able to take care of himself while I'm gone?"

"You have nothing to worry about," she said smiling, "you'll understand when you return."

She lifted her slender arm and once again motioned for him to follow her, and with one last look at the dilapidated cottage he turned around and started walking.

The ground proffered very little resistance and they moved quite easily through the desolate space and although he couldn't figure out in which direction they were heading, it seemed that the girl knew where they were going. She looked straight ahead and walked with a certain assurance, like someone who had already walked the same route countless times, and she never once stopped to get her bearings.

At some point he stopped and looked back over his shoulder, but although he stared in all directions there was nothing to see.

It was as if the cottage had been fully absorbed by the colourless space.

He thought about mentioning it to the girl, but she was already way ahead of him and continued to move quickly across the compact, but strangely pliable surface.

Somewhat concerned that he might be left behind in the vacuous space he quickly began moving towards her.

When they had been walking for quite a while she finally slowed down and pointed to something in the near distance.

"Look over there," she said.

He could barely make out what she was pointing at, but when they got closer he saw that they were heading towards a rather large rectangular opening in the surface.

When they reached the sharp edge of the long narrow aperture, they stopped and looked down.

Although there was nothing to measure it against, he reckoned the opening was about twelve feet long and about six feet wide.

In the all-encompassing homogenized whiteness, it was almost impossible to differentiate between the surface and what lay beneath, but he nevertheless recognized a set of steep milk white steps leading into a space deep below.

The monochrome walls surrounding the steps were as blank as a piece of paper and like the steps they disappeared in the white abyss. "Come!"

The girl languorously gestured with her hand and slowly walked down the first couple of steps.

He glanced around at the vacant surroundings, before he stepped down from the surface and followed her into the adamantine chasm.

They slowly descended the white stairs and after a long quiet descent, the wall in front of them, that he had been gazing at for a while, seemed to mysteriously dissolve and what appeared to be a massive white plateau spread out in front of them.

An unending colorless sky spread above them and in the far distance a greenish blue plane, lively as only the interminable waves of an ocean can be, met the sharp edge of the white edge of the white immobile mass.

A long narrow weather-beaten pier protruded from beyond the pristine surface, and continued far into the water. The light grey wood and structure of the pier reminded him of the crisscrossed shadowy lines of trees on the blanket of snow and he automatically reached for his notebook, but remembered that he'd left it behind in the cottage.

He slowly lowered his hand when something beyond the bounds of possibility caught his attention.

At the very end of the pier, almost lost against the colourless sky, two small figures dressed in white were standing side by side looking out across the animated sea.

The taller of the two had an arm securely wrapped around the shoulder of the smaller one and even from that distance he could see the long flaxen hair cascading down their backs like honeyed waterfalls.

At first he was positive that his eyes were deceiving him, but the longer he disbelievingly gazed at the image, the stronger it became, until it solidified deep within his soul.

He put his head in his hands, fell on his knees and began to weep.

After a while he noticed a small hand resting on his shoulder and he heard the familiar genial voice whisper close to his ear:

"It's time."

He stood up, quietly dried his eyes on his shirt sleeve and looked at the two unmistakable figures in the distance.

Then he determinedly stepped onto the pier and began walking towards the end.

Like ice crystals dissolving on a window pane in the warming rays of the sun, he slowly evanesced in a colourless embrace.

Acknowledgements

I would like to thank my editor and friend Kavi Montanaro for his guidance, insightful advice and patience in the writing of this book. Without the countless conversations and his unwavering enthusiasm for the desolate tale of Ambrosius C Moerk one can only speculate on how this narrative would have presented itself.

I am forever indebted to Kyle Louis Fletcher for lending his time and his marvelously creative talent to the cover design and artwork of this book.

Thanks also to Christian O'Connor for his astute caffeine induced input and his sharp eyes.

I would also like to give my sincere thanks to Jesper Magnusson to whom this book is dedicated. His changeless loyalty and friendship during the last couple of decades has been next to none and is very much appreciated.

Finally; I would like to thank my wife Helen for her endless optimism, her never failing words of reassurance and her invaluable support throughout the entire process, and my girls for their patience and sympathetic awareness of their dad's literary affliction.

Baskerville is a serif typeface designed in the 1750s by John Baskerville (1706–1775) in Birmingham, England and cut into metal by John Handy. Baskerville is classified as a transitional typeface, intended as a refinement of what are now called old-style typefaces of the period. Baskerville increased the contrast between thick and thin strokes, making the serifs sharper and more tapered, and shifted the axis of rounded letters to a more vertical position. These changes created a greater consistency in size and form.

 ANGRY OWL

CPSIA information can be obtained
at www.ICGtesting.com
Printed in the USA
BVHW031202200621
609990BV00017B/298

9 781975 746124